"MAGICAL."

—*Cosmopolitan*

"A sensitive, lyrical work that explores the universal timelessness of love . . . leaves the reader feeling touched by magic." —*Rocky Mountain News*

"Mystical and sensual . . . A charming, lyrical novel." —*Buzz*

"Filled with hope and wisdom, with richly imagined characters, and with the mystery of life and the magic of place." —*Cape Cod Times*

"LYRICAL, MAGICAL, and extravagantly sensual—a rich, enchanting tale." —*Juneau Empire*

"Lane von Herzen renders the small ways in which couples fall in love acutely and with great sympathy." —*Publishers Weekly*

"There are stylistic and thematic similarities to the work of both Alice Hoffman and Anne Tyler, but von Herzen's poetic and insightful writing is her own." —*Library Journal*

LANE VON HERZEN, author of *Copper Crown* (Plume), is a recent recipient of a fellowship from the National Endowment for the Arts. She was awarded the Los Angeles Arts Council Prize in fiction and received her M.F.A. from the writing program at the University of California, Irvine. A native of Texas, she now lives in California with her husband and son.

LANE VON HERZEN

The Unfastened Heart

———•———

A PLUME BOOK

PLUME
Published by the Penguin Group
Penguin Books USA Inc., 375 Hudson Street, New York, New York 10014, U.S.A.
Penguin Books Ltd, 27 Wrights Lane, London W8 5TZ, England
Penguin Books Australia Ltd, Ringwood, Victoria, Australia
Penguin Books Canada Ltd, 10 Alcorn Avenue, Toronto, Ontario, Canada M4V 3B2
Penguin Books (N.Z.) Ltd, 182–190 Wairau Road, Auckland 10, New Zealand

Penguin Books Ltd, Registered Offices: Harmondsworth, Middlesex, England

Published by Plume, an imprint of Dutton Signet,
a division of Penguin Books USA Inc.
Previously published in a Dutton edition.

First Plume Printing, November, 1995
10 9 8 7 6 5 4 3 2

 REGISTERED TRADEMARK—MARCA REGISTRADA

The Library of Congress has catalogued the Dutton edition as follows:

Von Herzen, Lane.
    The unfastened heart / Lane von Herzen.
        p.   cm.
    ISBN 0-525-93890-7 (hc.)
    ISBN 0-452-27290-4 (pbk.)
    1. Love—California—Fiction.   I. Title.
PS3572.O45U5   1994
813'.54—dc20   94–8535
                                                        CIP
                                                        AC

Printed in the United States of America

PUBLISHER'S NOTE
This is a work of fiction. Names, characters, places, and incidents either are the
product of the author's imagination or are used fictitiously, and any resemblance
to actual persons, living or dead, events, or locales is entirely coincidental.

BOOKS ARE AVAILABLE AT QUANTITY DISCOUNTS WHEN USED TO PROMOTE PRODUCTS
OR SERVICES. FOR INFORMATION PLEASE WRITE TO PREMIUM MARKETING DIVISION,
PENGUIN BOOKS USA INC., 375 HUDSON STREET, NEW YORK, NEW YORK 10014.

For Ken, the first breathing miracle I knew,
generous, bright-souled, longed for, loved.

Your children are not your children.
They are the sons and daughters of Life's
  longing for itself.
—KAHLIL GIBRAN

PART ONE

———◆———

A Breath, a Quake,
a Dream

ANNA DE LA SENDA knew what magic was, and so did the Lovelorn Women who gathered in her home once a week. My Cordojo Women, Anna called them, for their hungry, brilliant, swollen hearts and the clarity with which they beat. All of them knew about magic without quite having seen it themselves. It was what crackled in the summer air like static, turning the streetlights on and off at random. It was what made the fish in the koi ponds move like mermaids and phantoms, kissing one another and then dissolving into nothing. It was what made the lilies open their throats at night and sing their silent white songs. It was the anticipation of everything destined and impossible, and it had invaded the neighborhood like a weather from another world.

Each Sunday, the Cordojo Women followed Anna home from church. There was India Perry, whose hat dripped with imitation fruits and sprays of colored netting; Dove Pairlee, who bobbed and preened from the middle of her invisible perfume cloud; Maxine Ridgeway and her daughter, Emily D., who tripped forward with so many halts and jolts that they radiated a fear of losing their footing; and Esther Lee, who, in her encroaching deafness, smiled in trembling sweetness at every passerby, wondering whether they had greeted her or not.

The Lovelorn Women journeyed like pilgrims to Anna de la Senda's living room and there had their spirits soothed. Through measures of friendship and privacy, laughter and sorrow, explanation and silence, their edges were softened, their griefs were mitigated, their souls were led into bloom like rare indoor flowers, breathtaking and awkward and luxuriant all at once. Their hearts stopped aching, if only for a little while. They knew what it was to belong.

In May, Dove Pairlee had fallen off her diet, though it had not been her fault, as she would be the first to reveal. Then when summer arrived in California with all its white, violent heat, she began to suffer in earnest. She sat prettily beside Anna de la Senda's picture window, panting behind a Spanish fan.

"I wouldn't have fallen off it except for my birthday and that cake all of you baked for me," she said.

"But you asked us to bake you a cake," Maxine Ridgeway said.

"I did?" Dove Pairlee asked the question with exaggerated innocence, which she always did when she felt too polite to contradict.

"You said you'd just die from desolation if you didn't have a cake with butter cream frosting on it," Maxine Ridgeway said.

"I'm sure I didn't," Dove Pairlee said. "Why would I ask for such a thing when butter cream isn't even my favorite?" She thrust her fan into the air in front of Maxine's face, as though it were the proof of what she was saying, undeniable in the light of day.

"Try not to worry about the extra weight," Anna de la Senda said. "There is nothing wrong with the generous bosom that comes with it."

Dove Pairlee pulled her fan back into her lap. She had wanted to say something more to Maxine, but Anna had commented on precisely what her innermost worries were, and her intended words had disappeared in a hot breath of air.

"Do you really think my bosom is . . ."

"Generous!" Anna said. "Voluptuous! I have never heard a man complain about that."

The Lovelorn Women giggled, their midriffs jouncing happily. India Perry was gluing artificial fruit onto the brim of a glossy straw hat—dangling green grapes, pears in yellow clusters.

"That's right, Anna," India said. "And you want to know something that kind of ties in with what you're saying? I sell a lot more big-fruited hats than any other kind. Apples, pears, grapefruits—those are the most popular."

"Oh, India!" Dove Pairlee laughed. "How could you say such a thing?"

"I might try cantaloupe next year," India said.

Esther Lee shifted uncomfortably in her seat. She tried valiantly to understand why everyone else was having such a good time. "Did you say antelope?" she asked.

"Cantaloupe!" India shouted.

"Oh," Esther Lee said. "Because I really couldn't see wearing an antelope on my head."

"Too dangerous," Anna de la Senda shouted toward her.

"Exactly," Esther Lee said, satisfied that she had been, for the first time in days, fully understood.

ANNA DE LA SENDA lived for love. Not her own, but other people's. She took on counseling patients of all ages and attitudes, of all dilemmas and doubts, and she spoke with them in their living rooms about the health of their concealed hearts. In return, they paid her with what they could, with cash or avocados, with money orders or cotton cloth. The currency didn't matter to her. What mattered was the healing of the brokenhearted. She had a way of peering through the skin of her patients to look at the aches inside. In another world, she would have been a seer, a *vidente*; in this world, she called herself a woman of faith.

As a professed Catholic, she attended not only Saturday Mass, but also Saturday services at the Jewish temple on Glenallen Avenue, and Sunday services at the Methodist and Episcopal churches in Saxon Hill. Wisdom could be found everywhere that people looked after their souls. That thought buoyed her up each time it came to her.

In her house, the wooden statues of the saints lived in a silent crowd on shelves designed for them especially. Their robes pooled downward in the colors of jewels; their hair glanced over their shoulders in gleaming humility. Saint Jude raised his arm toward the sky without looking at it, as though the miracle he sought would at any moment drop from heaven into his open hand. Saints Catherine and Teresa, the matrons of marriage and longing, stood on the topmost shelf, so that their prayers of intervention would have a shorter distance to travel when they rose like vapors to seek the ears of God. Because after faith itself, love was the most consuming enigma in the minds of the people. Anna de la Senda had known this since her childhood, as an intuition, as a natural gift. Love was what people wanted most desperately to fall into or out of; love was what they wished most fervently to transform or create or erase; love was what gave them the will often to live and sometimes to die; to bear their children and to fight their rivals, to sing and celebrate and sometimes mourn, and always, always, to understand anew the great deserts of loneliness in which so many disappeared.

Even her friends, the Cordojo Women, had all come to her eventually with questions of love, questions such as: why was Maxine Ridgeway's husband stepping out on her, why had Emily D. lost her voice for a whole year beginning one Valentine's Day, why did Dove Pairlee have the profound failing of choosing lovers who were secretly, fatally ill? Anna de la Senda had addressed all of these mysteries in one way or another, with persistently surprising results. But that was the way of the world,

Anna de la Senda said. The truest answers were never what you expected.

Anna's house itself was testament to the precious accidents of life. Dandelions and giant poppies spotted her long-fringed lawn, and at the borders, where there ought to have been hedges, there were bright piles of kumquats, dropped from the ripening trees. The shutters flew away from their mountings at odd angles, surprised and scattered and appealingly askew.

Inside, there was kitsch and treasured chaos. The walls stood covered with maps and antique tapestries, all framed with gilt edges, the glass coverings disposed of. The windows were flung open and frozen in a state of flagrant wonder, their jambs having been painted over too many times to count. And through four of their portholes stretched the aging, leafy limbs of the trees in the yard, as though, in their mutual age and experience, the greenery and the house had simply linked hands, irrevocably, by mute and magical consent. The outside of Anna's house remained stunningly silent, but the inside nearly spilled over with the sounds of wind chimes and the singing of birds, open-throated and joyful in their giant, copper cages. The birds had been only a recent addition, but it seemed to Anna, just as it did to everyone who passed through her front door, that they had always been there. Their presence left a bitter, pungent smell in the air, a smell halfway between citrus and chalk, and Anna liked to tell people that this was the smell of the very earth, with its fertility and sourness inseparable from one another, just like life itself. It was the odor of sweetness that Anna turned away from, the sickly, hanging odor of air fresheners and wreaths that poured out of the rooms of the dead and the dying. Anna had first smelled it in her childhood, and never again would she associate sweet scents with what was innocent, with what was healthy and in its place.

Sweetness had been in the air on the night the birds had first come to her, when they had all seemed certainly dead, their claws and feathers singed, laid out in dark animal bundles on her living room carpet. They had all been perched on the power lines when lightning struck. There had been a white, scorched fracturing of the sky, a concussion of all the perceivable world, and then nothing, just silence and the thin, fear-tipped smell of smoke. Outside, the finches and the mourning doves had all fallen from the wire, hurtling down onto the grass like large, living hailstones, breathless and blackened. Anna and her daughter, Mariela, had run out onto the lawn, their dresses flapping behind them like sails, to fill wicker baskets with the still-warm bodies, their wings limp and falling open like rags, frayed at the borders.

The two of them had already begun shrouding the birds in tiny embroidered handkerchiefs when the first gray dove revived. In the beginning, it was nothing more than a shivering throat, a fluttering, tufted breast; but later, it was a warbling, a flush and stuttering of wings, an uncertain ascent to the curtain rods and the casements. Anna de la Senda strapped Popsicle sticks to the broken nibs of their feet and the crooked-edged bones beneath their brilliant feathers. She placed them in high, dome-shaped, copper cages with seed and suet and purified water, and she waited for them to remember how to sing.

So the house became one of unlikely hope, of miraculous revival, and Mariela was as much a part of it as its leaf-filled windows and its myriad crucifixes. Her existence itself was proof of a higher intervention since Anna de la Senda, in her youth, had been diagnosed by three physicians as barren. Her ovaries were stunted, they had said. Her tubes had grown away from her uterus in two half-formed thoughts, unsure of what direction they ought to take. Anna had imagined them drifting in the water of her abdomen like stray bits of seaweed, half alive and listless, likely at any moment to detach from their floor and lose all meaning in the world. But Mariela had taken root in spite of this frailty, had anchored herself to Anna's being with no intention of letting go, the beauty of her willfulness manifesting itself even then—so much was she like her father.

At Mariela's birth, an iridescent, silver-slick caul had covered her head and one shoulder and arm. In the darkness of Anna's bedroom, the infant had glowed like a seraph, casting her own light. Anna took it as a sign that the child had received a second look from God while still in the womb. A sign that He Himself had been moved by this creation. Forever after that first glimpse, Anna had thought of her daughter as Mariela the Shining.

Now, in the summer of her eighteenth year, Mariela shone with the expectation of love. Anna did not yet know whom she anticipated being loved by. It could have been any one of a dozen men. But Anna knew it to be someone in the neighborhood, someone on Raborn Way most likely—a fact which Anna determined from the hypnotic, half-fevered way that Mariela had begun to stare out of the windows facing east, as though willing him to appear on the sidewalk outside. She summoned him relentlessly, with the concentration of a telepath. Come, she said silently. Can't you hear my voice calling you?

All spring long, Mariela had strayed to the borders of the Lovelorn Women, flitting past their meetings like a sudden specter, willow-thin and otherworldly, rising up the stairs to the safety of her bedroom with barely a backward glance. Perhaps she sensed for the first time that she was meant for something other than their sorrow. Perhaps their complaints became petty and distasteful in the light of new love. Whatever the case, her remoteness made her seem all the more beautiful to the women gathered in her mother's living room. Whenever they caught sight of her passing by, dreamlike and exotic, their teacups trembled on their lips; the skin on the backs of their necks prickled with alertness and benevolent envy. *I was once like her,* they said to themselves, knowing all the while that this wasn't quite true. Because whatever relationship they had once had to beauty, it had never been a connection so unaffected and pure as Mariela's. No, she was something different, an entirely unique species of girl, set apart from them by a multitude of blessings too abundant to count.

"Mariela never talks to us anymore," Dove Pairlee mourned out loud one day.

"It's not only you," Anna said. "She says very little to anybody."

"Has she fallen for somebody?" Maxine Ridgeway said. "Falling for somebody will make a girl silent. That's the way it did with Emily D. when she received that valentine from Mr. Secret Admirer. Don't you remember? She couldn't speak two words in a row for a year."

Emily D., who sat next to her mother, Maxine, crossed and uncrossed her legs, trying to remember what she had been told about being ladylike under pressure. She chewed the inside of her cheeks with a gentle nervousness, like a flustered rabbit.

"Love deserves silence," Anna said. "The young know this best. When we grow older, we forget."

Everyone turned toward Emily D., wondering for a moment if it was possible that she knew something about love that had escaped them. Her glance fell to the floor in her girlish embarrassment. Her glasses magnified her eyes into two swimming, self-conscious orbs, her eyelashes growing from the edges in moistened shocks. She looked as though she had tasted whole portions of regret when no one was looking, and seeing this now, the Cordojo Women leaned over to pat her knees and stroke her hair and lay their hands on the bare places of her arms. Growing up didn't come simply to anyone. When they thought about it, they could remember.

Through the picture window, Anna watched the tulip tree turn its leaves over in the wind. Two men walked underneath it, appearing in the peripheral vision of the Cordojo Women simultaneously, as if by their collective sight. The eyes of Dove Pairlee and Maxine Ridgeway and Emily D. and India Perry and Esther Lee all fastened upon their moving forms with a fixed intensity, comparing them to other men they had known, men they couldn't help but recall.

"It's that widower man with his son," Dove Pairlee said.

"I don't know why you call him *that widower man* when you know perfectly well what his name is," Maxine Ridgeway said.

"Because he wears his mourning like a coat," Anna said. "It hangs in the air around him."

"That's Dr. Ettinger," Esther Lee said. "I don't know what all the confusion is about."

"Dr. Clifford Ettinger," India Perry said. "He told me his first name the day he diagnosed my lumbago."

"You must have asked him," Dove Pairlee said.

"It's possible that I did," India Perry said.

Dove Pairlee gave a small snort of triumph, readjusting her bosom over her lap. "A man like that does not give out his first name unless asked."

"It's possible that I asked him, and then again, it's possible that I didn't," India Perry said. "I don't recall."

"A gentleman knows what's polite," Dove Pairlee said. "And anybody can know just by looking that that widower man is a gentleman. It tells in the way he shines his shoes."

It was true that Clifford Ettinger's shoes were as polished as a pair of waxed fruits, thick-skinned and reflective and ripe to the eye. He took pride in seeing to the details, even long after their meaningfulness, and the meaningfulness of many parts of his life had ceased to be apparent. His son, Addison, seemed to feel that this confusion was only temporary, that meaning and purpose had lost their rightful places only since Marjorie Ettinger's death, and that, given enough time, the cheerful physics of life would reappear.

Clifford had named this, in the privacy of his thoughts, Addison's paperweight theory. He had an idea that his son conceived of grief in terms of a clear plastic bubble over a miniature winter scene. Calamity caused the bubble to be shaken and brought fragments of a snowy chaos to the ceiling of the world. Order became obscured; sense disappeared behind a swirling, seamless storm. But eventually, the snow would drift to the bottom of the world again, and the landscape as it had been would emerge unchanged.

Addison conceived of everything too simply, Clifford thought. It was one of the qualities that had allowed him to become a writer. Who else could distill the complex universe into a few neatly balanced pages of prose? In the world of art, tragedy was always foreshadowed, and loose ends always woven together. In the world that Clifford Ettinger had witnessed, sadness was seldom so contained.

While Clifford walked under the dreamy arms of Anna de la Senda's trees, he felt their abundant leaves kissing the top of his hair. For all I know, Addison could be right, he told himself. Perhaps I am living in a small, domed world, feeling the snow pile up on top of my head. He did not glance to the left and so he did not see the six women considering him on the other side of the picture window, now dappled with fading sun and shade as the afternoon stretched toward the darker hours. And neither did he see his son, Addison, as he waved to a girl who leaned out of a pair of shutters upstairs, olive-skinned and exuberant and with a look of saintly ecstasy on her face. "At last," she seemed to be saying. "At last, at last, at last."

———

"HE'S GOING to be in search of another wife," Dove Pairlee said. She brought one hand up to the back of her teased cascade of ash-blond hair and plucked at the curls there, straightening and releasing their studied, frothy coils one at a time.

"It's too soon," Anna said. "The first one died only a year ago, and other women are still nothing more than shadows."

"But afterwards," Dove Pairlee said. "After he's gotten over it, then I imagine he's going to be in want of somebody else, don't you?"

Dove and India and Esther Lee and Maxine and Emily D. all waited for Anna's answer. Her knowledge about matters of the heart was unsurpassed, and several of the women felt, and Dove especially, that Anna might not only predict whether Clifford Ettinger would marry again, but that she might also intuit the identity of his future wife. And who was to say that it might not turn out to be one of the Cordojo Women, waiting for just such a miracle to transform her life?

"I'm not certain that he will ever get over it," Anna said.

"Why do you say that?" India said.

"He has the walk of the condemned. You saw it yourself," Anna said. "His destination holds no consequence for him now."

"Now, Anna, I can't agree," Esther Lee said. With two fingers, gingerly, she pressed her hearing aid farther into her ear. It disappeared prettily, like a piece of pink taffy. "Only God can see who walks like the damned."

The Cordojo Women sighed and cleared their throats and smiled at one another. Whose turn was it to correct Esther, they seemed to be asking. But then Anna, as she often did, made the awkwardness disappear.

"Yes, Esther," she said. "Of course, you're right. We can't judge with the eyes of God." Anna stood and, folding the tea cozy over the empty copper pot, carried it out of the room as though it were a large, embroidered purse, inconvenient but beloved.

"Anna is such an angel," India Perry said as soon as Anna had left them alone.

"She's always willing to admit a mistake," Esther agreed.

"Yes, and she hardly ever makes one," Maxine Ridgeway said.

"She helps everybody else with their problems and she never mentions her own," Emily D. said.

The Lovelorn Women could hear Anna in the kitchen, filling up the copper kettle to make a fresh pot of tea. Anna and her birds sang back and forth to each other in short, punctuated twitters of music that collected at the ceilings with the echoes of a gentle, animal laughter. Through the side window, the kumquat tree unfurled its fingers in green hopefulness, as if the birds were beckoning in a language it knew.

"When Clifford Ettinger gets done with his first wife's passing, he's going to make some woman quite a find," Dove Pairlee said.

"Well, you just got over Orie Rush," Maxine said. "And before that it was that taxidermist. What was his name?"

"Haydon Moffet," Dove said. She spoke the words with her lips curled over, as though they had brought a certain unpleasant memory into her mouth.

"I'd say you've been busy," Maxine said. "I think it's about time you gave yourself a rest."

"I think so too," India Perry said. "Give some other one of us a chance."

"We've all been without a man longer than you!" Esther Lee shouted.

"All right, let's be fair about it," Maxine said. "Which one of us has been without a man the longest?"

The Cordojo Women rolled their eyes around in their heads and thought. How difficult it was to put a measure on their yearning. The names of seasons and whole untouched years hesitated on their lips, waiting to be confessed.

"It has been the entire spring for me," Dove Pairlee said, finally.

"Six years on my part," Esther Lee said.

"Six and a quarter," India Perry said.

"I'm too young to put in," Emily D. said.

"Then I'm the grand prize winner," Maxine Ridgeway said. "Love has cheated me the longest, and Clifford Ettinger is my reward." The lines on Maxine's face strained upward toward optimism, hovering in the vicinity of that perspective for several tremulous moments. Her hand rested on her throat like a great, pale moth, portentous and alive.

"How long has it been?" Esther Lee said.

"Seven years," Maxine said. "Seven years with no man even holding my hand!"

A murmur of appreciation passed back and forth between the women in the circle. That's right, they said under their breaths. It had been seven years since Maxine had divorced her husband. Imagine the unending loneliness. Imagine the number of days and nights.

"But there *is* someone here who has been alone for longer than seven years," a small voice uttered.

Although Maxine sat directly next to the speaker, she did not seem to have heard. Instead, it was the other women who turned toward Emily D., asking her to speak up, to repeat her words, to explain just what she meant.

"I'm sorry, Mother," Emily D. said to Maxine, "but Mariela

told me last month that Anna hasn't had a date with a man since Cristobal.''

India Perry raised the white pearl netting on her hat, as though she were trying to see beyond it into the whole of Anna's past. "I remember Cristobal," she said. "He left just before the earthquake took the roof off the old Methodist church." She sucked her lips inside her mouth, concentrating. "He looked just like Clark Gable, except naturally that he was much darker complected. Which is where Mariela gets it from. That was twelve years ago."

Maxine's face lapsed back into its habitual expression, saddened by the forces of a perpetual gravity. She could hardly even muster annoyance over the fact that it had been her own daughter who had spoiled her chances. Emily D., in Maxine's view, had always been fatally honest, had always believed that only good could come of the truth.

"Well, I'll give Clifford over to Anna, then," Maxine said. "I won't make a fuss."

"We'll do something for Anna for a change," Dove said. She clapped her hands together in her childish excitement.

"She'll never go along with it if we tell her," India said. "She told me herself that there could never be another man like Cristobal."

"No, no, we'll keep it a secret," Dove said. Then, looking around her with a face of unmasked doubt, she said, "Can all of you keep it a secret?"

"Of course!" Maxine protested.

"I know I can," India Perry said.

"None of us will tell her," Emily D. said.

At that moment, Anna de la Senda appeared in the doorway of the living room. Her face shone with a layer of steam, as though she had just then stepped out of the bath. In one hand was the tea-cozy purse, newly hot and bulging and ready to be shared.

"Tell me what?" Anna said.

"Tell her what?" Esther Lee said, being delighted, as she always was, that someone else had asked first.

THIS IS what the note said:

> *Dear Dr. Ettinger,*
>   *Since we have been neighbors for the last nineteen years, would you help me prune my tulip trees? And the kumquats, too? They are growing through half the windows of my house, and I am being overtaken. There is only my daughter and myself here, and we are quite unable to climb to the higher branches. Please intervene at your earliest opportunity.*
>
> *Yours expectantly,*
>
> *Anna de la Senda*
> *238 Raborn*

India had written these words on a piece of ecru, half-transparent rice paper, with the edges unfinished and elegant. Maxine had dictated them to her over the phone, speaking with the careful slowness she might have used with a child. Maxine thought it crucial that India transcribe the letter exactly as it had been composed. The tone was both vulnerable and insistent, she thought, and it was not the kind of appeal that could be ignored. India wrapped the note like a scroll around the handle of a basket of fresh figs, and then secured the paper with a slim red satin ribbon. She had only to walk two and a half blocks to get from her home to Clifford Ettinger's front doorway, passing Anna's along the route. The errand gave her a surreptitious thrill, seeing as she felt gratitude toward her friend beyond all measure. She once would have given up life altogether had it not been for Anna, who began her ministry of tending to the needy just as India discovered what the nature of need was.

India had led an unexamined life until the age of forty-three, when, examining it for the first time in the soulful, breathless glare of day, she nearly abandoned it for the here-after. That was the year that India's only child, Ethan, had moved away with his wife and son to Texas, the year he had told her to stop telephoning him once a week, he was getting along fine without her coddling him the way she liked to do, the year she tried to tell him, but could not, that she had just had a hysterectomy and wasn't sure she could survive the hollowness it left, that she was mostly calling because she needed to hear the sound of his breath, to make sure that he, her child, was still living, still whole.

Anna had been the only person on the face of the green globe who knew what was the matter with India. And knowing it, she had done something about it. Anna had put a name on India's malady: The Desperation of the Bearer, she had called it. For it she had prescribed a membership in the Cordojo club, a commitment which meant hot tea on some days and plump cinnamon claws on others, which meant the celebration of birthdays and the praising of minor triumphs, which meant wild laughter and admitted grief, and which always, always meant healing whispers for the aching heart. In addition to their Sunday meetings, Anna had walked to India's home at ten p.m. every night for a year. There, the two of them lit a candle in front of a pearly blue ceramic statuette of the Holy Virgin, a gift that Anna had made to India impulsively one day, before she understood why the pale blue figure reminded her so compellingly, each time she looked at it, of her too-frail, doe-eyed neighbor with the exotic name. They knelt in front of the sainted Mother, hands pressed together like children in the dark, and they prayed to her that she might take away the emptiness that India carried with her, that she might turn India's son, Ethan, into a man who could someday give back what he had received, that she might show her compassion over the disappearance of the womb and its labors and bestow on India an understanding of what had happened to her. After they stood up off the carpet and straightened their skirts, India always used to say something like,

"Do you really think she might have heard, Anna? Because

you know I'm not Catholic, and I can really imagine that that might disqualify me altogether."

"No, no," Anna would say. "The Mother doesn't like to meddle with the inconsequentials. She hears everyone who speaks to her from a sainted heart."

Gradually, with their daily, fervent supplications to the miraculous world of redemption, India recovered the will she had lost. She began to feel a mending taking place in those mysterious regions of her abdomen where, for so long, she had only felt the sear of phantom pain. The hills and awkward hollows of her stomach grew muted, less pronounced, evened out by the erosion and slides that were the weather within her. And her son, having received an anonymous letter from someone in her own neighborhood, Marbury Park, began to call her once a month to ask her was her health maintaining and was there anything he could send. India, in the first flush of her high spirits, took up embroidery, then rug-hooking, then hat-making. Her doe eyes grew wider in her delight at the possibilities contained within the simple condition of life. What had happened to her had been a divine intervention, she liked to say. Nothing less. And Anna had been the agent of it all.

Now, she left the fruit basket on the doctor's flagstone steps, the figs plump and sticky-skinned in the morning heat. While she hurried away, she felt a vague and gleeful guilt in the notches of her spine. What if one of the neighbors had seen her? But no, she reassured herself. She had worn one of her popular green-grape hats with all the clusters dangling off the rim. Last year, she had sold seventy-one of those very hats to Marbury Park women alone. Now, no disguise could be more anonymous.

———————

CLIFFORD ETTINGER stepped out of his front door at nine o'clock on his way to water his dead wife's roses. Up until six months ago, he had known nothing about tending roses, had never had any ambition to learn. But now, he prayed to God that he could keep them alive. He swore out loud at the snails that turned their leaves into a green skeletal lace, casting the impression of loss beside the stark, tongued, wild-colored blooms that had seemed to rise out of nothing but his wife's vigilance. Compared to the care she had given them, his efforts were stunted and fearful. He was driven to prune and fertilize, to water and mulch, out of a sheer terror at the prospect of witnessing another death, of standing idly by in the face of the withering, the caving-in. So that when the roses bloomed outward in their colors of saffron and tangerine, salmon and Christmas red, what he mostly felt was a sense of grateful relief. Marjorie would have felt that he had done her justice in preserving what she had made. And he wanted more than anything else now to do Marjorie justice—now that he had failed in preventing her departure from him, now that he had not been able to keep her from all harm.

Each morning during that whole month of June, Clifford had cut the most beautiful rose in the garden—a task that Marjorie had always cherished—in order to float it in a crystal bowl on the dining room table. That day, a flower on the Handel bush had caught his eye—pink-tipped and lavish, unwound like a maze from its center. He cupped the bloom in both hands like a great and fragile nest, the stem trailing down between his palms. But on the steps, he tripped and fell, cracking his knee against a long flagstone in an effort not to crush the rose. It wasn't until he came to rest, sprawled on his stony stairs, that he first understood the cause of his fall. There, on the lawn, was the overturned basket, the figs scattered around it like small, plump moles, motionless and blind and almost concealed by the bright strands of grass. And rolling down the walkway on the breath of a minor wind was a curled sheet of paper, skittering like a strange albino leaf along the steps he had just taken.

———◦•◦———

MARIELA THE Shining wore a white like the template of her soul. In the early morning, she floated through the hallways of her mother's house as though her feet were no longer necessary to her, as though they were the bare, elongated weights that God had designed for her in order that she should not fly away from the earth and into the plenitude of heaven before it was His will. Her nightgown, one that Anna had given her on her eighteenth birthday, was overlarge, and it gathered in great bunches and pleats underneath the silk sash and again behind her, on the floor, where it moved forward like a bridal train, waiting for a maid to pick it up by its glimmering edge.

Something had awoken the birds, and they shrieked in the darkness of their cloth-covered cages, knowing the day had begun without them. In Anna's room, Mariela walked through the air thick with magic and dreams in order to wake her mother. Anna slept with her auburn hair fanned over the pillow in a youthful, luxurious nest. Her mouth was flung open with wonder, and in the outer corners of her closed and trembling eyelids nestled her habitual tears—tears shed for the sorrows of others, Mariela had always thought.

"Mother," Mariela whispered in the air above Anna's head. She touched her mother's open hand, the fingers half-cupped as though waiting for something to hold, and Anna came awake immediately. Her eyes were wet, but focused, and as she sat up in bed, her hair fell into an attractive, haphazard shape behind her head.

"What is it?" Anna said.

"I don't know," Mariela said. "A noise woke me. The birds heard it, too."

"Was it a dream?"

"No," Mariela said.

"All right, then," Anna said. She brought her pale, freckled feet out from under the covers. They were the toes of an Irishwoman, so pale, so different from her daughter's. Anna did a quick dance under her housecoat and emerged from it wearing her plush, green-velvet robe like a pleasant, wrinkled, second skin. She trundled from room to room, not expecting to find anything but shadows and pretend goblins and the evidence of wind. For eighteen years she had done this, whenever Mariela had been frightened in the night. And Mariela had always been able to go back to sleep afterwards, after she felt assured that the intruder had been run off.

But Anna sensed that there was something different about that particular morning. The clock showed that it was only seven a.m., and yet the birds had turned raucous and craven. They battered their wings against their bars, and through the still, coal-blue light of the hour, their cages swung like lanterns held by a wild hand. And when Anna stopped to listen, she *did* hear something unusual. There was a curious whizzing and clack coming from somewhere above her, like the sound of two people wrestling on her roof.

When she entered the third bedroom, she saw the arms of the tulip tree thrashing against the window jamb. Behind them, there was a clipper and a handsaw and a man who stood wielding them from the topmost step of a twenty-foot ladder. He worked casually, as if he were balanced above his own property, surveying what he intended to be his manicured view.

"Stop!" Anna called. She forced her head past the indoor branches so that she could charge the man directly with his crime. He turned a stern, somewhat superior expression toward her. Although his ladder placed him at a point one or two feet above Anna, their faces hovered quite close.

"You should never approach someone working at a height in the manner you just did," he said. He turned away imperiously and began working again with his clippers, pruning off several short, flowering shoots and sending them spiraling downward.

"Stop what you are doing," Anna said, trying again.

"I realize you may object to the hour of the morning," the man said. "But I have people to look after, so it's either now or not at all."

"Get down from there," Anna said. It was something in the tone of her voice, some deep emerging threat, that made him turn. She had snatched two falling twigs out of the air and was now brandishing them in his direction like hapless, leafy swords, like startling vegetable extensions of her green-velveted arms.

"Hold on now," the man said, but just as he was saying it, Anna leaned forward and poked the bib of his overalls. The man seemed to hold his breath, because he kept completely silent for a moment while his neck flooded a dull, burnished red, and after that, the flesh of his cheeks and the outer, shellfish-curls of his ears turned dark also.

"I thought I was doing you a favor," he said finally.

"Well, you are presumptuous and mistaken," Anna said. "Now get down out of my tree before you fall that way or get pushed." She tried to lean forward again to brandish her twigs, but Mariela, afraid that her mother might fall from the window, had sunk her hands into her mother's green velvet skirts and was tugging them toward her, back into the safety of the room.

The man waved his clippers toward her in blatant self-defense. He began backing down the aluminum steps with a harried unsteadiness. His descent shook the upper branches of the tree, and six or seven buds jarred loose from their bunches and struck him like an alarming, material rain.

"This is what I get for coming to help you," he called up to her, bitterly now, his eyes gone small in his head.

"You're trespassing," Anna called back. "Remember that the next time you consider that this kind of vandalism could be a help to anybody!"

Anna kept her head out the window until she watched the man round the corner of the house, his clanking aluminum ladder dragging behind him like a prehistoric tail. Then she allowed Mariela to pull her back inside, her hair filled with crescent leaves and loose petals, her green ruffled sateen collar gaping open at the bosom to reveal her pink girlish nightgown underneath.

"Who was he?" Mariela said.

"A madman," Anna said, plucking the refuse from her hair.

"But who was he really?" Mariela said.

22

"Our neighbor, which is small comfort," Anna said. "Dr. Clifford Ettinger of the grand delusions."

———•◦•———

WHEN ANNA told the Cordojo Women what had happened to her, their faces turned glum and flaccid, as though someone had stuck a pin in each woman and then partially deflated her, right there in front of Anna's eyes.

"Did you really call him a vandal?" India Perry said. Her eyes were half-shut when she spoke, and Anna thought that for the first time India was showing the incurable tiredness of age.

"Yes, I did," Anna said. "And I don't know that I oughtn't to have called him worse. He was killing my trees, just killing them! He was shearing the limbs off them even while I told him not to do it!"

"Now Anna, I'm sure he didn't set out to kill your trees," Maxine Ridgeway said. "He probably thought he was being neighborly."

"Yes," Dove Pairlee said. "I've always thought that it's nice when a man goes out of his way."

"Neighbors prune one another's trees all the time," Maxine said.

Anna let go of a harassed, disappointed breath. "I think you've all lost your minds," she said. "And I would like to remind you, on the chance you've forgotten, that eligibility on the part of a man does not guarantee his sanity."

"Really, Anna, I don't think it's dignified to call a poor widower man insane just because he tried to trim your trees," Dove Pairlee said. Satisfied with her assertion, she raised another forkful of cherry-chocolate jubilee to her mouth, taking care not to drip any on her splendid new lilies-of-the-valley silk.

"Honestly, Dove, I sometimes believe you would date Genghis Khan himself if he were alive and a single man," Anna said. She could feel her downy hairs bristling on the curl of her neck, as though the soul of her anger had escaped her and was now flying around the room, creating a small wind.

Dove pointed her fork toward Anna in consternation. Her cheeks were still rounded with the last of a wedge of chocolate cake, and although she began to chew with desperate intensity, she could not seem to swallow. The Lovelorn Women watched for a few moments as she continued to struggle in silence. Then, Emily D. leaned forward, her bangs falling over her eyes with an awkwardness that was impossibly young, her shyness showing itself in the patches of red and white that clearly colored her throat.

"I think we've all left the track from where we started," she said, half-whispering, her words coming out with a strange childlike wisdom. "Because Genghis Khan is not alive and Clifford Ettinger is not Genghis Khan."

THE LORD Tennyson Home for Persons Retired and Dignified celebrated its annual Children's Day in style. It was the one day out of the year on which Clifford Ettinger could reasonably consider himself a child. He was fifty-two years old, his knees ached in rainy weather, and a bald spot the size of a silver dollar gleamed pink and planetary on the crown of his head. But on that day, with the float of pastel balloons in the air, with the spoon races and the ring toss and the ridiculous pink bouffants of cotton candy, with all these things, and with the resilient, bemused expression that lived somewhere in the heart of his mother's face whenever she turned to look on him, Clifford remembered what it was to be someone's child. And he found the memory strange and comforting.

Addison had come to spend the day, too, and he and Clifford walked behind Earline Ettinger's wheelchair across the home's languorous, extravagant lawn which rolled down from the mansion itself in a still, green, retreating sea. Where the grounds leveled out into even plains of color, silent flocks of white-headed men and women stood around polished chess boards, anticipating the sequence of moves with the subtle, seasoned concentration of a group of diplomats.

"Why aren't you playing in the tournament, Mother?" Clifford said.

"I like real competition," Earline said. "The men can't stand it."

"Because you give them a run for their money?" Addison said.

"Because I beat them, if you want to know," she said. "I'm too smart to lose honestly, and I'm too brazen to lose any other way."

"A man who can't take being beaten is no man," Addison said.

"Addison, come around here and look me in the eyes," Earline said. Clifford stopped pushing the wheelchair, and Addison loped around the side. His hair had been combed into a careful ducktail at the back of his head, but when he turned around, his expression was uncomposed, all the uncertainty collecting at the edges of his tentative mouth.

"Huh," Earline said, her eyes gone narrow in revelation. "You're younger than I thought."

"That's all right, Grandmother," Addison said. "If I were any older, I'd distress you more."

"Yes, you would," Earline said. She waved him off then, as if by flourishing her hands in the air in front of his form, Addison would, like a magician's assistant, obediently disappear. And in fact he walked away without complaint, smiling over his shoulder at her natural audacity, liking her even as she dismissed him. He moved off toward the east lawn where a raffle was being held and a solid throng of expectant people clasped their fresh yellow tickets like so many nuggets of possible gold. Before he disappeared into the crowd, he shot his hand up into the air, as if greeting someone on the other side. But Clifford and Earline suspected that this signal was really intended for them, the good-bye of the young, said while turned away and at a distance, where the ties between people were almost, but not entirely, invisible.

———•◦•———

"THE WHEELCHAIR race starts in fifteen minutes," Earline said. "We'd better get over there to register."

"Mother, I don't want to run in any race this year," Clifford said. "I told you that before I came."

"Well, why in the world not?"

"I'm not in any kind of shape to do it," he said. "I'm middle-aged, for God's sake."

"Don't expect me to feel sorry for you," Earline said. "I've *been* middle-aged, remember. I've been there and gone."

"Mother, I'm not going to do this unless you insist."

"I insist," she said.

"Why?"

"I've wagered two hundred dollars that we're going to win; that's why. And I never was one to throw away a good bet."

"No, you never were," Clifford said.

"Not in all my life."

Clifford and Earline were assigned the number seventeen, which they wore emblazoned on two great orange fluorescent bibs. Earline plucked at the sleeves of Clifford's polo shirt until he rolled them up, ridiculously, to simulate a racing jersey. She whispered to him about the course, as if to speak in normal tones would be to give away their tactical advantage. She threw particularly fierce looks to a lilac-haired, lipless woman in the wheelchair to her right, who appeared to be listing to the side in an attempt to overhear.

"The key is not to run behind me all the way to the bottom of the hill," Earline was saying. "When the chair starts going fast enough, you just come around front and ride."

"Don't you think that's a little reckless, Mother? Who is going to steer?" Clifford said.

"On the way back up the incline, there are no tricks," she said. "Whoever has got the most brawn will be gaining, so you've got to gather your lead in the beginning." Earline paused for a moment, staring critically at Clifford's biceps, her eyes traveling their pale circumference. She seemed about to comment, but just as she opened her mouth, all the tension there withered away and an unexpected, embarrassed, soulful smile took its place. She had caught the eye of someone in the crowd, and Clifford, following her gaze, found at the other end of it a round-shouldered old man in a seersucker suit. His eyelids were winking and popping with insinuating delight and his lips were mouthing a series of words that Clifford could not make out, but which he strongly suspected would have ignited something in him akin to rage. Earline took the attention all in her stride, waving a few girlish fingers in the man's direction, and nodding her head as if to say she understood just what he meant.

———————

ADDISON WAVED to Mariela de la Senda, but she, floating on the far side of the raffle players, her hair falling over her face in a wash of violet-black, was turned away from him and did not see. She hovered at the edge of her mother's booth, a four-cornered stand of plywood with the words *Counseling and Friendship* traveling across a cloth banner at the top. Anna sat across from Opal Pairlee, the conspicuously robust mother of Dove, and held her pink, mournful hand in one of her own.

"I just don't think it's right that she should blame me for her putting on the weight," Opal was saying.

"She's upset, that's what," Anna said, and with her free hand she stroked Opal's wrist, stroked it with a sleepy, motherly carelessness, as though it were the neck of some stray creature, laid bare with its loneliness.

"Now, don't try to soften it," Opal said. "I know blame when I hear it, and it was blame she heaped onto me, like coals upon my head. She said how could I teach my children self-control when the very notion of it had escaped me from my first born days. She said . . ." and Opal would have continued but for the new distraction in Anna's eyes, flooding them a different color. Anna's thoughts had drifted into another sphere, and Opal was again alone with her guilt, voluptuous and stifling in the air of June.

What had stolen Anna's concentration was the sudden, piercing conviction that Mariela had just wandered away from the booth in the company of a man, someone with a long-limbed, fervent stride and pale, carefully cut clothes, someone familiar. Anna could just now reconfigure his shape, blurry and imposing in the periphery of her sight, as he had walked away with her daughter. She felt, fluttering under her ribs, the wings of a mother's fear.

Across the lawn, a collective shout went up from a crowd, sailing above their heads in a long sound of exhilaration and intent. A passerby took hold of Opal's free hand. "It's the wheelchair race!" she said. "We're not too late to catch it."

Opal rocked herself up out of her seat, her shimmering, plump, jade silk dress showing creases on the back that branched out indelibly, like a tree rooting downward. Her breath became audible with the exertion of standing; it came out blustery and fundamental, like the sound of a private storm. "Why don't we go over to the race, Anna?" she said. "Along the way, you can tell me what I ought to do about Dove."

———•◦•———

CLIFFORD ETTINGER was not sure what it was about the race that, once begun, made him want to win. Some animal desperation climbed into his throat and lodged itself there, refusing to be swallowed. The tips of his fingers tingled and turned white, blanching in equal parts of determination and fear. While he ran behind the pale form of Earline, erect and bobbing in her chair, it seemed to him that he would not be able to stand it if a single runner passed him. It seemed to him that the solid lump of desperation in his throat would grow too large for him to continue breathing, and that he would fall over dead on the spot, expired from sheer incapacity.

Earline's hairpins fell out along the ride, and her familiar French bun collapsed, leaving her hair to fly backward from her shoulders in thin, stark-white shocks, mussed and strangely young. What a dear exasperating head she had, filled with ideas about the world as it should be, the world as it was not. She might have been a queen, presuming as she did that everyone awaited her pronouncements for living. And it was true that she had passed her flair for the judgmental along to Clifford, as he would very occasionally, in moments of profound duress, admit. He even recalled this to himself in a vague, unarticulated way as he pushed her chair uphill on the day of the race, with his legs turning to numb, rubbery sticks underneath him, and his breath filling all the air around him with its continuous, needful noise. In a way, he thought, he was rushing around behind the specter of his own infirmity, there in the wheelchair; he was racing behind the form of his own old age, determined and fragile, disheveled and intractable. Earline was he, with another twenty-five years gone past him, years which would be filled with only God knew what, because Clifford could only imagine them as a lengthy void, an uncertain punishment, an existence without Marjorie in it. And it was this thought that made him run faster than he ought to have been able to run, as though he were wheeling the prospect of his grief into oblivion, sending away what preyed on him with his wild burst of effort, unrestrained, flying, half-insane.

Clifford did not realize it when he reached the finish line. He ran right past it and kept on running. A ribbon of innocent, sky-blue crepe paper flowed across his mother's shoulders for a time, draped like the sash of a beauty queen, and then drifted away. And then small groups of people clotted the path in front of him, turning toward him as he approached, and slowed down, and adopted a stiff, lightly injured walk. A crowd of the elderly engulfed him, chortling their congratulations, putting delicate hands on his back, like the brush of individual leaves, barely felt before they dropped away. Faces bloomed toward him and then passed, vulnerable in their age, wrinkled in their pleasure. He recognized no one except a single, unmistakable woman, much younger than the rest, her generous hair spilling away from her face in an auburn, upturned splash, her expression fixed securely on him with a half-smile of curiosity. It took him a moment to grasp where he had seen her before: leaning toward him through the upper arms of a tulip tree, poking at him with a snapped-off branch. When Clifford turned to look on her again, he saw that she had entered a stream of pastel-haired ladies that, with delicate, inalterable insistence, carried her away.

———•◦•———

MARIELA HAD tried to discern what love was made of, but love was not easily decipherable. It was a quickened heart, a trembling mouth, a breath, a quake, a dream. It was physical and metaphysical, territorial and saintly. It was sacrificing and jealous, maudlin and profound, well-anticipated and entirely unpredictable, and she found it in all its various guises at the end of a long loneliness that she had thought would last her lifetime.

She and Addison Ettinger melted ice cubes in their mouths in a tent that was reserved for the sale of homemade chocolates. The proprietor, a resident of the Tennyson Home, had stepped out, and no one in the neighboring tents knew when she would be back. Addison quickly discovered that underneath the sheets of semisweet scallop shells and stars and miniature treasure chests were trays of ice, placed there to prevent the chocolate from melting. The two of them plucked out the cool, transparent cubes from their houses, as astonishing as colorless diamonds, and sucked them quietly for a while. Their mouths contorted into oddly sensuous shapes, with their lips protruding into a wish for kisses. Clear, glassy beads of perspiration streaked across Addison's temples and passed over the narrow nape of Mariela's neck, as though some internal part of each of them had begun to cry and the sweating simply marked the extrusion of the tears.

"Come out with me on Saturday," Addison said.

Mariela shook her head no. She stared at the chocolate stars laid out on the tin tray. In the late-day heat, they began to melt into small sienna pools, edgeless, shapeless mounds of sweetness, their attractive purpose lost.

"Why not?" Addison said.

"Mother doesn't know about you yet," Mariela said. "I was

going to say something last week, and then your father tried to cut back our trees, so . . ."

"He what?"

"He decided our trees needed cutting back. I don't know why," Mariela said. "But my mother almost fell out a second-story window arguing with him about it. So I thought I would wait a while before saying anything."

"All right," Addison said. He uncurled his long, tapered index finger and, with it, traced the shape of Mariela's face. Above her high forehead, a widow's peak dipped in a startling, black point, so that when Addison traced her hairline, he seemed to be outlining a giant heart. "And when you tell her about me, what are you going to say?"

"I'm going to say, 'Mother, I have found out about love.'"

"And she'll know what you mean?" Addison said. He pulled a fresh ice cube from its slot and began tracing Mariela's face again, leaving a narrow path of ice water behind his motion.

"She'll know," Mariela said.

Addison nodded his head. The ice had melted into a minute invisible shard, and it slid from his fingertips into the palm of his hand, where it instantly liquefied. He was taller than Mariela by seven inches, and so it was always a willful struggle to reach her mouth. He bent his knees, his back, his neck in unison and separately, in forced calm and then resounding frustration, all in search of a simple kiss. When he straightened, he usually found that he had lifted her off the ground, her feet newly dangling, her laughter bright in his ears, her eyes closed against the spectacle of it. Mariela had a truer sense of decorum than he did, but she would allow herself to be led out of it by someone she trusted implicitly enough. And Addison, for some reason blessed and unknown to him, was someone she trusted from the beginning.

They had grown up in adjacent homes, but as neighborhood children, they had been anonymous to one another. The

Ettingers' estate, which really *was* an estate, possessed long, rolling, flawless lawns spread like a great dirndl skirt around the body of a three-story Victorian manor. It stood on the extreme edge of Saxon Hill proper, a district in which all the houses were more than plain houses, and all the grounds were more than plain grounds. Addison had not been born to the Ettingers and to Saxon Hill proper; he had been adopted into them as a baby. But he grew under their protection with a natural, irrepressible exuberance, never giving pause to the question of what it was to belong, because when it came to belonging, Addison simply did.

The de la Sendas' house, however, was simply a house; their lawn was simply a lawn. Their shutters needed painting, and their dandelions needed rooting out, and their tulip trees grew through open windows. They lived just at the border of the Saxon Hill South district, in which the community was resolutely, indisputably located in the middle class. And, for some reason which Addison and Mariela could not now remember, for some reason which perhaps they had never known, the children had never played outside of their own district, had never even carelessly wandered over the invisible boundaries of money that had been drawn around them.

When Addison and Mariela dreamed of the years they had lost, however, they were mostly mistaken. Five years separated their ages, and until very recently, Addison would have looked at Mariela only to conclude that she was hopelessly mired in her childhood. No one knew what precisely was the moment when Mariela had torn away from her adolescence to become a haunting, otherworldly being who ate dreams for sustenance and flew from one place to another on invisible wings. But Addison was certain that that reckoning had come and gone, that the existence Mariela had shed was now a wizened, desiccated chrysalis hanging by an insect's thread, that the woman she had become left a mysterious brightness in the world, a silver, saintly shining which he saw even when his eyes were closed.

Under the chocolatier's tent, Mariela stiffened suddenly. Somewhere, above the burble and hum of the flowing crowd, her mother's voice had found her. Mariela could hear it through the loose walls of blue canvas, approaching her even as she concentrated on its sound.

"Sometimes, a daughter needs to blame her mother," Anna's voice was saying. "Sometimes, it is the only way she knows to unburden herself."

"Well, that may be so," a woman answered. Mariela recognized Opal Pairlee's voice. "But this isn't the first time Dove has claimed that the worst part of her life is entirely my fault."

"Not the first time nor the last," Anna said. "But Dove isn't intentionally cruel. She's depressed. There's a difference."

The voices came to rest just outside the door of the tent. Mariela waited for them to pass by, but they did not. "It's my mother," she whispered into Addison's ear, wondering when the words would take effect.

"There?" Addison said, pointing at the entry.

"Yes," Mariela nodded.

The two of them disengaged, their arms hanging uselessly at their sides for several moments before they took up the task of rearranging the disarray they had made of one another. Mariela's hair tangled downward in a passionate, black-fisted nest; and her lips were swollen from being kissed, their edges turned pink and ragged in the daylight, as though the seams of her containment had been torn, and she could no longer fit inside the modest shape of her former self. Addison's shirt had come untucked, and he could not seem to tuck it back in. The tails wagged loose at his waistband, mocking and creased. Mariela used the hem of her skirt to dry his face, from which poured the waters of longing and frustration. And she had not quite finished mopping them away when Opal Pairlee, lumberous and addled, walked into the concessionaire's tent and began promptly to scream.

"My chocolates! My chocolates!" she called out. She lifted the tins filled with the rows of stars and shells and treasure chests which had all melted into indiscriminate lumps of sweetness, dark and artless where they lay. Anna de la Senda appeared soon after, her mouth fallen open in expectation and alarm, her hands raised above her head as though to catch the plummeting sky. When Anna first saw Mariela and Addison, disheveled and disheartened, their desire marked on their faces like a fresh insanity, it was hard to say what happened to her. Perhaps she faded a little, her face turning to ash in her visible, leaking disappointment. Or perhaps she simply melted, as if she too were a confection in the heat, the details of her arms being lost as they were lowered, the shape of her astonished mouth blurring into some other form, indecipherable, fleeting, smoothed away into a pool of sadness that was luminous and new.

————•◦•————

ANNA DE LA SENDA did not exactly disapprove of Addison. She feared him. She feared what his presence implied about her daughter's womanhood, her unconcealed beauty in the sight of men, her unexpected readiness for the terrors and tremors of love. How comfortable it had been to know Mariela as the shining child, wondrous, vestigial, obedient, chosen. But the world never allowed anything to stay the same, not even the best things, not even the innocent. And Anna knew that she could not wish to prevent her daughter's awakening to a sensual life. She had merely wished to delay it, indefinitely, perhaps until the time of her own death. A blind notion, ignorant of everything she had learned life to be: impatient, desirous, hungry for itself. So, seeing Mariela under Opal's chocolatier tent that day, Anna saw what she had seen before. The knotted hair, the swollen lips, the cheeks stippled with hot embarrassment— Anna had observed all these things in her own mirror many years ago, after nights with Cristobal, when touch became a complex language and words became unnecessary. How could she deny her daughter what she herself could not resist?

No, Anna did what Cristobal had taught her to do in times of crisis. She prayed to St. Catherine of Alexandria for blessings in love and she waited for a sign to appear to her. On the fifth day of her prayer, a pot of vermicelli noodles burned on the stove, and when she tried to scrub the pan clean, she noticed that a word had appeared in the sinuous, charred patterns at the aluminum base. *Sorrow*, the noodle script said, and Anna felt that she had her answer. Her prayer for blessings had been refused, and Mariela and Addison would suffer before they could be joined in the eyes of God. Mariela, who knew that her mother prayed to the saints on her behalf, asked daily whether Anna had had a sign from them. But Anna always said, "Not yet, darling," even after the message had come to her in the vermicelli, singed and indelible. A girl such as Mariela, whose faith was her sustenance and whose feet grew angel's wings at night, could not withstand the rebuke, could not bear the anticipation of her downfall. Better to let her have her hope, Anna thought. Perhaps the noodles had made a mistake.

Addison began coming to the house every day, tentatively at first, his hands jammed awkwardly against the inner seams of his pockets, his fingers so long that they could never be completely concealed. They were always crawling out of things, like small animals, cramped and half-blind as they emerged from their hiding places. Later, as Addison learned the ways of the house and the people inside it, he made less of an effort to control his hands. They roamed freely through the air while he spoke, gesturing, white-boned, talkative birds, not unlike the tapered finches that perched in copper cages at the rafters. Their wings were always fanning open with sudden excitement.

Anna wondered how long this would last, this attentiveness on Addison's part, this clear effort to win her approval of him. Two months? Three? He was a boy just out of college with nothing to do but practice his writing and learn about love. When the summer was over, he would surely have other things to think about. Mariela would have been the distraction of a single season out of the year, her daughter, her greatest miracle, Mariela the Shining. The thought of it turned Anna's world to a desert with a black wind howling over the top. The devastation of such a thing.

Whatever she thought about them, though, Anna had to admit that Mariela and Addison were beautiful together. They were dark, both of them, like they had just come off a ship from the southern hemisphere, and they were wildly optimistic about everything with the kind of optimism particular to youth, effortless, irrepressible, fringed with laughter at either end. And the summer, with its powers of metamorphosis that reminded Anna of magic tricks, had transformed the two of them from the children they really were, lanky-limbed and awkward, their ears too big on their heads, into the lovers they promised to grow up to be, suddenly sleek in the way they walked across a room, as though their bodies had become something wild and feline overnight, predatory and self-conscious and primally attractive.

The summer had been the season of transformation for as long as Anna could remember. The time of strange winds touching rooftops with their brilliant, ragged fingers, the time of magnolia trees dropping their blossoms in a giant, white, throw-away glory, the time of Cristobal de la Senda's first arrival in Marbury Park, his goodness painted on his forehead in his small, fish-shaped birthmark, swimming toward the black, steady sea that was his hair. How quickly Anna had changed from a girl to a lover in Cristobal's presence, how willingly she had changed her name to Anna de la Senda for him, how eagerly she had adopted his complex beliefs, his full-blown Catholicism, his brightly painted saints who were bound to intercede on her behalf. As though the girl she had been before him, Ann McCafferty, Protestant by descent, uncertain by temperament, parentless and unattached by circumstance, had died a soundless, metaphysical death in a landscape no one could remember. As though, in her place, a woman had been born full-grown, complex and ethnic, willful and understanding, religious and mystical, passionate and pregnant. A simple exchange had never been so drastic or so welcome.

PART TWO

Goldenrod Worry

THE ROSES grew heavy and jewel-like at the borders of the Ettingers' lawn. In the evenings, they turned their faces downward in frothy weariness and collapse, and waited for the sprinklers to turn on at their feet in the modest fountains that meant restoration. Every other Sunday, Clifford cut a rose at six p.m. in addition to the one he had cut in the morning, because that was the day his mother came out to the house for dinner, her pocketbook as large as a shopping bag filling up her lap, her hair having been brushed into a French twist by the beautician at the Lord Tennyson Home who liked to tease Earline's strands into a state of high confusion before she had finished. Hanna, Clifford's thick-waisted, syrup-voiced cook, always made a special effort on second Sundays, filling the table with the colorful, subtly spiced dishes she was now accustomed to receiving compliments for. A salad of papaya and avocado and pine nuts and butter lettuce, a turkey with brandied plums and fresh ground ginger root mixed into the stuffing, a homemade sherbet made with mint from her garden, a salmon baked en croute, with a whirlpool of Florentine greens and crushed pecans turning in a creamy layer at the fish's center, a chocolate and raspberry Sacher torte for dessert, with the cake layers alternating between dark and light.

These were the terms in which Hanna had described the particular menu for one Sunday in June. Clifford had listened to her at first in a state of casual distraction, but had become interested in spite of himself. Hanna's voice was thick with an alto huskiness, and she had a minor slur, a cautious finessing of all her S's, which made her speech a pleasurable puzzle to him. He admired the way she navigated herself through the phrase "raspberry Sacher torte for dessert," her angular blond head straining upward in the effort of concentration that was required, as though she were reciting a lesson before a very tall schoolmaster. And in fact, he had always had the impression that Hanna was straining to please him, ever since she had come to work at the house, in the early months of Marjorie's illness. Possibly, she felt sorry for him, felt worried over the nervous, pinched-up way he bore his grief. Possibly, she had prepared all those delicate meals as a means of succor. Possibly, she was now a little in love with him, though Clifford dismissed this thought before it had time to settle in his mind.

He glanced through the scrim of the chiffon curtains, swelling and thinning again in the vagaries of the evening wind, and he wondered why his mother was late. Usually, a van from the Lord Tennyson Home dropped off both Earline and her wheelchair at no later than six-thirty and returned at ten to pick her up. So Clifford was surprised to see her arrive that night in the passenger seat of a bright yellow convertible, a yellow that would have been the color of some obscene, as-yet-undiscovered fruit, he thought. And this notion was reinforced by Clifford's recognition of the driver as the same winking, insinuating, offensive man who had mouthed a secret message to his mother before the start of the wheelchair race, two weeks prior. Now, he was wearing a cotton plaid suit and grinning like a thief for no apparent reason.

"Clifford!" Earline called from the car. "This is Stewart Souther. He is going to have dinner with us."

Clifford was able, with effort, to extend his hand. When Stewart Souther, who insisted that everyone call him Stew, had wrung his fingers dry, Clifford turned and walked away from the two of them, into the house, to tell Hanna that he was sorry, very sorry, for the inconvenience, but there would be a stranger with them at the table.

———

EARLINE HAD brought along with her the first-place trophy for the wheelchair race, a silver-plated representation of Hermes, with Clifford's name and her own engraved in the pyramid base. She fished it out of her giant-sized handbag after Hanna had served the mint sherbet, and she placed it squarely on the table for everyone to admire.

"I think you should keep the trophy here," Earline said. "You earned it, Clifford. You know you did."

"That's right, Dad," Addison said.

Clifford shrugged churlishly, his posture uneven, as if he were a sudden boy. "What did you do with the proceeds from your bet?" he said.

"Hmm?" Earline said.

"What did you do with the money you won?" he said.

Earline daubed at her lips with a napkin, even though her mouth was perfectly clean. "Oh that," she said. "I didn't need the money. I gave it away to a friend."

Clifford couldn't be sure, but he thought he saw his mother glance quickly in Stewart's direction when she got to the part about the unnamed friend. And there was some minute gesture on Stewart's part, too, an odd suspension of his sherbet spoon while a pale green drop of the contents fell off into his lap. Stewart, of course, was precisely the type to take money from the elderly and the wheelchair-bound. When he had complimented Clifford on his home, he had referred to it as a "magnificent property," as though he were imagining it written up in a real estate advertisement, as though he were calculating the asking price. It was possible that Earline had even used her own money to buy Stewart his howling-yellow convertible, since the car was by far the newest thing about him.

"I understand you're adopted, Addison," Stewart said. "Imagine that." There was something about the fact that he found hard to believe. He shook his head earnestly while he spoke.

"Yes," Addison said. "Imagine that." Irony visited the edges of his voice, camouflaged and quiet.

"I mean, you've got the next best thing here to winning the jackpot," Stewart said.

"How's that?" Addison said.

"Oh, come on," Stewart said. His eyes were winking and blinking again, asserting some connection between their activity and Stewart's own savviness in the world. "How many cast-off kids are going to get set up like this?"

Addison laid down his spoon with considerable care at the edge of his plate. He wore a smile of infinite tolerance and dislike, his lips pulled too far toward the corners of his face. "I grew up in this family," he said. "When you grow up as part of a family, you don't look at it as 'getting set up.' "

"All right, all right," Stewart laughed. "You look at it however you like. Abstraction is the prerogative of the rich."

"Bullshit," Clifford said.

"Excuse me. What did you say?" Stewart said. He appeared to have something caught in his throat, because he grumbled and coughed in consternation. Clifford thought it was probably a salmon bone, as thin and transparent as a fishing line, but he offered no assistance.

"Bullshit," Earline repeated, glad to clarify the situation. "My son said 'Bullshit.' "

"Well, you can dismiss some very impressive theories with that one word," Stewart said.

"I'm not in danger of it tonight," Clifford said.

"I am merely pointing out to you—"

"You are merely pointing out to me that you know nothing

about my family, although you think you know a very great deal," Clifford said. He was glad now to ride over Stewart's voice until it stopped. When Hanna tried to remove Clifford's plate, he was surprised to find that he had been holding on to it with one hand, insistently, as though that piece of porcelain had become a necessary part of him, an extension he must not relinquish.

"That's not entirely true," Earline said. "I've told Stew quite a few things about the family."

"God help us all," Clifford said.

"She did, and I like to think I'm worthy of the trust," Stewart said. "I myself know what it's like to suffer a loss."

"Oh?" Addison said.

Clifford was holding onto his porcelain plate more tightly now, encircling it with one arm, shelteringly. He had the impression that at any moment Stewart was going to speak Marjorie's name, and he was not certain whether he could bear the infamy of that. A family's grief should never be made known to manipulative, plaid-suited shysters such as the one who was now eating from his table. Never in a thousand Sundays.

"But we can't let these things derail us permanently," Stewart said. He placed special emphasis on the word derail.

"Stew, I wouldn't say any more about it," Earline said.

"Oh no, I wasn't going to mention her directly," he said.

Clifford couldn't be sure of when exactly his plate broke into pieces, of whether it was immediately after Stewart spoke or whether it was during. But the dish certainly separated into three distinct segments at about that time, the leftover Florentine sauce flowing along the cracks to make a miniature green river, viscous and unexpected, that joined the austere china plains.

"Get out of my house," Clifford said.

"Clifford," Earline said.

"Don't fight me, Mother. Just take your guest and leave."

Hanna entered the room with a blessed quickness and wheeled Earline into the foyer. Stewart walked behind them, confounded, red-faced, still clearing his throat. The two of them murmured apologies to one another, though it was clear from their feeble tenor that no one felt truly at fault.

"I'm sorry for my son's behavior," Earline said.

"No, no, I regret that I brought up the subject," Stewart said.

"Well, there shouldn't be anything offensive in the subject itself," Earline said. "We can't exactly place a moratorium on conversation." She adjusted her lace shawl about her shoulders, as if trying to extract some genuine warmth from it for the first time.

Their voices echoed faintly off the high walls, rebounding into the distant rooms they had just fled. Back at the dining table, Clifford and Addison could hear every word, and they sat perfectly still to be sure not to obscure the sound. They wanted to understand the debacle in its entirety, with every minor insult in its place, every insensitivity remembered.

Now, there was the jangle of Stewart's keys in his hand, the clop-clop of Hanna's shoes on the tiles, rhythmic and horse-like.

"I am sorry you are leaving unexpectedly," Hanna said to them. Her words carried a cool propriety unaffected by her lisp.

"Clifford needs to get into counseling, Hanna," Earline said. "Don't you think that would help?"

Later, when recalling the evening's events, Clifford could not be sure whether Hanna had responded, because it was at precisely that moment that he yelled out, "I will not suffer fools!" He made sure that his voice was loud enough for them to hear, even on the chance that they had already reached the driveway, and were wrestling with the doors of Stewart's strange-fruit convertible.

Hanna returned to clear the table, with the exception of Clifford's fractured plate, with its Florentine rivers and porcelain plains which he still held onto with mournful determination, as though their configuration contained a message for him, a secret, inscrutable sign. And he remained in his place after Hanna had left for the night and Addison had gone to bed, after the chimes on the grandfather clock had swung so low that its parts stopped moving altogether and the only sound that could be heard was the desultory whisper of Clifford's own breath, sailing over his landscaped dish like weather over a distant world.

———•◦•———

A LETTER from Earline reached Clifford on Wednesday, the handwriting exceptionally shaky and hunchbacked, as it always was when Earline hadn't gotten enough rest and a subsequent tremor invaded her fingers.

Dear Clifford,

This last time was really a spectacle, wasn't it. I'm still angry with you for throwing us out, I don't mind telling you. If you get used to cutting off discourse that way, dictator-fashion, you'll run out of people who'll tell you what they think, and then you'll be long gone and lost.

Of course, Stew is a fool. I don't need anyone to point this out for me. He is aggravating and contentious and he knows how to find a sore spot and walk on it. But I like an old man to drive me around in a convertible and who else am I going to get. There's all that fuss and bother with the wheelchair, and then he's got to carry me to places where the chair won't go, and there aren't many fellows who are willing to do it. That's the plain-Jane truth about it. And if he requires a little spending money at the end of the month, what's the difference to me or you. Loneliness would bankrupt me a hundred times faster.

What happened with Marjorie was an earth-shaking thing, and I've known that every time I've looked into your face for the last year. Maybe I thought you would take it like I did when your father passed on. I prayed a prayer for his soul and I got on with my business. But where was the love in that. You don't puff up your grief with something that isn't there. You were lucky to have a marriage where one of

*you was diminished without the other. But now, don't cherish
your diminishment, don't worship your lack.*

*Promise you'll talk to someone about this, even if it's not
me. My friend that lives next door, Opal Pairlee, likes a counselor that came to the Children's Day at the Home. Anna
something is her name, and Opal says you can call her any-
time, she won't mind, at 670-3437.*

That's all for now. Lovingly,

Mother.

ANNA BEGAN to bake cakes for Saint Catherine, seeking to gain
her favor. They had an egg batter with golden currants, pista-
chios, and pieces of broken chocolate bars mixed throughout,
and she steamed them in coffee cans until they were high, moist
towers of tenderness, ethereal enough even for Saint Catherine,
who was accustomed to the food of lovers. Anna set out the
cakes at night and by morning only a few crumbs remained,
scattered over the Persian carpet. Perhaps the finches came
down from their cages in the interval of darkness and consumed
the cakes themselves, but if that were true, it must have been
the spirit of Saint Catherine that opened their copper doors to
release them, and it must have been she that ushered them back
inside once the last currant had been eaten. Anna did not question the disappearance of her cakes; she only knew that her
offering had been accepted, that with enough offerings, she
might gain a gift of intercession and secure a happier future
for Mariela. These were the things that Cristobal had taught
her; these were the customs of the faith they had shared.

Early in the morning, Anna's hands were sunk deep in the
new batter for her saint cakes when the telephone rang. Ordi-
narily, she would have cleaned her fingers before answering,
but Anna sensed that there was something unusual about this
call, something urgent and strife-ridden about the way it had
interrupted her baking, crying at intervals with an animate
voice. So, when she picked up the receiver, it was with dough-

covered, dinosaur hands, great flaps of floury paste hanging off her wrists as though she were shedding some thick, reptilian skin.

"Hello, it's Anna," she said. She waved her unoccupied dinosaur hand in the direction of the birds, urging them to be quiet. But the birds pretended not to see her and continued their chatter.

"I . . . I understand you're a counselor," the man said. He sounded uncertain, as if he suspected he had misdialed, as if he feared he had reached an aviary.

"Oh yes, I counsel many people," Anna said. "Many people with all kinds of troubles, some of them beyond imagining. I don't turn anyone away."

"Maybe I could come speak with you," the man said. It was then that Anna recognized something in the voice, an inflection or an enunciation, or perhaps the way the sentence rolled downhill at the end.

"Fine. And may I have your name, please?" Anna asked the question with a warm routineness, like a secretary who is writing appointments into a book, one after the other, all her curiosity withered away.

"Clifford Ettinger," he said, spelling it out for her afterwards.

Anna turned toward her northern sitting room window, the telephone almost stumbling off of the table as she moved. On top of the tended hill, the Ettingers' house rose like a lady, cream-faced and spacious, her doe-eyed windows revealing nothing but distant grace. "I can see you on Saturday at noon," she said.

"All right," Clifford said. "What is the address?"

Anna stepped out of the cord that had spiraled around her leg, performing a small, jiggle-footed dance while she thought of what to say. "I prefer to make a house call on the first visit," she said. "People are more comfortable in their own homes. They feel less constrained in what they can talk about."

"That's acceptable to me," Clifford said. "But I live out on the edge of Saxon Hill. Is that too far for you to drive?"

"No, no, it's not too far," Anna said. "I assure you it's not."

After she hung up the phone, Anna wondered whether she should have revealed herself to him, whether she should have said *I am the woman with the overgrown trees and the resurrected birds and could I call you right back because I have great gobs of sweet dough hanging off my hands.* But no, he would never have agreed to meet with her in that case, and if there was anything Anna knew, it was that the fates had willed her to counsel with this man.

THE FIRST time that Clifford saw his son with the beautiful Latina girl, he pretended he hadn't seen anything at all. The two of them had shared a picnic of cold chicken and buttermilk biscuits, sitting cross-legged in the slight, unsheared valley that lay just outside the easy realm of the Ettingers' share of land. The couple hadn't touched one another as far as Clifford could discern, and that was what he had intently looked for, and what would have sent him into a frenzy of filial correction if he had found it. At the age of twenty-three, Addison was too old now for sexual indiscrimination. That was the sort of thing that would end up in misunderstanding, in resentful abandonment, in drawn-out paternity suits. But there had been no touching, and so Clifford concluded that the haunting girl with the lambent face was a minor acquaintance, a hanger-on, perhaps some teenager whom Addison was tutoring on her writing.

The next time Clifford saw them together, though, they were kissing in his living room, the girl partially reclined on the length of the couch, one of her bare, olive-skinned legs protruding from the gathers of her skirt as naturally as one curled stamen falls out of a summer lily. And Addison was there above her, his hair on end like Einstein, his breathing genuinely labored, so that Clifford felt ridiculously cruel when he turned on the overhead lights. As if there were anything more to see, he thought ruefully, just before he moved the switch.

"Addison!" In his embarrassment, his voice was booming. "I heard you down here. I was worried."

Addison did not get up from his place on the couch. He sat up in stubborn straightness and with one hand tried to press his hair back in place, but he did not get up. Beside him, the girl tucked her legs up underneath her like a child. In the light, Clifford was struck by her extraordinary face, by its premature womanliness, its shy and fateful longing.

"Nothing to worry about," Addison said. "We're keeping the burglars away."

"Oh, okay. Well, let's keep the lights on anyway. Will you see to that?"

"I will," Addison said.

So Clifford had retreated. He had left them to their own devices, plainly regretful of the fact that Addison was no longer a high-schooler and couldn't anymore be cowed.

The next morning, a Saturday, when Addison revealed the girl's full name, Clifford offered his most strenuous, insurmountable, incredulous objection. "You'd better stop this right here," he said. "Because I'll tell you something, and it may not be common knowledge, but I'll tell you that if this girl is who I think she is, then her mother is a wild, untreatable madwoman. Capable of violence, and I can say so firsthand. Just think about *that.*"

———————

ANNA HAD stopped mistrusting her neighbor on the day she saw him running the wheelchair race, long-legged and desperate, driven and bewildered. He ran as if he were being chased by an unseeable terror, fanged and hollow-eyed, and Anna thought she knew what it was. As for the incident that day in the treetops, that was nothing more than a man thrashing in the mouth of the grief that threatened to swallow him whole. A sorrowful man was prone to the erratic. Like Don Quixote, he jousted with windmills, he summoned invisible armies to his side, he struggled for his life among the tentacle-branches of the great tulip tree. Anna forgave him his respectable delusions, just as she had forgiven others theirs. Now, he was asking for her help, and she would offer it in the gentlest ways she knew.

On Saturday, the sky rose up like a fine blue balloon, pastel and momentous, halcyon and round. Anna dressed in a dark paisley suit, with the paisleys schooling across it like so many intricate fishes pressed onto a fabric sea. With a navy scarf, she made an open, somber rose, anchoring it to a hollow spot in her hair. Because the walk was short, she chose her high-heeled shoes, which reminded her of miniature ships with two snub-nosed bows, stream-lined and capable in their shape. It took her less than four minutes to walk the distance between her own front door and Clifford Ettinger's, but by the time she arrived, she had partly withered in the heat. Her tiny ship shoes were wet at the insole, and her auburn bangs had shifted to prickle her eyelids with their brush-point ends.

Clifford Ettinger opened the door himself, and, recognizing her with tired-eyed, defensive surprise, began to balk.

"Look, I don't know what you want," he said. "But you've come at a bad time. I'm expecting someone any minute now."

"I want to apologize for the other day," Anna said.

"Oh?" Clifford said. He widened the opening of the door, not far enough for her to pass through, but far enough for them to regard one another head to toe in free evaluation. He might have been a guard to some inner sanctum, deliberating over the quality of the bribe he had been offered.

"Yes," Anna said. "I hadn't anticipated that you would come so early in the morning. My daughter thought that someone was trying to break in. We were frightened."

"You nearly pushed me off my ladder," Clifford said.

"I'm so sorry for that," Anna said. She cocked her head to one side and smiled at him like a womanly elf, red-headed and spry and charming for all her faults. "A temper is a terrible thing, don't you think? My father was an Irishman, and that explains almost all the trouble I manufacture for myself."

Clifford couldn't seem to think of anything to say in reply.

Perhaps he was worried about agreeing too heartily and thereby insulting her father. His eyebrows crawled together over the bridge of his nose, joined in some mutual, nameless worry.

"May I come in?" Anna said. "I don't mean to push myself on you, but you did say on the phone that noon was an acceptable time."

"On the phone?" Clifford said.

"Yes, when we spoke on the phone," she said. "About the counseling you were considering."

Clifford repeated her words to the air, silently, trying to interpret their meanings anew. His eyes focused neither on the near nor far-off ground, but somewhere on the obscure middle distance in which obstacles first become visible. "That was you that I was talking to?" he said.

"That was me," she said. "Anna de la Senda." Anna placed one of her hands against the door, a fragile, white starfish pushing at its polished surface. She walked forward into the foyer, stepping delicately over the creamy, marble tiles as though trying not to make too much sound. Clifford followed her in obvious distress.

"But I had no idea who you were," he said. "I couldn't possibly talk to you about the personal details of my life."

"Why not?" Anna said.

"We're neighbors," he said.

"We're strangers," she corrected. "So what if we happen to live next door?"

Anna had made her way to the living room now, where she promptly sat in the brocade high-back chair. Everything was so disturbingly clean in this house, she thought, so antiseptically white. Nowhere was there a sign of the chaos that was life, with its scattered books and birdseed, with its windows open to the world. They would have a lot to discuss, the two of them; they would have many simple discoveries to make.

"I don't know about this," Clifford said.

"What's not to know?" Anna said. "You asked if I could help you. Let's see if I can."

Clifford could not seem to sit down. He paced the open spaces in front of her, wandering from one window to the next and looking out, like a man who suspects he is under siege.

"What do you want me to talk to you about?" he said helplessly.

"Talk to me about what you wish for and can no longer have," Anna said.

———•◦•———

CLIFFORD ETTINGER shared out his secrets one at a time, with a tender, exaggerated, trembling carefulness. It was as though he were handling uncooked eggs, their shells as thin as cellophane, their golden, ineffable contents unimaginably valuable in the impoverished world. Anna listened to him with her head tilted in wonder. She concentrated on concealing the signs of her pity, not because she wanted to, but because she knew instinctively that Clifford would eschew pity wherever he recognized its face, momentous and maudlin and unbearably powerful, looking at him straight on.

The secrets were these: a hairbrush, a crystal doorknob, a handful of soil. The brush was a Mason-Pearson, large sized, with boar's hair bristles that shot upward in sturdy quills. Contained within it lay a silky bed of Marjorie Ettinger's hair, seal-colored and wistful, fairy-tale-ish and long. Marjorie had liked to hold on to the handle in the last of her months, to hold on to it and to remember what it was like to have hair, how she used to brush it out at night without the fear of pulling too hard or discovering the loose, uprooted hanks left over afterwards. Hair that could be braided and teased and mussed and kissed, all in the name of life.

Now, Clifford could not bring himself to throw the old brush away. Sometimes, he stuck his fingers in between the bristles to remember what her hair had felt like, slightly cooler than the air, luxuriant and seamless, and smelling remotely of a tropical oil. And to touch it made him tremble with the loss. He shook, too, when he remembered Marjorie's alabaster head, naked and wigless where it rested on the pillow each night. She looked so vulnerable and transported, an angel asleep on an earth-bound bed. It infuriated him that she had left with so little of a struggle.

The crystal doorknob was Marjorie's quiet talisman. At first, she had it installed on her office door at the welfare registry. She enjoyed the idea of the unlikely beauty, stationed there in an orb of possibility, a reminder of hope. And then, when she and Clifford married, she brought it home and affixed it to the door of their bedroom where it shone like an impossible diamond, sensual and ideal, a collector of light. Now, when Clifford looked on it, it was nothing other than an emblem of his sorrow, a perpetual and solid tear which he could no longer bring himself to touch. Instead, the door stood consistently agape, as if appalled that the bedroom contained no vision or gesture that was worth concealing anymore, as if astonished that, after so long, loneliness had found its way back.

The handful of dirt was Clifford's own doing. It was the same handful that he was supposed to have thrown down onto Marjorie's casket where it lay at the bottom of the grave. Dust to dust. Except that Clifford's fist would not open to let go of the soil. He had clutched it with an involuntary grip during the entire limousine ride that carried him back to Raborn Way, and there, he had sifted it onto the beds of two Pilgrim rosebushes, lean and flowerless. But what Clifford could not stop thinking about now was that Marjorie's grave was missing his handful of consent. He had taken it away with him for selfish reasons, and there was no bringing it back. He had withheld what counted when it came to Marjorie, even in her death. And could there be any forgiveness for a thing such as that?

Clifford did not look at Anna while he told her the particulars of his sorrow. He gazed out the panes of the window, his breath so close that it left a fog on the glass. His eyes stared unfocused, unblinking, the wetness there being dammed up by the rim of his lower eyelids. When Anna first spoke, he seemed surprised at her very presence, shocked that someone else had overheard the character of his secret burdens. He had counted them his private knowledge for so long.

"Did you cut back your roses in the winter?" Anna said. She stood up from the satin high-back chair and joined Clifford at the window. He didn't answer her. At the borders of the lawn, the serried bushes were sunning themselves, their bright, many-tongued blossoms yawning gorgeously under the light.

"They look so frightening when they're pruned at first," she said. "Just sticks and thorns. And barely alive. Do you remember?"

He blinked just once, but when he did, the dams under his eyes broke, streaming their transparent ruin. Anna thought for a moment that he was going to speak, but he had merely opened his mouth in need of air.

"You will survive this, Clifford," she said. "Some things in this world are made more beautiful by their losses. Rosebushes. Autumn. The plains after flooding. A man such as you."

THE FOURTH of July fell on Sunday that year. The Cordojo Women ate rhubarb pie at the picnic table under Anna's kumquat trees. The ice cubes chimed together in the double-high lemonade glasses, and dozens of yellow and black swallowtail butterflies collected around the small pools where the sugared juice had spilled. India Perry decided that artificial butterflies would be just the thing to add to her new line of ladies' hats. Anna watched while Dove Pairlee reached into her pocketbook to sneak a piece of chocolate, a dark, misshapen, fluted lump, one of Opal's leftovers.

"I don't ever remember July being so hot," Dove said when she had finished swallowing. On the lower edge of her lips, a smear of chocolate remained, wet and careless and clear to all the Cordojo Women who looked her way.

"July isn't any hotter this year," Maxine Ridgeway said.

"You're just suffering because you've got more natural insulation."

Dove smiled coquettishly for a moment, as if she had been complimented, but then her expression flew away from her, leaving her face a dour blank. Her heaviness was, in fact, overtaking her. Her clothes had begun to fit her like sausage casings, with no imaginable space in which the contents might shift or breathe. And at her elbows and knees, profound creases marked her flesh, as if her limbs were fitted together with a series of interlocking pieces, like those of a bendable doll.

"Why don't you cut back, dear?" Esther Lee said. She patted Dove on her bulging back.

"Oh, it's easy for you to criticize," Dove said. "But none of you know the sum total of my trials. There's just so much a solitary woman can bear."

"What haven't you told us?" Anna said.

Dove pulled a pink embroidered handkerchief from her purse and pressed it to her eyes. She whimpered her distress, a last resort for a woman who could not cry at will. "Orie Rush got sick in the springtime, and just last week—and it's hard to believe for a man of his vigor—but just last week, he passed on."

"Dove Pairlee!" India said. "Were you still infatuated with that man?"

"No, I wasn't," Dove said.

"Were you keeping company with him?" Esther Lee said. "No."

"Did you love him?" Anna said.

"No, I did not," Dove said. "But I must have doomed him all the same."

The Lovelorn Women groaned in disbelief. Everyone talked at once, trying to make their protests heard. India Perry, with a broad, emphatic gesture of her arm, knocked over her glass of lemonade, and a dozen more swallowtail butterflies appeared in the air above it, clamoring in colorful frenzy. Esther Lee turned off her hearing aid, determined not to listen to any more nonsense.

"Now don't try to tell me I'm mistaken," Dove said. "Because I've had enough of that. Any woman who's seen seven gentleman friends dead and buried had ought to know it's more than just coincidence."

"Dove," Anna said. "How old was Orie Rush?"

Dove's open handkerchief had picked up a spot of the chocolate that stained her lips, and she was now pressing a series of dry, studious kisses onto the cloth. "Seventy-nine," she said.

"Well, I hate to put it to you," Anna said, "but seventy-nine-year-old men die every day."

"This is different," Dove said. "This is just the last in a long line."

"And how many of those men were what the general public might call elderly?" Maxine said.

"They were vigorous, all of them," Dove said.

"How many of those vigorous men were over the age of seventy-five?" Maxine said.

"That's not the point," Dove said.

"All seven," Maxine said.

Anna tried to keep silent for as long as she could. Above them, the kumquat tree spread out its arms indulgently, tolerant of their heartfelt squabbles, their illogical recriminations. The Cordojo Women had been through this all before. Dove simply gravitated toward the elderly and ailing because she had a widow envy, a need to be recognized as the holder of maximum grief. The day that Dove was not at the center of the world as she saw it was the day she would cease to exist. If only Anna could break her of her habit of meeting men through her mother at the Lord Tennyson Home for Persons Retired and Dignified. But Dove would not tolerate anybody putting restrictions on her love life. The possibility of a new affair was all that she got out of bed for in the morning, as everyone knew. She proclaimed this with her fearless necklines and polished nails, and with the enormous envelope of perfume that she sealed herself inside of.

"Right now, you think there won't be other men," Anna said. "But love always renews itself. You won't be left alone."

Dove put away her handkerchief and said no more about it. Often, Anna's words had that effect on her, hypnotic, immediate, the salve of a mother's comfort.

The Cordojo Women talked and napped in the shade until twilight. The trees towered off into the sky in flagrant, green expansion, the branches wheeling away from the centers in living spokes. But the kumquats and tulip trees were emptied of birdsong, the only sounds there coming from the way the leaves shushed against one another in the bare, developing transfer of air. From inside the house, the trills of the finches and sparrows and gray mourning doves emerged like notes from a music box, the beauty contained, lidded, held in delicate reserve. The Cordojo Women lit the ends of Roman candles and made private wishes under the showers of their iridescent sparks.

Maxine Ridgeway wished that she might find love.

Emily D. wished that she might find love.

Esther Lee wished that she might find love.

Dove Pairlee wished that she might find love.

India Perry wished that she might find love.

Anna de la Senda wished that Clifford Ettinger might find love, since he was in more earnest need of it than anyone she had ever known.

———•———

IN SAXON Hill South, the children liked to play Hackysack in the street, standing in circles, bony-kneed and concentrating, while the sack bounded between them with an energy that was mystic and uncontained. The patterns of the sun sifted through the trees, spotting the children's backs with irregular points of light that turned their small bodies coltish and wild, as though they had been half-transformed into Appaloosas. But even when their skins were metaphoric and painted, the children were still children; their mistakes still struck them as worth crying over. So when, back in May, a group of them accidentally hurled their Hackysack into the Ettingers' white Horstmann's rosebushes, they all came crying to Mariela the Shining, where she sat peeling apples on the porch.

They had barely explained their predicament to her before she agreed to help them, because Mariela possessed a soul that understood the agonies of children, that knew the poignancy to them of even their minor losses. She waded into the Horstmann's bush, her arms held high above her head to preserve them from the wash of thorns. The brambles shifted in an uneasy net as she moved past, the mesh waiting to close. She retrieved the Hackysack from the bush's center and threw it out toward the clear space on the lawn, a hapless, cloth fish for the children to carry away with them. But Mariela herself was trapped, neck-high in a still, green tangle of vegetation, the thorns all pressing her with the sharpness of needles or of animal teeth. The children had all gone and she, in her helpless embarrassment, did not dream of calling out.

So that is how Addison found her, the girl he could not even recognize as his neighbor, and the one he would never again forget; lambent and black-eyed, distraught and vaguely feral, she waited at the center of her trap until he found a pair of garden clippers with which he cut her exit. The scratches traveled over her limbs in long, curling, red-rimmed vines, and he made her come into the house with him, her feet bare and muddied where they stood on the pristine, marble tile, while he traced a clear gel of antiseptic ointment over the welted paths.

"Don't think of how it hurts," Addison said when she flinched. "Think of something else. Your favorite food."

Mariela closed her eyes, consenting to the distraction.

"What is it?" Addison said.

"Ambrosia salad," Mariela said.

Addison said nothing in reply, but what he thought was, "Oh, ambrosia salad. What else could it possibly be?"

So IT started in the way that most loves start, namelessly and by accident, with that jolt you receive when you recognize someone you are about to know.

Mariela could not recall how many days it was exactly before Addison laid her hair over the front of one shoulder, thick-stranded and violet-black and mussed as if by sleep, and placed his mouth at the nape of her neck in order to kiss her there, with excruciating slowness, as if he might only be allowed this one time. She had gone to meet him at the edge of the Marbury citrus groves, as he had asked. Over their heads, the globes of late fruit clustered together, blue and gleaming in the filter of night. The oranges bowed the branches on which they weighed, hanging in silent profusion, burdensome and sweet.

But Mariela did not know how many days it was before Addison kissed her; and she did not know how much time it was exactly before she pulled away from him, and fanned her hair again over her back, and walked off across Marbury's heavy grove toward Raborn Way and her home, knowing he would follow, knowing it without turning around, without uttering a solitary word, knowing it simply by the manner in which he had touched her, with a serious, unmistakable will, with a silent, tangible intent. She did know that all through the remainder of the night, the notion of time altered and collapsed whenever she tried to take hold of it with her mind. How long did it take a man to undress in the dark of her room with her helping him? How long did it take them to admit to one another that they were both virgins, and how long after that to make the admission no longer true? How long did it take her to fall asleep in a naked embrace, and how long did it take her to dream that she understood what romantic love was, wholly and miraculously, for the first time in her life?

In the stories that her friends had told her of their first experiences making love, there was always a certain horror when it was over, a profound and resonant sorrow when the boy got up to leave the bed—an event which almost invariably took place too soon. The girl was left lying in a nest of torn-up sheets, chilled and regretful and near-desolate with the sense of fresh, unspeakable loss. But this was not a pattern that marked her own life.

Because Addison Ettinger never left her bed that whole

night, and even into the broad, light-drenched hours of the morning. Instead, he held her to him in sleep, his limbs flung over her in an unconscious embrace. There were moments in the night when she woke, uncomfortable and confined and over-warm in the cage he had made for her, but she became gradually accustomed to the intimacy she found there. Like a stray cat, she balked at being held too long, but later, in relenting, wondered how she had survived any other way.

In the morning, with the new air spilling in across the window seams and the quilt gathered in a feathery mountain that covered only their feet, Anna de la Senda knocked at the door. Addison, hearing her, rolled off the edge of the bed in a movement of desperation and grace. So that when Anna entered, her green velvet bathrobe sagging on the floor behind her, there was only Mariela, naked and trembling on the white field of the mattress, reaching for the bedclothes and finding them scattered.

"Mariela," Anna said. "What's happened?"

"What do you mean?" she said.

"I had a dream about you last night," Anna said. "You sprouted green wings and flew away over the rooftops."

"It sounds like a wonderful dream," Mariela said. She was standing now, wrapped up in a wrinkled sheet. For a moment, she worried that her mother would see Addison's sleek leather shoe, stranded by itself in the center of the hardwood floor. But no, Anna was envisioning Mariela in flight, picturing her winging away over Marbury's orange grove and the Methodist Church, over the lush village park and the streets that led away from it in the pattern of a star. She could see nothing else.

"No, it wasn't wonderful," Anna said. "I kept telling you to come down, but you just ignored me, you just . . . you just . . ." Her voice turned tremulous and shallow and then broke apart into weeping.

"Mother," Mariela said. "It was only a dream."

"Don't protect me with untruths," Anna said. "I know you better than anyone else in the world."

"That's the way it should be with a mother," Mariela said.

But Anna wept all the while she was speaking, childish and free, disconsolate and deaf.

"You won't tell me what's happened?" Anna said.

"In a little while," Mariela said. She led her mother out of the room, holding on to her trembling hand. In the kitchen, Mariela would make fresh coffee, buttermilk muffins, a creamy egg soufflé. "In a little while everything will be all right."

ADDISON WANTED to be a writer more than anything else on the known earth. This is what he confided to Mariela one night in the cover of the citrus grove, with the Santa Rosa mountains rising in the distance like dinosaurs, jagged-backed and blue. Mariela wore a white eyelet dress, off-the-shoulder, like a beautiful peasant. She strolled among the shadowed, orderly forest of trees, lighting the boughs inexplicably from underneath.

"How long have you wanted to be a writer?" Mariela said.

"Forever," Addison said. His hands drifted up into the smaller trees, fidgeting there as if searching for the oranges that had been picked last week.

"Oh, you will be one, then," she said.

"How do you know?" he said.

"Sometimes I can see into the future," Mariela said. "It's a gift my mother has passed down to me."

Addison tried to study Mariela's face, to see whether she was teasing him, but all he discerned there was an innocent clarity, an upward-looking, clear-eyed conviction, as though she had just left off reading from a bible. No, there was never anything about her that wasn't sincere.

"And what have you wanted to be forever?" he said.

"With you," she said.

Addison's hands floated down from the trees and settled on the girl standing by him. She had sprung full-blown from the mind of some genius and first touched the earth here in the middle of his lucky life.

"But I meant something you have wanted for yourself," he said. "Something personal."

"That's what I meant, too," Mariela said. "Don't you understand?"

———•·•———

EVERYTHING SHE learned about him, she learned at night: his wants, his pains, the rhythms of his breath while he dreamt. She found stories of his that had been published in university magazines, stacked inside shirt boxes at the back of his closet. She found an old wrist splint and a chess trophy and three photographs of what must have been his mother as a little girl, seated on somebody's polished porch swing.

Addison slept through all the times she rummaged through his things, slept through them unshakably, his senses closed to the ongoing world. He worshiped his sleep, she realized. He went to it each night with a reverence toward what he would find there, his hands flared wide with surprise over the sheets, his mouth tapped open with private wonder. Several times she had tried to wake him with her questions—how many times had his work been published before and how long had it been since he'd broken his wrist and where had his mother grown up with her ribboned hair and her patent leather shoes. But he couldn't be roused—not with touching or cold washcloths or his name spoken urgently into his ear.

There were consequences to loving your sleep too much, though. Once, Mariela couldn't wake him up after several hours at the beach. The sand had piled itself into his hair, and his lips had gone dry with salt, and his skin had begun to mottle and burn. In the end, she had had to lay herself down on top of him, her hair tented over his face in a protective drape, her arms and legs and torso pressed into the configuration of his, assuming his silhouette as her own, becoming the shadow that cooled him. That evening, when his sunburn had brought on a fever, Mariela had made him take a bath in cold milk and sliced cucumbers, which drew the heat away from him until the liquid turned as tepid as soup, steaming from the surface. When all the cucumbers wilted and sank, it was the sign that his cure was complete.

"My mother used to cover me in apple butter after a sunburn," Addison said.

"Apple butter can work, too," Mariela said.

She was blotting him dry from his bath, swabbing the rumpled towel against his skin gingerly, as if she were afraid she might erase him.

"It takes a long time to spread on, though," she said.

"Oh, my mother didn't mind taking her time," Addison said. "When I think about it, she took her time with everything except dying."

"She did?" Mariela said. "I wonder why."

Addison shrugged. There was milk crying in pale streams down his back, and cucumbers were fastened to his limbs like fish scales, green and glistening as Mariela peeled them away. He mourned his loss like a dragon, his head lolling low, his internal heat doused and drained off.

"After the funeral, when I went back to school, I found a note from her waiting in my mailbox. She'd had Hanna post it the week before," Addison said. "She wrote about leaving us in an oblique sort of way. I think, for her own reasons, she didn't want to prolong it."

Later, in his room he pulled a piece of stationery out of his bedside table and handed it to Mariela. Its border was embossed with long-stemmed lilies, slim-necked and perpetual. It read,

Dear Addison,

 When you were a little boy, you weren't afraid of anything. Not strangers or ghouls or bad-tasting medicine. Nothing at all. There was something philosophical about it, as if you had simply made up your mind not to let life worry you. That seems important to me now, that making up of one's mind.

 I think it will be beautiful where I'm going next. There's

no advance information available, but the best places are al-
ways the ones nobody knows about. Don't you think that's
true?

Love always and ever,

M.

———•◦•———

MARJORIE ETTINGER died in May, in the bedroom with the yellow wallpaper that showed roses blooming out of upside-down
bonnets. From that room, she could see the Santa Rosa mountains in the first light of morning, rolling over from their motionless sleep with their stunning, angular, flush-tipped bodies,
momentous and hopeful, in spite of what they knew. She had
asked to be moved there after she and Clifford could no longer
make love; it was her way of lengthening the tether between
them, of extending it to her own remote, wallpapered island
and asking Clifford to see that she inhabited that place, quite
necessarily, by herself.

Clifford found himself telling these things to Anna de la
Senda on her weekly visits to his home. He had tried and failed
to restrain his galloping grief. What was it about this wide-eyed
woman with the muted red hair and the oddly Spanish name
that made him have to tell her everything? She came into his
home wearing her bold-print dresses, her ankles wobbling over
the high heels she was evidently not used to balancing on, and
he treated her like his confessor, his all-knowing, beneficent,
unpredictable healer. He revealed to her the excesses and de-
ficiencies of his loss in insights that occurred to him for the first
time even as he spoke.

Thank goodness, he said, that Marjorie knew enough not
to leave him alone, that so many years ago, from her welfare
office in San Diego, she had foreseen the need for Addison.
Because without his son, Clifford would never have survived the
artificial quiet that had invaded his life. That much was certain.
His child had been his salvation.

It was hard to remember that he had been against Addison in the beginning. Not Addison himself, but the idea of Addison. There was the invasion of their well-heeled privacy to consider; there was the constant flux that a child would import into the home. And then, to adopt a baby from such a disadvantaged couple was a risk in and of itself. What if the mother had not had sufficient care during the pregnancy? What if, much later, with whole years passed by, there were mental infirmities that cropped up? These were the questions that Clifford had asked.

"And what did Marjorie answer?" Anna said.

"She told me to stop worrying about whether the baby would measure up, because she had *seen* the baby with her own two eyes, and she knew everything about him she needed to know."

"Did that satisfy you?" Anna said.

"No, but it didn't matter," Clifford said. "She satisfied me. Her unreasonable generosity satisfied me."

Anna had brought over two extra saint cakes, and Hanna had laid them out on a porcelain server, slicing them like jelly rolls into neat, even pucks. Clifford helped himself to a piece. In spite of his best efforts, the cake generated a steady rain of crumbs onto his lap. But he ate it anyway with an air of boyish satisfaction, managing successfully, for the moment at least, to ignore the growing mess.

"Addison goes to see her sometimes," Clifford said. "The birth mother."

"He knows her?" Anna said.

"Marjorie wanted it that way," he said. "She said he wasn't through with his need for a mother, and she couldn't stand the thought of his going without." Clifford studied the pattern of crumbs in his lap as though he were trying to name a constellation, scattered and chaotic against the blue of his napkin.

"She went straight up to the child welfare office, and they still knew her there, and she opened the records over one of the lunch hours," he went on. "She didn't ask anybody about it; she just did it. When you're dying, the word *wait* drops right out of your vocabulary. You get certain ideas about what has to be taken care of, and you won't let anyone delay you. That's the way Marjorie was."

"Yes," Anna said. "My mother died when I was eight years old, and I remember how it was. Every day is a last chance for something. Kisses, gifts given, tokens of remembrance."

Clifford slid into awkward silence. He seemed to be startled by the presence of someone else's past in the same room with his own. He suddenly handed Anna a second piece of cake, using a paper doily as a clamp. Anna took this as a gesture of sympathy, a baffling, unexpected mark of goodwill. She felt inexplicably embarrassed by it.

"Well," she said. "Addison still goes to see the mother?"

"Once a month when he's home. I don't know why."

"Maybe . . ."

"There must be reasons," he said. "She's begun to rely on him probably. She has, and her other children, too. Addison's always carting things over to them. Boxes of food. Books they're not interested in. Clothes he's bought brand-new at the department store."

"Maybe he's begun to care for her," Anna said.

"No," Clifford said. "No. What's behind it is obligation. Addison knows who his mother was, and that's something he won't forget."

———

MAXINE RIDGEWAY had been married twice, the second time to a raging philanderer with an eye toward girls who still stood at the edge of their adolescence, their faces turned to pure, bewildered cameos of mortification, as though they had been caught bathing in a private lake. He had even gone so far as to approach his own stepdaughter, Emily D., once sending her an unsigned Valentine that read, *I have admired you for so long.* Emily D. had retreated into an obscure, nail-biting silence, her overgrown bangs descending like a fine, impenetrable veil over her eyes, until the marriage had self-destructed the following year. Only Mariela and Anna de la Senda had known about the implicit threat that moved inside the Ridgeway house, because Emily D., despite their urgings, could not bring herself to tell her mother, her opinionated, fragile-hearted, gray-at-the-crown mother, whose hands shook uncontrollably when she thought of another divorce. But all of them had survived the uncertainty of that time, and in the end, Emily D. was able to locate again her mislaid voice, and whisper new words to the world that had gone on without her.

Now, Emily D. loved to spend the summer afternoons with Mariela, sitting cross-legged by the open windows, the tulip trees laying their small, immobile fingers against the girls' hair. This careless house on Raborn Way with the ancient, peeling paint and the crooked, unlocked door was a place where secrets were entrusted, where confidences were honored, and Emily D. felt safer within its walls than she did anyplace else that she had willingly passed an hour. And then, too, Mariela's was a magical life, replete with frank yearning and unearthly reverence, both collecting in the air about her like an aura. Emily D. imagined that she could occasionally see it, the aura, shimmering in the iridescent air that encircled Mariela's head. It was a transparent sphere, gold and dusty in the light; it was the outline of some miraculous planet. Emily D. liked to sit as close to Mariela as she could, hoping for a blessing by reason of proximity.

Often, when Addison arrived at the de la Senda house, he would find the two girls crowded on the window seat, whispering into one another's ears as if they were still children who understood blind devotion, who had just come in from playing jump rope in the school yard, their heads still swimming with rhymes. But when they saw Addison, their womanliness returned to them, suddenly and profoundly and without a trace of regret. They crossed their legs and they smoothed their hair, and their giggles became the laughter of women, even and transformed where it left their mouths. To Addison, the change was magic each and every time he witnessed it. It was the passage of whole years compressed into a single moment in time; it was the private joys of an entire childhood dispensed without a backward glance. It was the direct intrusion of the self-conscious upon the naive, and at the end of it, there was the lovely, mystical girl on Mariela's part, and there was the awkward, silent girl on Emily D.'s. The distance that had unfolded itself between them was difficult and uncrossable, but that did not change the fact that the girls still gazed affectionately at one another across the divide, wondering what power it was that had gifted them so unevenly.

In July, Addison brought Mariela and Emily D. along with him on a car ride to Baston, where the streets all ran like rivers of lava, glutinous and boiling, in dark paths across the world. Addison's car was filled with bags of groceries—cold cartons of milk and almost-ripe black plums, avocados, artichokes, and Porterhouse steaks wrapped in brown butcher paper. In the back seat, Emily D. balanced three dozen eggs on her lap, her face colored with such genuine effort that she might have produced them herself, one at a time, on the long ride from Marbury Park. Addison saw her bouncing in her fragile predicament every time he checked the rearview mirror; he surprised himself with his feeling of fatherly concern. Emily D. was only five years younger than he, and yet she looked like she could do with a modicum of protection. Mariela, by contrast, was beautifully self-possessed, sitting there next to him with plums in her arms. The fruits' endless glossed-over skin seemed related somehow to her own. When she opened the window a sliver, a high, syrupy scent threaded its way over to Addison's side of the car, and he recalled with delight that she always smelled of one fruit or another, of oranges hanging in a grove or of plums clustering in a sack, of the bounty that went with them, of the physical hunger they so simply inspired.

Addison took a turn toward the foothills, which stretched out raw and brown after whole months without rain, and entered a neighborhood where the houses were stark and eyeless and bleached the color of bones. In the yards sat occasional cactus pots and cement paths, or blank-faced residents sitting at their shadeless doorsteps. The trees, where they grew, came up stunted and parched, their roots bound up inside wooden, slatted barrels. And everywhere, everywhere, was the glare of the sky, glinting off the smattering of mica in the pavement, bleaching the scenery to brilliance and dust.

Addison's mother lived here, bandy-legged and wizened, the most undeniable part of her beauty siphoned away. She had borne three other children, prematurely aged like herself, and they stared at Addison whenever he came, their faces like ciphers, inscrutable and closed to him. The oldest, Bernard, was just two years younger than Addison. At the age of ten, he had lost two fingers while playing on a Jensen oil jack, but other than this, he appeared to be the self-same image of his more privileged brother—as tall, as black-headed, as preoccupied with the movements of his hands. And the similarities were not lost on the two of them. They studied one another with a curiosity that took the form of sullenness in Bernard and furtiveness in Addison. Neither one could look straight on at the life he could have led.

Only Bernard and his mother, Rita, were at home on the day that Addison and Mariela and Emily D. came to visit. Rita smiled at them, the skin under her eyes wrinkling like tissue paper, pressed into hundreds of indelible folds.

"We was hoping it'd be you," she said to Addison. She spoke with a forced, manly depth, the result of the way she had swallowed the smoke of her cigarettes for so many years.

"There are steaks," Addison said, carrying the sacks of groceries past her and into the kitchen. "Porterhouse. I chose them very carefully."

"Terrific," Rita said. "Because I love Porthouse."

"Porterhouse, he said," Bernard murmured. "You don't even know what he's talking about, do you."

Mariela and Emily D. reached the door then, hesitating outside of the screen. Bernard swung it slowly open, appraising them with his wordless, impermeable stare. His eyes were nearly squinted shut, as if the girls threatened to bring the outdoor glare with them to the inside of the house, as if they themselves were the source of what was unbearable about the earth.

"Brother, you bring us so many things," Bernard said.

"Just the food," Addison said. "It's really not so much."

When she saw the girls, Rita's eyes expanded, claiming more of the ragged territory of her face. "Who are your girl-friends?" she said. Her words carried the sound of delight and insinuation at the same time.

"This is Mariela de la Senda," Addison said. He reached out his hand to touch Mariela's violet-black hair as she passed him on her way into the kitchen. The gesture was involuntary and overtly tender, and Addison thrust the venturesome hand into his pants pocket as soon as he realized that it acted with a will of its own. "And this is Emily D. Ridgeway," he said, nodding toward Emily's mousy form, which still balanced the egg cartons precariously.

"Mariela and Emily. Those are princess names," Rita said admiringly.

"So Ma, when did you ever know a princess?" Bernard said.

Rita sat down in the nearest available chair as if she had been pushed. Her legs folded under her woodenly, like a mar-ionette's. It occurred to Addison for the first time that she had been drinking, that that wandering, diffused expression she wore was simply the mask of gin.

"Just because I didn't know a princess, it doesn't mean I can't recognize a couple of them when they walk into my own home," Rita said.

Mariela and Emily D. stood silently, at a loss for something to do while their royalty was being discussed. Behind them, the light of the kitchen window illuminated their forms through their dirndl skirts, passing through the cotton folds, to outline their legs, astonishingly young in shape and clearly used to be-ing concealed.

"We can't stay," Addison said.

"That's all right, 'cause we can't ask you to stay," Bernard said. "Ma's got her boyfriend coming over, don't you Ma. And she don't like anybody in the house at a time like that. Not even me." Bernard pointed laughingly at himself. He seemed to realize only afterward that he had used his left hand, the hand with just three fingers remaining. His palm shrunk into a loose, concealing fist and disappeared behind his back. It was the retreat of a creature that understood its own shame.

When Addison bent over to kiss Rita good-bye, he was surprised to see that her chin trembled, gingerly, undeniably, shaking with the forces it tried to hold back. Above it, she bit her lip. "You turned out beautiful," she said. "I never told you that before."

"Thanks," Addison said. He looked at his mother, child-sized and ancient, desiccated and crying where she sat before him. He felt, unreasonably, that he ought to have been able to keep her from this, that he ought to have protected her from some unnameable crime that had been perpetrated against her years ago.

"Really," she said. "You did."

Outside, Addison shielded his eyes from the scattered white light of the sky. At the heads of the foothills, clouds gathered like clots of cream, luxuriant and solid against the hollow atmosphere. Addison held the car doors for Mariela and Emily D., and then walked around front to the driver's side. But Bernard was there, leaning against the door handle, indolent and powerful and asking for something even before he spoke.

"You like giving us things, brother?" he said.

"I like giving what I choose to give," Addison said.

"What you choose to give," Bernard said. He pressed his lips forward in mock frustration, as though he were rearranging things inside his mouth. "That's a disappointment, you know?"

"Well," Addison shrugged, but he said nothing else. He could think of no explanation or apology he felt like offering.

"Because I thought you was giving us what we needed," Bernard said.

"I'm not?" Addison said.

Bernard took his maimed hand out of his pocket and laid it against the car window, as if setting it on a glass display. Inside the car, the girls turned their heads in the other direction, straining for something to look at even though there was nothing. A long-haired cat digging a cool nest in the earth. A pair of blue pillowcases trembling on a wash line. Bernard's hand was still pressed against the glass, still displaying his dismemberment.

"There's other things I need more than a couple of steaks," Bernard said. "Like I need a car more than anything."

Addison smiled a smile of discomfort, his lips pulled into a narrow, tense wire with upward crooks at both ends.

"Hey, I ain't saying you *got* to give me a car. I'm saying think about it. Think about it 'cause I could really make something of myself if I had one."

Bernard stepped to the side then, his demand made, his challenge finished. Addison opened the door and dove in.

"I'd take what you've got right there, even," Bernard called out, meaning the Volvo, Addison's Volvo, which was just that minute carrying them down the driveway.

Addison waved to Bernard, mostly out of a silly relief over having escaped him. There had been a great, twisting hunger behind his brother's eyes—not a hunger of the metaphorical kind, but something else, something tangible and pressured and gathering itself inside his mind. So much so that, standing before him, Addison had experienced the real fear of being eaten alive, one piece at a time, a notion which had not occurred to him since he had been a child, fleeing through the landscape of a bad dream, with a Tyrannosaurus rex pounding after him. Of course, the problem with Bernard was that he did not have the impenetrable chicken flesh of an ancient reptile, but that he looked nearly identical to Addison. There was the same half-dimple in the middle of their chins, the same vein that stood out on their foreheads when they laughed for a long time or held their breaths. So, when Addison faced the ruthless, immeasurable hunger that shaped his brother's intent, he had the impression of facing a fearsome incarnation of himself, stripped, unvarnished, elemental and true. There weren't many spectacles that could have inspired in him a more desperate desire for escape.

He had been moving along the highway for fifteen minutes before Mariela reached over and placed her hand on his arm.

The weight of it was tentative and small-bodied, as if instead of her hand she had placed a small bird upon him, soft-footed and sleeping.

"There's no hurry," she said. "I'm not worried about getting back, and I don't think Emily D. is either."

"No, I'm not," Emily D. said.

It took him a moment to understand that they were talking about his driving. The angled, red tail of the speedometer pointed to eighty-five. He pulled his foot back from the gas pedal and watched while the continuous fluid that was the blurred trees and housetops and gold-haired hills broke into so many separate distinguishable pieces, passing his sight now in clumps, irregularly, in small portraits of a peaceable world.

"I'm sorry," he said. But Mariela just smiled in that generous, vague, otherworldly way that said she already knew.

———•◆•———

MARIELA BAKED a doll cake for her mother in honor of her forty-third birthday. The skirts were forget-me-not blue and bowl-shaped, and they had great festoons of white ribbon icing tiered around the circumference. The doll, which was only inserted into the center of the cake after the layers had been turned out and sculpted, had been chosen especially for her auburn, up-turned hair and for the fact that she, when filled up with water, would cry real tears out of her calm, jewel eyes. Tears for the sorrows of others, Mariela thought. When the Cordojo Women first saw her, they gasped with amazement.

"She's the perfect image of Anna!" India said. "How did you ever make her so real?"

"Look how prettily the blue sets off her hair," Dove said. "Anna, if you wore a blue like that, it would do the same thing for you."

"Mariela, why did you go to all the trouble to fashion something that we're just going to eat right up in five minutes?" Maxine said.

She didn't ask the question harshly. The truth of the matter was that she simply wanted to hear Mariela speak. The girl had floated at the periphery of the Lovelorn Women for too long, and now they missed her gentle perception and her shining ways; they missed the whisper of her voice when she spoke her secrets to them, and they missed the way her face blushed warm afterwards, out of shyness instead of shame. Because what would a girl so pure ever have to be ashamed of? How could such a one as she know anything but blessings when they came to her? Now, the Cordojo Women all turned to her expectantly, waiting to hear words of the old innocence they loved so well.

"We will eat the cake in five minutes, it's true," Mariela said. "But it's impossible to eat the memory of the cake. And I need to give a memory or two to the mother who has filled up my mind with them, with the best of them. It's unfair that she has handed me so many."

"Aaahh," Maxine sighed. "She's grateful and she's still so young. Did you hear what she said just now?" She poked her daughter, Emily D., in the ribs.

"Yes," Emily D. said. She turned toward her mother a look of vapid naiveté, as though she had entirely missed the point.

Anna sat encircled by her friends. For once, she waited on no one; she carried no pots of tea or china cups or sugar lumps or lemons. Her hands looked strangely empty when they were free from her ministrations. They slept on her lap like two alabaster fairies, cool and pulsing and possessed of a magic life. On the coffee table, there were gifts wrapped in colored foils and tissues, their ribbons frothing past the edges in a collection of curlicue tails and satin lethargy. Each one, when she opened it, contained a minor surprise, a pleasant, unanticipated shock that made her eyelids flutter in girlish response. From India Perry, a crimson-velvet-covered book of love poems, with selections from Shelley and Browning and the sonnets of Shakespeare. From Maxine Ridgeway and Emily D., an extra-dry bottle of Mumm's champagne, slim-necked and broad-hipped and looking oddly like Maxine herself, in all her ungilded richness. From Esther Lee, two tickets to a Mozart concert at the Hollywood Bowl in September. From Dove Pairlee, a black silk voile nightgown with a portrait collar and a hemline of scalloped lace.

"But I'm forty-three years old," Anna said, blinking. "How can I put all these gifts to use by myself?"

"They're not meant for you by yourself," Esther Lee said.

"No?" Anna puzzled over the array of presents in her lap, trying to comprehend something in them other than the obvious.

"Now we won't let you be coy about it any more," Dove said. "You're supposed to enjoy all these things with your doctor friend from across the way." Dove pointed breathlessly out the window in the direction of the Ettingers'.

"You've gone to see him every Saturday for seven weeks in a row," India said. "Don't deny it because you'll just embarrass yourself. I've seen you from my roof."

Anna, where she sat in her chair, opened and closed her mouth so many times that it appeared she had forgotten the mechanics of breathing. The Cordojo Women laughed and clapped their hands at the face of her astonishment. It delighted them to think that Anna's powers of perception had been, however subtly, transferred to them, that her heart-healing talents had been shared all around. Now, they could counsel the counselor, with all the rewards inherent in such an act. They felt the same way as grown children do, who, on becoming financially successful for the first time in their lives, send their parents on an Atlantic cruise in a luxury-class cabin filled with bon voyage bouquets. They felt precocious and nurturing, extravagant and justified.

Anna could have taken all this away by telling them what was plain and true, but when she opened her mouth to speak, there was no sound that ascended. The hollow between her lips became a cavern, devoid of explanations and the air that could have carried them. She was incapable of disillusioning those she loved. And even if it had been otherwise, there were her professional ethics to keep her silent. She could never divulge without his express consent that Clifford Ettinger was being counseled. And from a man who was so fiercely, unbendingly private, she would never ask it.

"You've been holding out on us," Dove Pairlee said. She tossed her head of ash-blond curls and they trembled sweetly like a cut and styled salad.

"Well, I have gone to see him, but it's not like you think," Anna said.

"All right, then, how is it?" Maxine said.

"We're neighbors, for heaven's sake," Anna said. "Neighbors have things to discuss. Not to mention the fact that Mariela is seeing Addison Ettinger. That's enough of a subject for parents to come together over."

The Lovelorn Women turned to look at Mariela, whose eyes had grown solemn and glistening with this last revelation. Love for her was still a miracle, fragile, untainted, perfectly whole, and it hurt her to expose it to the examinations of others, to their probing analyses and their classifications of the soul. Who knew whether love might not be altered in the dissection, scarred invisibly by the workings of gossip? Anna and the rest of the Cordojo Women saw her timidity and stepped gingerly back from the treasure it protected. They, too, remembered what it was to feel the tender places in their own expanding hearts; they, too, recalled the value of being separate from a world that had forgotten enchantment.

"Mariela and Addison are a very fortunate pair," Emily D. said finally. Everyone present whispered their agreement, even Anna, who began to imagine that the vermicelli noodles had never once written sorrow, but that she had simply drawn this illusion from a dream or a novel or the story of someone else's life.

———•◦•———

ANNA GAVE Clifford her prescription for his grief: one day of living for one day of mourning. For each day he clung to Marjorie's bristle brush, studying the hair it held, he must also spend a day at the beach, barefoot and unharried, and with a kite string in his hands. For each day he pained over the teardrop doorknob, petrified and permanent on the face of his bedroom door, he must also pass his time at a horse show or a movie festival or the season's county fair. One hour of grief for one hour of life. It was a bargain between the part of him that had given up entirely and the part of him that waited for an explanation that would make sense of it all. Clifford agreed only reluctantly to the trade-offs it implied, to the planning and the effort and the conscious recreation.

"I will help you in the beginning," Anna said.

"How?" Clifford said.

"Next Saturday, we'll go for a hike in the mountains," she said. "Just to remember what the air is like in so high a place. Just to recall what the view is like from the top."

Clifford leaned his head on one hand, carefully balancing its weight. His eyes roamed his living room ceiling, seeming to search it for an undisclosed flaw. But then they returned to look directly at Anna's own. "I pick the mountain," he said.

ON SUNDAY, Clifford picked up his mother, Earline, at the Tennyson Home and drove her to McArthur's for brunch. Outside, the sun peppered through the trees to make Main Street into a dappled, wavering way. The wind skipped around in the mint-green quince trees and brought a pleasurable, hard-edged coolness into the slow-moving lower reaches of the air, scenting them with summer. McArthur's was fronted with great, beveled-glass windows that looked out onto the lazy thoroughfare and beyond it, onto the stony, implacable skin of St. James' Episcopal Church. Clifford and Earline sat staring out at the view. Above them, a set of gargantuan mahogany-bladed ceiling fans clung motionless and antique to the overhead as if they were a family of prehistoric dragonflies.

"But really, life's not much worth living without a little romance in it," Earline was saying. Her hair was pulled back into its usual French twist, but at the crown of her head, the strands had separated into distinct furrows, the delicate shell color of her scalp rising like a flood from underneath. In a few years more, Clifford thought, she would be almost completely bald, as bald as she probably had been as a baby, nearly sexless and overwhelmingly coy, the embodiment of confusing contrasts.

"That's ridiculous," Clifford said. "Do you have any idea how many people you're condemning with that single statement?"

"You mean I'm condemning you," Earline said.

The waitress interrupted them for a moment to place two shallow bowls of steaming lobster bisque in front of them. The broth was thick and viscous-looking, as though someone had pureed peaches into it and decided to call it soup. At that instant, everything occurred to Clifford as a deception, as a careful misrepresentation of what it really was.

"I don't see how you can call yourself a feminist and then go spouting off those maxims about romance and the meaning of life," Clifford said.

"I'm complex." Earline shrugged.

"You're hypocritical," Clifford said.

Earline stared into her lap with a glassy-eyed, injured apathy that made Clifford wonder whether she waited for an apology, and beyond that, whether he ought to give it. "Actually," she said, "I was just hoping you might have taken an interest in someone."

"Why didn't you just ask me, Mother?"

"You would never have told me if I had asked you directly, and you know that perfectly well," Earline said.

"Only because there's nothing to tell."

"Well, I don't know why you should refuse to even *consider* taking an interest," she said. She was ladling the bisque onto itself, creating slight hillocks and knolls that were in a perpetual state of erosion within the borders of her dish. Occasionally, she ate a spoonful, consuming it with gusto, as if she were a hill-eating giant.

"You can't just decide to take an interest in someone," Clifford said. "It's not some elective you use to fill up your schedule."

"Well, that depends on the parties involved," Earline said.

"The parties?" Clifford said.

"Stew Souther is an elective," she said.

"I won't argue with you there."

Across the street, the bells of St. James' Episcopal Church began to ring. The sound of them fell down onto the open spaces below the steeple, spilling out with a familiar, high-pitched ache that washed up against McArthur's windows and then passed through to the other side. Clifford briefly imagined that he was back at school, discussing electives with his mother and submitting to her inquisitions on the subject of love. They had been all over the topic one hundred times, with her dragging him up the slippery slope. And maybe this was what mothers were meant to do: force their sons into staring at their own loneliness.

Earline had begun speaking again, her incisive, off-center intelligence focusing itself entirely on him. "You should forget about whether your interest is natural or cultivated," she was saying. "In the end, that's a question you won't even remember." She went on, but Clifford's attention meandered away from the table, in search of alternative voices. At the table behind him, a couple of men were discussing the difficulties of finding a girlfriend. Clifford had seen this happen many times before—the contagious spread of conversation in public places, with everyone feeling their own observations were original. Still, he couldn't help listening to what they had to say. He hoped for a masculine insight which he could wrap up like a nugget and carry away with him.

"I'm not interested in a woman who's been married before. I can tell you that much."

"Why not?"

"Well you've got to ask yourself, is this somebody who can see things through? Is this somebody who can hang in there with you even when it's not convenient?"

"I don't know. I don't go along with you on that. There're a lot of divorced people who are going to try harder the second time around."

"You think so?"

"Absolutely. And it can work the other way, you know. Plenty of women are going to take one look at you and walk the other way because you *haven't* been married."

"Come on. At thirty-six?"

"Really."

"Plenty of guys haven't been married by thirty-six."

The smart one didn't answer. A silence intruded on them —one filled up with the mute turbulence of self-doubt, Clifford thought. He resisted the adolescent urge to turn around in his chair and see what the two men looked like. One or the other of them would be sure to catch him staring, and then they would kill what was left of their conversation prematurely, by mutual and merciless consent. The only way you could profitably eavesdrop anymore was as a blind man, with your sense of hearing the only thing you relied on.

When the men began talking again, Clifford at first had difficulty understanding them.

"The one in blue."

"No, definitely not."

"I don't see why."

"It's the false eyelashes. They're a definite detractor."

"Are you sure those are false?"

"No question. She's got that tarantula look."

Clifford casually scanned the restaurant for a woman in blue with tarantula eyes, but he found no one who even barely approached the description. There was one elderly woman whose hair reflected blue in the indoor light, but that was all. Then he realized the men had been discussing passersby on the street outside. St. James' Church was just concluding its eleven o'clock service and the people inside flowed out over the stone steps in subtly knotted bunches, with pairs and threes descending together. A woman in blue had just turned her back to Clifford's view and strolled away.

"What about her?"

"Which one?"

"Just in front of those ladies with the crazy hats."

"The one in white?"

"That's her."

"I like her. She's probably forty, but she walks like a twenty-year-old."

"You noticed."

Clifford had found the woman they were talking about. She trotted forward before a surge of oddly dressed companions, the group of them moving in and out of the freckles of light. She wore a sleeveless, white linen dress and she swung her arms like she understood the full range of her grace. She walked like a woman who knew she was leading. She turned toward McArthur's as she crossed Main Street, and when she did so, Clifford was astonished to admit to himself that she was someone he knew, that she was Anna de la Senda, fresh and independent and quixotic and lovely.

Behind him, the two faceless men continued their commentary.

"But you never get to meet women like that, you know?"

"True."

"Their lives are chock-full without you, and there is always, always some guy waiting in the wings."

———•◦•———

CLIFFORD HAD never actually seen the inside of the de la Senda house before. Maybe he had peered in through the upstairs windows while balancing on an aluminum ladder, but he had never been escorted through the front door as a guest to see for himself the exuberant disarray within. And Anna realized that her housekeeping habits would dawn on him with something of a shock. So, on the Saturday that Clifford had arranged to pick her up for a hike in the mountains, Anna rose early and began to clean.

Across the hardwood floors lay a fine covering of birdseed

which the finches had kicked from their overhead trays, and this needed to be swept up into odd-sized pyramids of millet and sorghum and then to be carted away. The shelves that housed Anna's panoply of saints needed dusting. The devotional candles had melted into amorphous mounds of wax at the feet of the statuettes, and these needed to be scraped from their holders with butter knives and then replaced. The coffee cans in which she had baked the night before were stacked in the sink, waiting to be washed. Stuck to the refrigerator with heart-shaped magnets were several photographs of Mariela and Addison, their arms wrapped so tightly around one another that it appeared they were locked together, inextricably, in the desperate fusion of Siamese twins. These, she gathered together and hid away in a drawer. Who knew how much Clifford Ettinger realized of the love that thrived between their children? Certainly, it was best not to force him into discovering it through a series of snapshots that decorated her kitchen. This was the respect of one parent for another, she told herself.

When Clifford stepped through the doorway at nine a.m., he did not seem to notice the trouble to which Anna had gone. He stood in the middle of the Persian throw rug and stared with perplexed wonder at the chaos and the bounty that surrounded him. Dried flowers sprouted out of ceramic wall sconces in purple profusion. Seven antique mismatched teacups had been relegated to a side table, in wait for the Cordojo Women who would come to drink out of them the next day. The mail of at least the last ten days stuffed the mouth of a large Chinese urn, the envelopes still and white like inanimate tongues. Anna followed Clifford's gaze as it skipped from one incomprehensible item to the next, widening or narrowing at the encroachment of so many things.

Finally, he settled on looking at the birdcages which were suspended above his head. Through the brass bars of one of them, he spied the figure of an auburn-haired doll that cried real tears, sitting on a bird swing that rocked gently back and forth. This was the effigy of Anna that had emerged from her eaten birthday cake, the token that had so touched the Lovelorn Women that they could not bear the thought of her being thrown away. So Mariela had set her in a cage with two mourning doves, propped upon the narrow swing, her porcelain legs still coated with icing and crumbs. There, her tears would fall to the greatest purpose, since, as everyone knew, the mourning doves were only capable of singing two distinct songs—one of longing and one of sorrow. Every day, Mariela replenished her cavities with water, so that she would not forget crying as the means of her sympathy, so that she would not dry up and wither, like the hard-hearted and the bankrupt.

But Anna could explain none of this to Clifford. Not now, while he still hungered for the logical before the meaningful, the visible before the sacred. For him, the tangible world held nothing particularly mystical underneath its skin. But such ignorance was meant to be lifted away, and this was what Anna so delicately set out to do.

Clifford drove them to the Santa Rosa mountains, sharp-shouldered and yawning and shrugging off the remnants of a violet-layered haze. The land between the sea and the foothills had been scrappy and barren, unable to sustain the requirements of anything green but the joshua trees, which grew in the profiles of beautiful cripples. In the sky, several wedges of cloud separated themselves from a pregnant white bank, floating off into the open spaces like listless offspring, newly emerged from a weightless womb. The whole world seemed to be leaning over Clifford and Anna, observing the two of them with its remote, implacable grace.

Mount Carillon had a footpath that wound around it like a brown, crumbling decoration. Couples studded the broad, ascending trail, holding one another's hands in wordless adoration, passing nuts and chocolate bars and what looked like waxed apples back and forth. The pairs smiled at Clifford and Anna when they passed by, knowing smiles, as if to say that they recognized in the two of them a devotion like their own, as if to say that they, all of them, were members of the same species, passionate, bohemian, with all the values in the right places, a species of people who knew what life was really about. Anna wondered whether the other hikers concluded that Clifford and she were husband and wife. Probably, they did. But the question itself made her feel that her head had lost its top and that the most rational part of her entire being was now quivering naked, exposed to the weather. Perhaps this feeling was simply due to the way the air thinned out as they climbed higher. Anna didn't know.

"What do you think of Addison and your girl?" Clifford said. Two tufts of hair had blown away from his temples and stood out rakish and confused at the sides of his head.

"I think they're wonderful," Anna said.

"But I mean together," Clifford said. "What do you think of their being together?"

"You know about them?" Anna said.

Clifford nodded, the tufts of his hair waving like antennae.

"How can you not know about them?" he said. "Addison wears it all over his face."

"Yes," Anna said. "Youth is transparent."

Clifford seemed to be watching her in expectation, waiting for the meat of what she had yet to say. When she glanced at him his eyebrows were crouched low over his eyes, waiting there with a tacit sternness and respect. Anna registered with a small shock that he was waiting for her to express an opinion in accordance with his own, that he anticipated an affirmation, as if together they were in the process of making a decision with repercussions to it.

"But it's summertime," Anna said. "It's so easy to fall in love in the summertime. Mariela and Addison haven't lived enough years to realize."

"Exactly," Clifford said. "They fall into these phases and then they fall out of them again. It's all an experiment. It's all one great trial run."

"You might be going too far," she said. "It's not as though they're pretending their lives."

"No, I didn't say pretending."

"Their feelings come to them genuinely," Anna said. "Urgently even."

"Which is exactly why they need some boundaries set," Clifford said. "I'm not in favor of condescending to them. I'm just in favor of guiding them along."

"Oh, I believe in guidance," Anna said.

"You do?"

"Oh, certainly," Anna said.

"Well, that's fine," Clifford said. "Because so do I."

The tension dropped out of his demeanor as suddenly and wholly as a yolk falling out of an egg, a thick sphere of goldenrod worry dropping away below them. He laughed with an unhindered satisfaction, like a man who has just closed a delicate negotiation. Anna wondered what in the world it was that they had just agreed to. Guidance, she had said. But what would such a word mean to a man like Clifford Ettinger? Anna tried momentarily to assume his mindset, elegant and linear, where every cause and effect in life was explicated except for one: Marjorie. From this vantage, the word *guidance* was trained and tight, a euphemism for control. She ought to have made him understand that she meant something else entirely, but Clifford had hiked ahead of her on the path, and when she called his name, he did not hear.

At the summit, there was a small café that catered to the skiers in winter and the humble traffic of outdoorsmen in the off-seasons. Anna and Clifford bought cappuccinos and buttered club sandwiches and consumed them at a table overlooking the steep, crab-grassy slope. Occasional bunches of June-berry shot out of the earth in white fountains, and the boulders that separated them were smooth and featureless, like the heads of bald, giant men, all facing the other way. Clifford watched Anna while she was eating. She felt the clear pressure of his eyes in every place they rested—her lips, her chin, the hollow of her throat.

"I don't know anything about you," he said.

"Pardon me?" Anna said.

But he knew she had heard, and he didn't bother repeating himself. Anna was daubing her lips on a paper napkin, hiding behind this minor propriety. Her lipstick traveled onto the gauzy white square in the shapes of young nasturtiums—stem-less, lavish, entirely self-sustaining.

"It's completely unfair," Clifford said. "I've told you every important thing that's ever happened to me, and the only thing I know about you is that you live next door."

"Untrue," Anna said. She laid down her napkin on the table and Clifford stared at the pattern of lips spread across it, sensuous strawberry blooms, flooded with suggestion.

"And that you don't like anyone to trim your trees," he said.

"You know the way I look at life," Anna offered.

"I know the way you want *me* to look at life," he said. "That's something entirely separate."

"No," she said. "Those who know me will tell you it's the same. I can't recommend any solution that I haven't tried myself."

"Stop being so full of wisdom for a minute, will you?" he said.

The wind caught up Anna's napkin and dangled it above their heads, birdlike and bright, its paper wings flapping. "All right," Anna said. "I'll try to act foolish for a little while." She reached up for the napkin, but it rose and swooped away.

"Fine," Clifford said. "Now while I have you with your guard down, tell me something about yourself."

"Ask me something you want to know," Anna said.

Clifford looked out over the slope, studying its bare spaces and rises, its scars and hidden marks. Anna had the feeling he had the question in his mind all the while, but was searching for the phrase to clothe it in. When his eyes stopped moving, he had found it.

"How long have you and your daughter been on your own?" he said.

"Twelve years," Anna said.

"Twelve years," he said. "That long."

"It's not what I expected," she said. "Being alone never is."

A piece of fringe from Anna's bangs fell down over one

eye and she neglected to move it away. Behind it, she withdrew into her womanly privacy, into the sightless, precious ache that carried the name of Cristobal. If she had had to locate the site of her injury, she would have picked the spot just under her sternum where her flesh turned ripe and soft and shapely despite the fact that there were no bones underneath to guide its direction. Mostly, the sensitivity that lay there remained asleep, hibernating and protected from whatever forces shook its cave. But there were moments, like this one, when her past was brought into question and the delicate place went into spasm, fluttering inside her abdomen like a strange and second heart. No one knew of its existence except herself. Not even Mariela. Not even the Cordojo Women. It struck Anna, and she thought it would have struck them, as unseemly that she contained this flaw. The generous shall not be needful. The healer shall not fall sick.

But when Anna and Clifford began their climb down the mountain, she could still feel her second heart beating, flip-flopping under her skin like a fish pulled up onto the dock. It moved in desperation and bewilderment, its mouth pumping in the empty air. Anna heard its rhythm before she heard any other, and set against it, the pace of her footfall was contrapuntal and disorienting, clumsy and ill-timed. The afternoon sun fractured itself against the limestone inclines, manufacturing images amid the light and shadow of the rock face: a cornucopia basket, a fetus curled in the shape of a three-quarter moon, a sphinx crouched and smiling in its gargantuan repose.

Anna lost her footing at about the time she saw the last of these pictures, stumbling over a tree root that crooked its woody knuckle in her path. She had sprained her ankle, Clifford said after he pulled off her shoe and sock and held her tiny alabaster foot in his hand. Above her bone, a lump was pushing up its rounded, purplish peak. It seemed to Anna slightly volcanic. The skin, where she touched it, was bitterly hot and its very existence appeared to derive from some trenchant, internal pressure, from the secret shifting of invisible sands.

Anna held onto Clifford's arm for half of the descent. But

then the last of the sun came to them as through a filter; the cicadas gathered and sang from the skins of the evergreens; the shadows consumed the visible world with their slack, unhinged mouths. Anna's good ankle grew tired and teetered underneath her and when it began to tremble uncontrollably, Clifford noticed. He picked Anna up altogether then, one arm underneath her back, the other underneath her knees, like men on the cover of the romance fictions that Dove Pairlee carried with her everywhere. One of those embossed, windswept clinches with the cleavage and the breathlessness and the raven-haired disarray. Anna didn't know why she thought of this except that she felt as disheveled and ridiculous as some of those moist-eyed maidens being hefted away into romantic nirvana. On her stomach, she held her empty shoe and sock, mementos of her awkwardness. Her injured foot waved freely in the open air, white and increasingly bulbous, the toenails polished the blue-red of bougainvilleas, which was startlingly close to the color of a wound.

Her small and ongoing nakedness embarrassed her. She had never intended that anyone but Mariela should have such an intimate glimpse of her foot. Not that it really mattered, of course. Perhaps what disturbed her more was the sense of being contained so completely within a man's grasp, or maybe the furtive pleasure she took in realizing that there was no need for her to worry about the burden of her weight, that Clifford was strong enough and that he would not complain or give out or tell funny stories about her afterwards. Because it was hard to think about Clifford Ettinger as a grieving patient while he was carrying her down off a mountain. It was hard not to think about him first and foremost as a man.

When they reached the car, he settled her in the passenger seat without her feet ever touching the ground, as if she had forgotten how to hold herself up, as if he wasn't taking any chances. Later, it occurred to Anna that this was precisely the way Clifford transported his mother, Earline. How many times had she seen the two of them through her window, Clifford carrying Earline back and forth across the threshold like some pale invalid bride? Often enough to know that it had long ceased to be awkward and uncertain between them, if ever it once was.

And there was another reason why carrying Anna off the mountain should not make an impression on Clifford. He was a doctor, after all. People were always confiding their infirmities to him, helplessly, nakedly requiring his assistance. All of that neediness might have been off-putting, but at least it wasn't personal. These were the reassurances Anna made to herself as they drove homeward to Marbury Park. From where she sat, the scenery flooded the windshield like debris in dark water, turning over on itself with inscrutable repetition. The cover seemed to have been lifted off the sky, because all the stars had withdrawn to an invisible distance, and the wind whipped up the clouds into a circling maelstrom with a hole at the center, as though someone were secretly siphoning them away. Clifford drove too quickly, passed cars on the right, negotiated turns without a proper margin. His eyebrows were in flight somewhere close to his hairline, making him look, even from the side, like he was in a state of perpetual surprise.

He was still wearing the same expression when he pulled up outside the de la Senda house, the birdcages swinging beyond the open windows like clear lanterns of light. The broad leaves of the tulip tree silvered in the wind, like schools of delicate fish, taking a sudden direction. Clifford carried Anna underneath their whispering transformations and onto the open porch. He said nothing, but his breath came and went in such a way that Anna could feel the ebb and pull of the air as it passed over the opening at her collar. It was a breath that was holding itself back from something, hesitatingly measured out in portions of restraint.

When Clifford began fumbling for the door handle, Anna said, "Oh no. No no. You don't need to carry me any farther."

"Well," Clifford said. He stopped trying to make his way inside, but he didn't put Anna down, either.

"I'm sorry about the hike," Anna said.

"Why are you sorry about it?"

"My ankle," she said.

Clifford raised his shoulders as much as was possible in an effort to shrug them. "You can't always be taking care of the rest of the world."

On the slatted floor of the porch, the shadows of Clifford and Anna were kissing. Perhaps it was only the angle of the outdoor lighting that brought their heads together in such a suggestive fusion. But Anna knew very well that shadows held reflections of the private will, and so it only surprised her minutely when, still kissing, the figures passed through the barrier of the front door and beyond, moving toward some place of seclusion and silence where the dark kept company with itself.

Outside, the real Clifford and Anna said good-bye, good night, see you next week, and set about the business of untangling themselves, one limb at a time and oh so gingerly, in an effort not to cause anybody any pain.

PART THREE

Streamlined,
a Changeling

ANNA'S CLAIRVOYANCE was an irregular gift, tattered and lovely at the edges, like a veil of antique lace. Sometimes, it enabled her to see past the coverings of things, to divine the essential contents that lay inside, silent and glittering, their existence concealed. She had known, for example, all the times that Mariela stole saint cakes from the pantry as a little girl. She had known it without even opening the frosted glass doors that swung like giant butterfly wings off the edge of the kitchen, without counting out the cakes that remained or trying to remember how many she had prepared the night before. She had known it without glancing at her daughter's face, dark-eyed and blissful and emptied of all earthly hungers. She had known, too, about the quiet, slow-moving dementia of Esther Lee's husband. She had sensed his illness before it ever adorned itself with symptoms, before it ever withered the fleshy fingers of his mind or supplied the nonsense notions that he had babbled over all day, before it ever drove

Esther Lee into a willful deafness in which blasphemy and bad news no longer needed to be acknowledged.

But in spite of her clear-sightedness, there were many things that Anna wished to discern which she could not. She wished to comprehend the particular hills and hollows that made up the landscape of Mariela's heart that summer, but Mariela had begun to hold her heart private and dear, the way she might cup her hands around a lit match. No longer would she confess her small delights, her lasting disappointments, her tender, ineffable revelations that life was like this or that. And Anna began to come to terms with the idea that the attachment of the mother to the child was necessarily, undeniably, stronger than that of the child to the mother. From that point onward, she would need Mariela more than Mariela would need her back; she would long for Mariela more than Mariela would long for her in return. Such were the asymmetries of love and aging, and Anna would try to accept them with the smallest amount of regret she could manage.

She remembered a folk tale that Cristobal had told her, long ago, before she had ever been able to imagine that he could speak an untruth. There was once a bird, he had said, who had three chicks which she planned to transport across a river. The first of them crawled onto the mother bird's back, and the two of them took flight. The mother beat her wings with urgent force to support her chick's weight in addition to her own. When they were halfway across the swollen, cold-flowing water, the mother asked her chick, "Will you love and care for me in my old age in the same way that I love and care for you now?" "Yes, Mother, I will," the chick replied. But the mother bird knew her chick to be a liar and she flung him off of her back and into the coursing river below. The bird re-trieved her second chick from the riverbank, and when they were halfway across the swollen, cold-flowing water, the mother again asked, "Will you love and care for me in my old age in the same way that I love and care for you now?" "Yes, Mother, I will," the second chick said. But the mother bird knew this chick also to be a liar, and she cast her off of her wings and into the churning river below. The bird picked up her third and final chick from the riverbank, and when they were halfway across the swollen, cold-flowing water, the mother asked for the last time, "Will you love and care for me in my old age in the same way that I love and care for you now?" "No, Mother, I cannot," the third chick replied. "I can only love and care for my own children in the same way that you love and care for me now." Satisfied that her chick would do as he said, the mother carried him to the safety of her new nest.

Cristobal had spoken wisely about everything—mothers and children and parables of loss. His words still sounded in Anna's mind as freshly as if he had just spoken them, yesterday or that morning or a moment ago. Something within his voice conspired to give the impression of timelessness. Perhaps it was simply the subjects he chose. He always ruminated on truths that would outlast him; he always spoke with the strange, relentless knowledge of the soul. Later, after he had left her to return to the small, sun-flooded village somewhere outside of Cuernavaca, Anna wondered whether it had all been a ruse, whether all his careful teachings had been part of some elaborate deception designed to draw her into his confidence. But no, a man does not sacrifice seven whole years of his life in order to perpetrate an emotional deceit. Where was the satisfaction in something like that? Where was the reward with which to escape? No, when Cristobal had said that he loved her, there had only been an ingenuous clarity in his eyes, there had only been that still, wondrous, welling-up of what he felt for her. That was what she would most remember. That was what she would hold firmly in her mind.

Clifford had begun asking questions about Cristobal, hesitant questions, careful ones. He approached the threshold of the other man's absence on tiptoe, gingerly, with a quiet curiosity about its importance in Anna's continuing life. In his own subdued, straightforward way, he seemed to imply a certain similarity between Anna's missing spouse and his own, as if Cristobal and Marjorie had disappeared into the same vast, invisible void that rendered them now unreachable. He moved with suddenness and skill between his inquiries about Cristobal and his revelations about Marjorie, as if the one very naturally brought to mind the other.

Anna realized that it was almost classic, this growing fascination on the part of the patient with the therapist's life, this need for him to say, "You and I are alike, Anna. You understand my life as I understand yours." It was part of the infatuation of friendship; it was part of the assignation of trust. So Anna could not understand her own reluctance to talk about Cristobal in Clifford's presence. She could not understand why it was painful to her in a shame-ridden, teenage, neck-prickling kind of way. As if a high school boyfriend had asked her to tell all about the boy she had gone steady with last year. It was a ludicrous comparison, of course, but that was just what it felt like exactly. Unequivocally secret, wildly disloyal, rife with embarrassment. She said to Clifford what she could not get away without saying, but nothing more. That he had been a house painter, that they had married after knowing one another for only four months, that at the end of seven years, he had left her to return to his home in Mexico. Because he missed it, because he dreamt about it, because he could imagine doing nothing else.

"And he just left you and your daughter behind?" Clifford said.

"Yes," Anna said.

"Did you want to go with him?" he said.

"Sometimes what you want isn't possible," Anna said.

Clifford's expression was pressed, straining toward the details that were left out. How could he? How could she? And what about the child? His questions wrote themselves over his face in sinewy script—ancient, insistent, confounded.

But everything about Cristobal had defied explanation—from his indelible intrusion into Anna's life to his unprepared flight from it. She could not justify what he had meant to her in the same way that she could not justify her faith in God. These attachments simply existed as a part of her being, inseparable from the fabric of her soul. Certainly, there were some people, one or two of the Cordojo Women, even, who would have preferred that Anna relegate Cristobal to the realm of admitted mistakes, who would have wished her to say that she had been foolish and naive in granting him such an easy reign over her life. But for Anna, he had been nothing less than an unexpected gift, a gratuitous happiness, a strikingly ample embodiment of her dreams. Never would she deny the generous reality of who he was, not even in retrospect, with all of his flaws chasing in his wake.

She had first met him on the day he arrived at 238 Raborn Way, assigned by the Marbury Park Homeworks Company to paint the interior of her house. Anna had been new to town, twenty-four years old, still wearing black as a token of the stark, tremulous mourning she undertook at the death of her father. Mr. Ian McCafferty had died in his sleep one night from the sheer, insupportable weight of his own desire to do so. He had been a widower for sixteen years and had sworn before Anna that sixteen was enough. When Anna had found him in his bed, he was splayed across the covers in diagonal splendor, the folds of his bathrobe arcing out from his sides like voluminous butterfly wings, dusty with flight. There was nothing she could have said in advance to prevent his willing exit, and yet the event infused her life with many unbearable echoes of inadequacy, of cringing, filial guilt. Somehow, she had expected that she would be able to provide her father with the reasons for continuing. She felt some unfathomable, silent rebuke contained in his ultimate turning away.

In his careless, single-minded confusion, he had left her with nearly as many debts as he had assets. After Anna honored all the outstanding bills, there were three thousand forty-seven dollars in the bank, and a stand-alone house in Marbury Park which, having once belonged to Mr. McCafferty's mother, was paid for free and clear. Anna planned to fix up that house and sell it, to take the proceeds along with her to San Francisco where she would put her masters degree in counseling to use and find work as a therapist. But then, Cristobal de la Senda appeared, with his step ladders and bristle brushes and gallons of peach satin paint, with his easy conversation and Caribbean complexion and his calm, trenchant wisdom for which he never asked anything in return. When he spoke to Anna, he looked at her longer than he should have. She did not know why she felt this, because, after all, what was so inappropriate about a long look? But she always had the sense that she was swimming toward him as their eyes met, passing through the intervening spaces head first, as if stroking toward him under water. As a precaution against the relentless heat, he often wore no shirt, and Anna found herself returning his stare when his back was turned, studying the way his skin glided over his shoulders as he swept the brush back and forth, the way the tips of his hair clung to his neck as if pulled there by some dauntless, preternatural attraction, the way his coloring looked glazed in the indoor light, basted with some sauce that was spread miraculously and even, thickened and gold-tinged and salty. With time, his form became monumental, impassable. It filled up Anna's house with the shape of inevitable yearning.

It was he who lifted Anna up out of her loneliness, out of her peerless, orphaned isolation. It was he who one day gave her a brightly colored dress to wear, a blue-green gauze with an off-the-shoulder collar, a dress made for a mermaid and not a mourner. And when she changed into it from her straight, silk, funeral dress, he asked her to promise never to wear black again, she looked so much more alive without it, so much more in the breathing world. She looked lovely outside of black; brilliant, glowing, surfaced from her soulful imprisonment. All this he told her, and so she assured him that she would never descend into her mourner's clothing again. It was a vow that only seemed rash in hindsight, many years later, when loss once more enveloped her like an old, well-known enemy, intrepid and worn and too quickly forgotten. At the time, though, in the middle of that blinding, heat-struck summer, with both her mother and her father in their deep, distant graves, Anna thought it was probable that she should never have any real, new cause for grief again, that there would only be the old griefs taken up in reprise, aching and far away, the precise shape of their sorrows turned familiar.

The first time they made love, they lay down together on the newsprint that covered the hardwood floor. Cristobal had asked that the windows be left open, and the cross-breeze moved through the house like a breath, picking up the corners of the newspapers surrounding them and then laying them back down again, languorously, like the movements of strange elephant ears. They traced one another's birthmarks and scars, Anna caressing the tiny rose-colored fish that swam toward his hairline, Cristobal outlining the white, Y-shaped keloids that marked the place on her palm where she had once been scalded. As if the movements of their fingers sought to take away the sign of the other's pain, to remove the token of the other's imperfection. Anna felt somehow healed under his hands, the most miraculously whole that she had been in the entire length of her young, bewildered, yearning life. So, it did not surprise her to learn, two months later, that a baby had taken hold that very first time despite her long-agreed-upon infertility, despite her seaweed ovaries and her shriveled womb. A baby had taken hold, Cristobal's and hers, and could there ever be a thing more splendorous than that?

When Cristobal sat up from the floor that first time, the newsprint had bled onto his back. All the letters were reversed, and Anna could read nothing but the section heading and a few of the proper names. The word ƧƎNIꓷꓷƎW appeared in an inch-high tattoo between his shoulder blades, and below it was a smudged, impressionistic picture of a bride and groom, their lower halves rooting downward in two amorphous tree trunks, like lovers from a myth, whose legs had cracked with wood and sap in the very instant they had wished for love without end.

———•◦•———

CRISTOBAL, WITHOUT seeming to try, without struggling or coaxing or pronouncing himself her teacher, transformed Ann into Anna in the space of a single summer, at the end of which they were married on the wave of Anna's ecstatic, newfound, beatified certainty that God in heaven ordained all things good. In point of fact, Cristobal could not pronounce the word *Ann* at all. The habits of his accent could not leave her name without a final flourish, and his embellishments caught on with the people of Marbury Park before Anna could say otherwise. Even the priest, Father Murphy, who was so precise with his language that he invited corrections on his readings of the Latin mass, called her Anna in the midst of his recitation of the wedding vows: Do you, Anna, take this man . . . ? She allowed her own renaming without a solitary misgiving or regret. She shed her former self as unequivocally and as thoroughly as she had shed her mourner's clothes. One day, she awoke and these things were no longer with her. They were warehoused or given to charity, or they were worn by the string-bound scarecrow out behind Mr. Marbury's vegetable stands. Anxious, twice-abandoned, barren Ann McCafferty had ceased to live and breathe in this world as she had known it. And in her place rose Anna de la Senda, expectant, religion-struck, beloved beyond her imagining.

Mariela was born in February, carried forth from the womb in a salty wave of water that broke with such suddenness and force that there was no time to travel to the hospital. The onset of the birth turned Anna rubber-kneed and clammy, her white, freckled feet trembling with such wild volatility on the mattress that it took Cristobal to hold them down. Anna touched Mariela for the first time when she was only half-emerged into the world. Covering her head and one of her tiny blue-gray arms was the brilliant, hooded caul, the sign of a favorable creation, the symbol that would make her always, in her mother's mind, Mariela the Shining. It was slippery to the touch, like clear egg whites or deep-sea jellyfish, viscous, protozoan, sticky with the makings of life. Anna would never forget the pleasure she felt in touching this still-warm mask, or in sliding it away to reveal the treasured, black-haired head of the baby who, with the very next push, would emerge complete and wiggling into the wide daylight, her body held forward in the hands of her father.

Under the influence of her parents' Catholicism and

candle-lighting, of their elaborate, homespun celebrations of Three Kings' Day and Candlemas, Cinqo de Mayo and the Day of the Dead, Mariela grew up to be a profoundly mystical child. She collected rosary beads and Greek myths with equal fervor, and she prayed on her knees each night with no reminder. For some reason unknown to anyone, she called her father by his Christian name. In the early years, though, *Cristobal* was too difficult a word for her. She approximated it by saying *crystal ball*, which was just as much as she could manage. "Crystal ball, what are we going to do today? Crystal ball, when will I be older than you? Crystal ball, dance with me while I stand on your toes." It was as though her father were an oracle she regularly consulted, a seer, all-knowing, a clear eye looking toward her future. Mariela believed he understood the very corners of the universe.

Together, the three of them made a life for themselves that was conventionally modest in its outer design and lavishly idiosyncratic in its private workings. Anna supported them all with her tender, burgeoning practice in counseling, an endeavor for which many of her patients paid her in trade or services, in six bags' worth of vine-ripened tomatoes or in three months' worth of gardening for her patchy, poppy-covered lawn. Cristobal painted houses and stained pieces of kitchen cabinetry and carved small statuettes of the blessed saints. Each week, he laid half of the money he had earned into Anna's hands. The other half he folded inside a white piece of paper, mailing it off to a long, six-lined address somewhere close to Cuernavaca which Anna imagined to be the residence of his mother, who would be white-haired and hearty and would overcook her rice in the same way that Cristobal did. But she never asked. Such were the privacies that she knew instinctively to respect. A person who did not speak freely of his origins would not wish to be questioned about them by another. Every revelation would have its own proper time.

In the interim, Anna lived in a state of perpetual, happy disorganization. Cristobal liked the windows left open day and night all the year round, and through them flew dragonflies on double cellophane wings and warm rain at a slant, and, when the dandelions went to seed in the yard, a thousand feathery flecks of drifting fertility. Anna made love with Cristobal in between her counseling appointments or when the dinner dishes still needed clearing from the table or in the blind, pitch-stained hours of the night, when to open the eyes was the same as to keep them closed and when the hands learned to see without seeing. In the moments when she reflected on it, Anna felt as if she had been transported into another life, one in which a husband and child filled up the best of her days, one in which her loneliness had been amputated, like the useless, extra appendage it was, leaving her transfigured, streamlined, a changeling. The only time she felt her old sorrow was in the morning, on first waking, when tears flooded her eyes with reasonless, daily profusion. She wept without understanding, like a vessel that water passes through. Cristobal always said that she cried for her patients, out of uncontainable empathy, because that was her God-given talent: to comprehend the losses of others as though they were her own. He ate her tears as they appeared. It was an act of patience and tenderness that Anna would always remember. His head lolled as he swallowed them, one at a time, looking like some hapless dragon pausing over a bitter meal. It would have strained her to consider the dimensions of his devotion. Like the universe, it seemed to hold no actual boundaries.

But everything as Anna had come to know it changed in the interval of one February day in the year that Mariela celebrated her sixth birthday, the same year that her first innocence fell like scales from her eyes while Anna watched with disbelief, unable, even temporarily, to look away from the wreckage that came to surround them. What happened was simply a knock on the door at 238 Raborn Way. Outside, on the shady, mud-patterned porch, a woman in a yellow gauze dress shouted something at Anna in Spanish. The words came out too quickly for Anna to understand. The woman kept gesturing at the house while she spoke, crazy, repetitive, back-handed gestures that seemed to warn of impending demolition.

"I don't know what you mean," Anna told her. "Speak more slowly. *Despacio.*"

But the woman could not help herself. The words fell out of her mouth in an effusive, agitated torrent, as if someone were directing a full-force spigot from a source at the base of her throat. Cristobal's name filled her sentences more than any other, and when Anna finally understood that the woman had a message for her husband, she led her inside the house and comforted her.

"It will be all right," Anna said with deliberate clarity. "I don't know what you're trying to say, but Cristobal will know. He'll know right away, and then we'll solve whatever the problem is. *No se angustie.*"

The two of them waited for an hour before Cristobal came home from work. The Spanish-speaking woman drank Anna's twice-warmed coffee, and lay down on the bolstered couch, slipping her sandals off before she did so. Under her cheekbones, there were well-shaped caverns that made her face elegant and worn and pitiably beautiful. Once, she cried, when Mariela came into the room to offer her a freshly peeled orange, bright and sectioned in a ceramic bowl. The tears fell out of her eyes at the corners, dripping onto the sofa cushion that supported her head in a sorrowful mixture of brine and mascara, confusion and duress.

Somehow, Anna felt sure that all of this was connected to Cristobal's mother—that the ancient, white-haired lady she had imagined picking avocados out of the trees in the hills of Cuernavaca was no longer hale and hearty and waiting for her son to introduce his new family to her. Probably, she had died—of pneumonia, of influenza, of one of those diseases that shouldn't have killed anyone anymore. And here was one of Cristobal's relatives, a cousin, a sister-in-law, a someone, calling him home for the impending funeral. Anna could sense the proportions of the tragedy, unexpected, impossible, irrevocable.

But, of course, she had never been so wrong about anything in all her life. Not with regard to the tragedy, but with regard to its fundamental content, its principal characters, its grossly flawed heroes, of which she apparently was one. Because the scene which began to play itself out before her was one that she never could have imagined, one that she could scarcely grasp even as it was in front of her, facing her straight on, monstrous and wrenching in all its effects.

It did not take Cristobal long to come to his confession— twenty-one minutes of arguing with the woman in an earsplitting rush of Spanish, and six minutes in the kitchen by himself, his head held up by his hands in a silent migraine of grief. Then he revealed to Anna what it was, that the woman, the woman there on the couch in the wrinkled gauze dress and the beautiful worn face, that she was his wife. His first wife, his real wife, the one he had been sending all the money to. He had only come to California in the first place to support her and the others. Short-term, they had agreed. But then, the money was so good that no one objected to his staying on longer. So, what was he to do? Hold himself in celibacy for all those years? A man had to have a life! Did Anna understand? A life! That was all he had wanted. He had never meant to harm her. Never, never in the wide, green world had he meant to harm her. He wanted her to understand. Was it possible that she could understand?

The words did a strange, muted violence to Anna. Just the sheer physical presence of them, there in the same room with her. They gathered in small, taloned heaps about her head, inanimate and dangerous, and making it difficult for her to walk from one end of the room to the other. The very air was treacherously full of unseen obstacles, of reasons and rationalizations and plain, raving lies. Mariela twined her thin, burnished arms around the circumference of Anna's thigh. She cried without comprehension, the long jet-colored lashes under her eyes clumping together in the same way that they did after she had been swimming. Anna coaxed her over to the three-tiered altar of the saints, where she pinched some soft wax off the lips of the votive candles and rolled out two small tepid plugs. These she inserted carefully into Mariela's seashell ears, into their beautiful pink curled edges, into the polished conch surface of their interior whorl, where Anna had intended that only the sounds of love should pass. Now, for an hour, Mariela would know only silence, only the unexpected, dislocated quiet that poured forth when her parents opened their mouths.

There was never any question but that Cristobal would go back with the woman to whatever far-off place she had journeyed from. The whole drama had been an exercise in retrieval, in the excruciating, latent, inevitable ways that a person could be called home. He transferred his clothes from the bureau into the dusty beds of two cardboard boxes. Anna thought that his shirts somehow retained his shape, even when they were empty, and she was sad to see them collapse carelessly into the containers, their arms flailing, as though they were being taken away against their will. The woman in the yellow gauze watched from the doorway. Her lips were set in a line of grim satisfaction, braced against one another, no longer capable of showing surprise. The neckline of her dress was lopsided, and at its straying base, Anna could make out a lacy, salmon-colored swatch of her bra, unabashedly embellished, as intricate as a doily. For all her weathered appearances, the woman was still lovely. Anna could admit this to herself, even then, at the time.

"Are there other children?" Anna asked.

Yes, Cristobal nodded, there were. He offered no further explanation and Anna didn't require it. She could see them in her mind's eye, their faces darkened with sun and heredity, their heads of hair so glossy and black that they would reflect clear pictures of the outer world: low sienna hills and avocado trees, old men who dozed in their wicker chairs on the sidewalks in front of their shops, little brown partridges that flocked together in the streets. It was all inexplicable and true. Somewhere, they existed, waiting for the return of Cristobal, a man they hardly remembered.

When he had gathered his belongings together, Cristobal walked out the door of Anna's house for the last possible time. The fish birthmark on his forehead suddenly looked to Anna like a brand, an emblem of his uncontrolled fertility, a warning to the women who paused over it. Anna hadn't known. And neither had the woman who now walked behind him, cardboard boxes weighing in her hands.

Mariela, with her wax-filled ears and her tearful bewilderment, called after him from the edge of the lawn. "Crystal ball!" she said. "Where are you going?"

AND WHAT was Anna left with after Cristobal had gone? Fourteen statues of the saints and the faith that lived inside them. A Spanish name, a belief in the miraculous, nine windows which would remain open for as long as she would live. A second heart which fluttered and stumbled underneath her first. Mariela the Shining, impossibly alive, indisputably angelic, suspended between the heavens and the earth with her strange unspoken knowledge of what it was to fly. No, Anna could not harbor a permanent anger for the man who had given her all of these. Even in the midst of his betrayal, she could find no room for regret. Later, there would be the rages and recriminations which she would become hoarse giving voice to, but never would she wish away those years of love and mysticism and the first, most extravagant putting down of her roots.

In the week following Cristobal's departure, Marbury Park felt its first earthquake in a decade. In different parts of town, the crystal teardrops of the chandeliers clinked together, the window boxes filled with lush, fat-bodied geraniums toppled from their ledges, the tiger cats and the spotted dogs and the molting parakeets all cried their cries of animal doom with the peculiar prescience that was their birthright. But the only substantial damage was sustained at the United Methodist Church, where the Mediterranean roof was shaken off completely, its earth-red ceramic tiles raining down onto the lawn like the broken teeth of a giant, a dozen of them at a time. During the weeks when the vestry board tried to raise the money to rebuild, the church held its services under the open, undiminished sky, with great bodies of clouds swimming silent and fish-like over the congregation's heads. Anna began to attend out of a kind of sympathy and stayed for the sheer loveliness of it. She knew what it was like, after all, to have the covering pried away from one's life, to be sitting out there, under the elements, praying for the shortness of the rainy season. But what she didn't expect was the beauty of a church without a roof, those four walls filled with wind and light, all the ribbons on the little girls' hats floating up off their backs as if some invisible hand were lifting them. What she didn't expect was the way the hymns were snatched up into the air above them, hungrily, their sounds being taken up by the atmosphere like a nourishment, as if there were a taste to those fleeting, tremulous pieces of song. Almost every disaster had its redemption, Anna realized. Almost every calamity had its cure.

———————

PERHAPS MARIELA never got over the missing man. Anna had always known this was a possibility. Perhaps she waited now for Addison to make his daily appearance in just the same way she had waited for Cristobal, standing just inside her open bedroom window, her eyes fixed on Raborn Way in a willful, glazed-over plea that he would come back after all. She could not bear the notion that she would not be returned to. Anna could sense these truths as clearly as if they had been written out for her on the translucent parchment of the soul.

Anna would have worried less about her daughter's attachment were it not for the sweet-scented aura that Mariela began to carry with her wherever she went. Her breath floated the fragrance of too many lilacs, as though secretly, in the privacy of her bedroom, she had been eating blossoms dozens at a time with a hunger that was wild and constant. Under the arms of her cast-off blouses, her perspiration left no trace. Instead, there was the faint, left-over smell of fruit, of orange groves and bottled plums, of pears set to soak in brandy. It all had something to do with Addison and Mariela coming together. Something about their union was turning Mariela into a vulnerable confection, perishable and easily bruised, ripening too quickly for comfort. Anna once tried to reassure herself with the thought that her daughter might simply have taken to wearing perfume. But when she had asked about it, Mariela's eyes had closed shut with astonishment and mirth.

"Perfume!" she said. "Why would I need to wear it?"

"No, no," Anna said. "It's not that I think you do."

"Perfume would be too much for someone like me."

"You already smell like flowers without it," Anna said.

"I do?"

"Yes," Anna said. "Even your hair."

Mariela shook her head with girlish amusement. "That's just what Addison says. *Even your hair.*"

So there was no way for Anna to tell her that the odor was frightening to a mother's senses, that it was unnatural and cloying and redolent of tragedy. But if Anna could have had her way, she would have cleansed Mariela in a bath of vinegar; she would have rinsed her hair with whipped egg whites and witch hazel; she would have rubbed the soles of her feet with powdered charcoal and crumbled chalk. All this, so that Mariela would smell the way she used to smell. Like the child, like the innocent, like the half-angel girl that she had once been.

———•◦•———

MARIELA AND Addison made love as though they were the only two people ever created for each other. They made love in their bedrooms without breathing, so as not to wake their parents. They made love on a blue lamb's wool afghan spread out under the trees in Marbury's orange grove. They made love next to the fish pond behind the public library, in which the koi moved in bright, languid ellipses of color: pumpkin and maize and palladium red. Mariela never felt so whole as when she was undressed, standing in front of him, her skin anticipating which part of her he would touch first.

Addison laid down his sorrows in front of Mariela because she made him a safe place. He told her how he worried that his writing would never amount to anything, that he might be just a dilettante, inconsistently talented, lacking the willpower to make something more of himself. And he listened while she told him that none of it was true, that she could not imagine how he trusted his own abiding gifts so little, that he would not stray because she would not permit him to stray; it was as fundamental as that.

Sometimes, he cried over the death of his mother, Marjorie, whose passing he was supposed to have recovered from. He let go of tears which struck the ground with audible force, huge tears, the size of gumdrops, which seemed too big to have originated at the corners of his eyes. He hid this grief from his father and everyone else who asked about it. In actuality, he could not even sense his grief in the presence of the others. Only by himself, or with Mariela, would it take on its inexhaustible life, thrumming hotly behind his temples, forcing the brine out of his eyes as if by some internal pump, involuntarily, unstoppably, draining him swollen-eyed and dry.

"She always used to sing these little nonsense rhymes to me," he said. "You know, when I was a boy."

"Rhymes?" Mariela said.

"Yes," he said. "Whenever we would pull up into the driveway, she would sing, 'Home again, home again, jiggety jog. Home with a prince and a boy and a frog.' "

"She did?" Mariela said.

"Yes," he said. "Have you ever heard that?"

Mariela shook her head no. The two of them sat on the ledge of the fish pond, partially dressed, their hair weeping over their foreheads in wet disarray. "She must have made it up for you," she said. "Tell me another one."

"There was one she used to say in the morning," he said. "It went, 'Wake up, wake up. The oatmeal's in the breakfast cup. The boy is young but well-brought-up. He must wake up.' "

They smiled wistfully, remembering what it was to hear nursery rhymes. Underneath them, the fish made slow figure eights, hypnotizingly, the tips of their fins as transparent as glass.

"The thing is, I had forgotten them until just the other day," he said. "I had left them behind completely, just like they were nothing. Can you believe that?"

"You can't hold every moment in your mind at once," Mariela said. "That's not possible."

"But I was so careless when I was younger," he said. "I was so careless about what she said to me and what she did for me. I thought to myself, *She's just my mother. Everybody has a mother. That's the way the world works.*"

"Everybody thinks that," Mariela said. "And then everybody finds out later that they were wrong."

"That's true, isn't it?" Addison said.

Mariela slipped into the water, the bloom of her skirt floating around her like a parasol. She waded over to where Addison sat and waited for him to touch her. Later, when he stepped into the pond beside her, the fish would kiss their ankles, as if they had been enchanted.

———•◦•———

MARIELA AND Emily D. sometimes made money by fashioning hat decorations for India Perry. They sat on her roof, stringing together artificial berries or the stems of silk nasturtiums or painting intricate designs onto the backs of cardboard swallowtail butterflies. Afterwards, they glued the objects in clusters of different combinations. India paid them four dollars an hour and provided them with unlimited amounts of iced tea and finger sandwiches. And the rooftop lent the best possible view of Saxon Hill South's comings and goings. From their perch, the girls could see Mrs. Friedrich sunbathing naked by her swimming pool, her knee-length chestnut hair arranged over her reclining form like Lady Godiva. They could see the glint of Mr. Laliberte's binoculars where they appeared at the lower edge of his balloon-shaded windows, directed invariably on the distant focus of Mrs. Friedrich. They could see Mr. Clifford Ettinger as he walked back and forth between the de la Senda house and his own, the silver-dollar-sized spot where he was balding at the crown of his head gradually darkening to a frustrated pink under the strength of the sun.

"What does Mr. Ettinger want with your mother?" Emily D. said. She held a string of plastic raspberries in the air and inspected them for regularity. One end of the rope was hidden within the folds of her skirt, and it looked for a moment as though she might have been examining her own tail, bulbous and exotic and painted a brilliant red.

"They're friends," Mariela said. "What does one friend want with another?"

The girls laughed at the silence that followed. Of course it was clear that Mr. Ettinger was thoroughly bothered about something and what bothered people most of the time was the uncontrollable course of their own quiet desire. But it wasn't right to joke about it too much. Both of them knew that very well. Because after three hours or four, they would have to come down off of India Perry's rooftop and walk around in the world again without any separateness, without any antiseptic distant elevation. And then they would think about their own desires and nothing about them would look humorous or fumbling. Not in the least little way.

Mariela and Emily D. put most of the money they earned into savings accounts for college. Emily D. was going to UCLA at the end of September, but Mariela thought she would delay her matriculation for another year. She needed more time to accumulate the tuition payments, and besides, she didn't believe in attending college before she had an idea of what she wanted to do there. She would have to go to the library and try out certain studies: clinical psychology, comparative literature, and there was a book on philosophy which Addison had told her she should read. Addison would help her. She was sure of that much.

A little of the money the girls earned went toward buying themselves things that they were too embarrassed to ask their mothers for. Emily D. bought a pair of sterling silver earrings which Maxine would have dismissed as suggestive and bohemian but which in Emily D.'s eyes were neither. And Mariela purchased an ethereal set of lingerie made out of a Bismarck gold lace with iridescent threads running through it. The cups of the bra were shaped like scallop shells and they fitted over her breasts so insistently that she had to purchase the size larger than her usual. Even so, her bosom appeared fuller than it had, as though all the lovemaking had made her body more generous and ample, as though it had caused her to ripen overnight.

"You're a mermaid!" Emily D. gasped when Mariela pulled her into the dressing room to see. "You're Venus in the shell!"

———

THERE WAS no use pushing Mariela toward a place she didn't want to go. It was like trying to retrain the arms of the bougainvillea where they fanned out along the side of the house. The stems had memorized their direction in advance of their growth, like a blueprint for the course of life. And if you grabbed hold of one of the stiff green tendrils and stapled it to the wall at a fresh angle, as often as not that part of the plant would willingly die, its carnelian red petals dropping to the ground all at once, in extravagant demise, in sudden martyrdom. Anna knew this about her daughter very well, so when it came to Mariela's future, she did not command; she merely suggested.

"I have a surprise for you," Anna told her. She was helping Mariela to set up a picnic in the shallow green valley that separated their house from the Ettingers'. Later, Addison would lope down the knoll from his front door, one crystal goblet clasped in each hand like a gentle bell, transparent and invaluable.

"What is it?" Mariela said.

"We have enough money for you to go away to school this year," Anna said. "Isn't it wonderful?"

Mariela knelt on the blue and white checkered tablecloth. She laid out a pie that had heart-shaped indentations sealing the edges of the crust. In the center, the dough rose like a

brown-sugared mountain, a sweet apple lava bubbling underneath.

"I don't know what you mean," Mariela said.

"The money for your tuition," Anna said. "It's there as
soon as you need it."

"Where did it come from?" Mariela said. She looked up
at Anna from her small nest of a picnic. Her eyes were gray-
black in the outdoor light, like a pair of luminous, onyx pieces,
and they had an expression in them that said they would always
find what they looked for.

Anna said nothing for a moment, because after all, what
was there to say? That the money had come in the form of a
loan from a neighbor who could well afford it? She could not
mention that much without finally coming to the name, Clifford
Ettinger, and to the worries she had in common with him. He
had even offered the cost of Mariela's tuition as an outright
gift, a present to ensure the separate futures of their children.
But Anna had stood by what was only forthcoming and ethical,
and so they had agreed on a loan. It was nothing other than a
bald attempt to circumvent youth and love, but having survived
both of these, Clifford had quietly claimed the right to inter-
fere.

"Don't you want to go?" Anna said.

"I don't know what I want to study yet," Mariela said. "I
told you that before." She turned her eyes on the Ettinger
house, scanning all the windows for a sign of Addison, for the
appearance that would mean her rescue.

"You don't need to know what to study in advance," Anna
said. "And that's really beside the point anyway."

"Why?"

"Because that's not what's stopping you from going," Anna
said. "And it's not the money either. Not anymore."

Mariela opened her mouth to speak and then closed it
again. She started over. "Do you always have to know everything
about me?" she said.

"Well, I have to at least pretend," Anna said. "That's what
parents do."

Mariela laughed. Her widow's peak rose up on her forehead as though it were registering its own surprise. "You're always pushing me out the door to college," she said. "But you wouldn't know what to do with yourself if I left you. Whose life could you ever be so nosy about but mine?"

"No one's," Anna said.

"You see?"

Addison stepped out his front door just then, the wine glasses dangling from his hands. Anna waved at him once before she walked away. She willed herself not to turn around for another glance at her daughter, Mariela the Shining, the prize that was being won away from her without even the transfer of her consent. In her mind's eye, she pictured the girl she now retreated from, bare-shouldered and miraculous, a dusky, lambent halo floating like a crown in the air behind her head. Addison walked toward her so naturally, as if she were meant for him, aura and all, as if he would not leave her when it suited him to do it, when amnesia scourged his heart and all he could remember was that there had once been a dark-haired girl who was scented with the ripeness of fruit. Mariela waited for him with an ecstatic stillness, the only movement being the nearly imperceptible flutter of life below her navel. The motion was vague, but Anna's internal sight found and held it. There, inside Mariela's private sea, was a minuscule, curling-edged fish of a child, transparent except for its two tiny eyes, which shone black like the start of deep treasure.

THERE WAS going to be a dinner party, complete with champagne in shallow glasses and porcelain swans for napkin holders and a six-course meal which Hanna would make, quite miraculously, with her two powdered, lonely hands. All of it was Clifford's idea, though no one knew why, since he had always professed to disapprove when outsiders sat down at the family table. He claimed to be celebrating something—good neighborliness or newfound friendships or something along that line—but Addison held on to the conviction that all of that was a pretense. Why, otherwise, would his father let Stewart Souther back into the house, with his plaid suits and insinuations and his undisguised hunger for other people's money? When had Clifford ever been quite that forgiving?

Addison began to see, though, that there were one or two aspects of his father which defied prediction. Where Clifford had always kept his surroundings in a compulsive order, now there were minor lapses, slight excursions into disarray. The rosebushes, which were in the midst of their growing season, had not been tended. The blooms were left to shrink and fade into brittle, brown whirligigs that would prevent September's buds from coming. Clifford's shoes went unpolished and his hair grew over the tips of his ears in a way that was fringed and tousled and vaguely artistic. He didn't always replace the reference books that he pulled from the shelves in the living room and they lay yawning open on the coffee tables and window ledges, their pages aged yellow by the daylight. Another few months of this and Addison would not recognize his father; and he was not at all sure that this was a bad thing.

Anna and Mariela arrived for dinner with flowers in their hands, imperial lilies and china asters and cool, frothing, blue larkspurs that grew in their haphazard garden with no separations between them. Hanna took the bouquets from them in the entryway, lisping her approval. When she returned from the kitchen a few minutes later, the flowers were arrayed unrecognizably in vases with glass pebbles clustered at the bottom. The stems had been shorn in half and all the lower leaves stripped away and the exuberant wildness in them had been lost. They could have been raised in a greenhouse, in orderly rows with automatic sprinklers and fertilizer administered via premixed drip. Addison took one look at them and thought it was a crime. However unintentional on Hanna's part, it was still a crime.

At dinner, everyone was paired by seating: Clifford with Anna, Addison with Mariela, Earline with Stewart. In between bites, Mariela was stared at from around the table with an eagerness that was involuntary. Because she was young and impossibly attractive, and because she seemed to float above her chair by a few inches in complete defiance of gravity. She had three forks to the left of her plate, and when the fish course arrived, she could not decide which one to use. It was a fault which everyone noticed, since she wore her confusion like a mask, frozen-featured and blushing. She wished she could drift away into the next room to be alone, but when she felt herself rising away from the floor, she held fast to the seat of her chair. For the rest of the evening, she had to use the furniture to anchor herself, to keep herself from rising up to the ceiling like a helium balloon. This was what love could do to you, she realized. It could turn you into an angel even when you didn't want to be one. It could fly you up to heaven even while you were craving the earth. Miraculous, outrageous, uncontrollable love. Mariela would have laughed out loud if she could.

Stewart had been uncharacteristically subdued all night, but when Hanna poured the burgundy wine, he insisted on making a toast. "Youth is beauty. Beauty is youth," he said. "That's all I know and all I need to know." He looked straight at Mariela while he spoke, his great glass globeful of wine balanced precariously over his head. He looked like an old troll, dwarfed and bristly and remarkably self-satisfied.

"I thought that was truth and beauty," Addison said.

"What's that?" Stewart said.

"You mixed up youth with truth."

"Did I?"

"Yes," Addison said.

Stewart sat down then, piqued and confused, wondering why it was that he was always contradicted in this house, when all he had tried to do was be sociable.

"You'd better not quote any poets to Addison," Earline said. "He's a writer, so it's his job to correct you."

"And why not?" Clifford said. "If he's going to get anywhere, he's got to be serious about it."

"Dad," Addison said.

"Well, you do," Clifford said. He ate the inside of his baked potato with methodical tenacity, as if he were preparing the hollowed-out jacket for some future use. "I told Addison that he'd better leave Marbury Park if he intends to accomplish anything."

"Why is that?" Earline said.

"Well, I just think it's hard to be a grown-up artist if you're still living in your home town," Clifford said. "It's too easy to live like you did as a child. The world comes to you the way it always has. By default."

"That's ridiculous," Earline said. "Home towns are made up of some of the most fascinating stories you'll find anywhere. What could be better for a writer?"

"And Marbury Park is such a wonderful place to live," Mariela said.

"Not really," Clifford said. "Not for a young person with ambition."

Mariela held on to her chair with a plainly desperate grip. If the evening lasted much longer, she felt sure that she would break into pieces, a halo, a wing, a tiny angelic foot, all of them floating skyward in inexorable retreat.

"We can have a hundred opinions of our own," Anna said. "But in the end everybody makes their own choice."

"That's right," Earline said. "And let's not leave love out of this either. Addison might not want to go off on his own so quickly now that there's love in the picture." She directed a reassuring smile toward Mariela. It was a frankly partisan gesture, one that said she hoped to have great-grandchildren during her lifetime.

Addison and Mariela turned conspicuously silent, their eyes lowered toward their steaming dishes of bread pudding and whipped cream. It amazed them that their parents could still do this, could still transform their most confidential hopes into objects for public debate. The whipped cream melted and swam downhill, making albino lakes where depressions had been. Only Stewart Souther spoke through the evening's end, commenting about what a tragedy it was that the middle class could no longer afford help like Hanna, who knew how to make bread pudding from a recipe that lived inside her head.

After everyone had gone home, Clifford and Addison drank iced coffees from high, perspiring glasses on the couch. Addison's free hand fidgeted on the sofa cushion, independently alive, his fingers long enough to reach into the next room if he unfurled them all the way.

"She's a nice girl," Clifford said.

"Mariela," Addison said.

"Yes."

Clifford never spoke her name, Addison noticed. In the beginning, he had thought it was out of a fear of getting it wrong. But now he saw that the omission was somehow purposeful. His father refused to say the word *Mariela* for the same reason he no longer mentioned his office receptionist, who had announced that she was quitting at the end of the summer: they were details that were on their way out of his life. He had merely dismissed them early, for reasons of efficiency, for the sake of plain expedience.

"But what?" Addison said.

"Hmm?"

"She's a nice girl, but what?" Addison said. "You weren't just going to leave it at that, were you?"

Clifford's eyebrows crept together and then fused, metamorphosing into one long hedge of concern. "I was going to tell you what I think you already know."

"Which is?"

"She's not the best you can do," Clifford said.

Addison set down his drink on the end table, the coffee rippling back and forth in opaque, teeter-totter waves. "What do you mean she's not the best I . . ."

"All I'm saying is . . ." Clifford tried to interrupt, but Addison was not having it. His hands started moving through the air as he spoke, emphatically, as if he were translating all of his words into simultaneous sign language.

"No. No. I really want you to explain this to me, Dad. I really want to hear this."

"She's not . . . she's just not . . . she's not at your level," Clifford said.

Addison crammed his hands under his knees. If he could only keep still long enough, his father would lay everything out in front of him, all the suppositions and unvoiced wants, all the stark requirements for Addison's adult life.

"Your mother and I raised you to have certain opportunities and to make your life with people who have had those opportunities, too," Clifford said.

"I don't believe that Mom would ever have said that."

"Well, I think she would have. And besides that, I'm saying it. You've got to think these things through years down the line," Clifford said. "You've got to think through the realities of just what things would be like."

"You can't possibly know what the realities are going to be like years down the line."

"Addison, you can make a pretty good guess," Clifford said. He managed to conjure a look that was beleaguered and childish at the same time. He took a thirsty draught from his iced coffee and when he lowered the glass, there was a milky mustache painted on his upper lip, doleful and symmetric, as if someone had drawn it on. "All I'm saying to you is, you've got a substantial share of your life off in the distance yet. You're twenty-three years old and you've got a decent crack at making something of yourself if you're serious about it. You're already published, for God's sake, and that's more than . . ."

"Stories," Addison said.

"Well, all right, now it's stories. Later on it'll be something more," Clifford said. "But you're talking about tying yourself to somebody who can't even make up her mind about whether she wants to go to college."

"She wants to go," Addison said.

"Are you sure about that?"

"Absolutely."

"You ask her," Clifford said.

Clifford's coffee mustache melted down onto his lip and he wiped it away. He walked over to the living room window, which was inexplicably open, and listened for the sad-throated birds which only sang at night. The windows always seemed to be flung open after Anna had passed through his house. He had never actually witnessed her raising them; he simply noticed the wind traveling through his rooms after she had left. It was as though the house exclaimed "Oh!" through its wide-windowed mouths when it felt the presence of Anna inside. Some part of Clifford, when in Anna's company, said the same thing. It was an irrepressible response, as natural as the need to look up at the sky during a total solar eclipse. And maybe this was what Addison felt when he saw the black-eyed wonder in the face of the Latina girl. That certain suffused shock in the marrow. But no, Addison was almost certainly too young to know what that was like. At the age of twenty-three, there was only the instinct of physical want.

"Have you thought about the kind of background she's got?" Clifford said.

"Dad . . ."

"No, I mean it. I mean, this is a girl whose father walked out on her when she was barely old enough to speak," Clifford said. "What kind of an impact do you think that could have?"

Addison joined his father at the window. At the border between Saxon Hill and Saxon Hill South, the gas lights abruptly stopped, marking the leaving-off of grace.

"Dad, what kind of life do you think I would have led if you and Mom hadn't adopted me?" Addison said.

"You're changing the subject," Clifford said.

"No, I'm not." Addison's hands were flying again in desperate motion, white and rapid like the backs of kites. With one of them, he struck Clifford's coffee glass where it rested on the sill and it fractured against the window jamb messily, the pieces and the liquid and the ice raining down onto the floor. No one moved toward it.

"You wouldn't have been the same person then," Clifford said. "And that's not what we're talking about right now."

"She can't help what's happened to her," Addison said.

"No, she can't," Clifford said. "That's just it. She can't help it at all."

Addison would have gone on, but he could think of nothing more to say. In his mouth, there was the taste of bitter soil, and words would not pass through it. He knelt down over the spill he had made and tried to make sense of it with his naked hands. After a moment, Clifford knelt down too and they tried to separate everything into two basic piles, one of glass and one of ice; but the light was confusing and their fingertips turned numb from the cold, and when they looked up from their work at the end, their embankment of glass had melted entirely away.

———

CLIFFORD PRODUCED pamphlets on writers' retreats, cabins in the mountains or the desert where artists sealed themselves away for whole months at a time. Thick-papered descriptions in bone and beige and pale shades of earth fell out of his pockets at the end of the day; they littered his nightstands and his magazine racks and the dashboard of his car. He approached Addison like a salesman, one arm thrust out, brochures at the ready, asking him to consider this or that feature, asking him to decide.

Addison would have turned him down flat if he possibly could have. He would have said, "Stop interfering. I'll look into it myself when the time comes." He would have said that and more if it hadn't been for the fact that pleasing his father seemed like something he ought to try hard to do. Ever since Marjorie had died, leaving the two of them alone together, it seemed to Addison that they ought to have agreed on the whole world and all its perturbations. The structure of their lives had for years and years been more fragile than they could have imagined. Each day had passed in more or less the same graceful fashion as the last, but that had been only luck. Families were destructible it turned out, wildly so, and after you knew that, you couldn't think about them as carelessly as you had before. You couldn't just turn to the only father you'd ever known and say stop meddling with me. What if he did stop? What if he stopped forever?

There were times when Addison could see things from his father's point of view, minor moments when Marbury Park looked cloistered from the rest of the world, cut off from real life in ways that were likely to last. And he knew that Clifford thought of Mariela as an extension of the setting—as limited and limiting, as flawed by her unseen boundaries. He sensed that Clifford feared the beautiful blackness of her hair, so ethnic and unfamiliar. He could not trust her mystery or her fatherlessness or the disorganized life she had been born into. Sooner or later, she would revert to her beginnings—impoverished, abandoned, directionless. Clifford had set out to prove that to Addison somehow, to uncover evidence of it that could not be denied.

Once, in trying to make conversation, Mariela had asked Clifford about a sketch on the living room wall. "Did you do this yourself?" she said, pointing at one edge ingenuously.

"The frame, you mean?" Clifford said.

"No," she said. "The picture."

"That's a Utrillo," he said. And then, when she showed no recognition, "French. The artist was . . . French."

She looked like she wanted to ask another question, but she didn't. She held her mouth slightly open while the uncertain air flowed in and out again. Addison thought to himself that even her confusion was something sensuous.

"Do you like it?" Addison said, to which she simply nodded.

After she had left, Clifford turned to his son. "She thinks Utrillo is someone we knew," he said. "A friend with a sketch pad."

"No, she doesn't," Addison said.

"I had the distinct impression . . ." Clifford began.

"And even if she did, it wouldn't be a crime," Addison said.

"Well, no," Clifford said. "Not a crime." But his voice held no conviction. He wandered around the borders of the room, closing all the windows even though the weather outside was spectacularly clear. Addison watched him, studying his stiff-shouldered effort to seal out the local air. Afterwards, he paused. "Ignorance isn't a crime very often," Clifford said. "That's something you'll find."

PART FOUR

---·•·---

The Skin
of Love

SOME THINGS tilted when you looked at them under the wrong kind of light. Atoms were that way. And love. Addison thought about Heisenberg's Uncertainty Principle. Examine the foundations of life too closely and they would shift and scatter and change their design.

Nothing about Mariela had altered except the way he had thought about her once or twice. She still enchanted him with her small flights and her illuminations and her bright, unspoken hopes. But sometimes when he kissed her now, a part of him stood back and regarded himself and her and the way they went together. A part of him stood at a remove and said, There I am looking like I'm in love.

———•·•———

IF THERE was one thing Addison could have changed about Mariela, it would have been the fact that she didn't seem to want anything for herself. He would have planted an ambition in her somewhere, a green, insistent desire that she could talk about when asked. That would have made her perfect for him, the perfect choice. And then, he could have imagined them passing long years together without their seeming long; he could have pictured their hair growing in more sparsely and their teeth fading in the direction of gray and the two of them not even remembering to notice. Because that's what he thought becoming older would be like if his wife was the perfect choice: not noticing, even once, that neither one of them was what they had been.

Instead, Mariela's ambitions all had to do with him. She wanted what he wanted. How many times had she answered his questions that way? She reminded him of a reflecting pool, always borrowing someone else's horizon.

"What do you want to do next year?" Addison asked her.

"Be with you," she said.

"But what do you want to do about college?" he said.

"What do you want me to do about it?" she said.

They went back and forth like that, with no end in sight, and still she didn't understand what he wanted from her. It was a game of echoes, of doublings, and Mariela never faulted. Of course, this kind of doubting on Addison's part was just what his father had intended all along. Addison knew that, in some oblique way, Clifford had arranged it. And even though Addison saw that this was sabotage, he could not ignore the justification for it: that Mariela was not the best he could do. What if that were true? Addison wasn't sure whether this assessment was one he could reasonably expect his father to make. Clifford knew about the constellations and cooking and cutting back roses and tending to sick people and what made good reading and grief. Clifford knew about almost everything, but did he know about love?

———•◦•———

ADDISON'S BROTHER, Bernard, visited Raborn Way on a night when the moon was a silver cup and what flowed out of it was hunger. He had gotten off the bus one stop too soon and by the time he reached the southern edge of Saxon Hill, a blister the size of a horse chestnut had surfaced on the curve of his heel. His clothes had been dulled with the dust of the Santa Ana winds to the color of sandstone, the color of deserts and ocean bottoms, of predators and prey. He walked along the sidewalk, passing into view under the aureoles of the gas lights and then turning invisible in the intervening stretches of dark.

Addison was on his way to meet Mariela in Marbury's orange grove when he saw Bernard slinking toward him down the street. He fought the impulse to cut across the neighbor's grounds and slip away without being seen. It would have been a simple solution, but Bernard would only have come back again, more desperate and determined than he had been at the beginning. Addison would have to turn him back sometime.

"You didn't bring us any food last week," Bernard said, when he was close enough for Addison to hear.

"I didn't plan on stopping by then," Addison said. "I was going to come over after Labor Day."

"That would've been late," Bernard said.

"Is there a problem?"

Bernard circled Addison at a steady distance, orbiting warily, out of reach of the light that fell from the closest street lamp.

"I'm low on cash," Bernard said. He held his bad hand in his pocket all the while, and Addison kept anticipating the threat-filled moment when he would pull it out. The stumps at the base of the fingers there made Addison flinch no matter how many times he saw them.

"A lot of people are low on cash," Addison said.

"Hey, I'm not a lot of people to you. I'm just one very important one," Bernard said. "You know what I'm saying?"

"I don't want to stand here arguing about it," Addison said.

"Nobody's forcing you," Bernard said.

But neither of them made a move to walk away. In the dark, they stared freely at their likeness in each other, at the physical familiarity that housed the soul of an infidel. Without an effort to preserve them, Addison thought, all the sacred meanings behind what it was to be human readily vanished. In the blackened street, two men facing each other off were beasts with hooded prehistoric eyes and sour breaths that ignited with flame. He wondered whether Bernard would kill him if he imagined he could get away with it. Probably he would.

Addison retrieved his wallet from his pocket and thumbed through the bills inside it.

"How much do you need?" Addison said.

"How much have you got?" Bernard said.

Addison handed over two hundred dollars, silently, the bills going limp in the wetness of his palm. Bernard counted it, the cleft below his mouth deepening into a point of sullenness, like a man who is resigned to being cheated.

"Okay," Bernard said, as if answering someone. He turned around and walked off without any further acknowledgment. Addison watched his diminishing form, appearing and disappearing from under the streetlights, and felt like he had just bribed someone to stay out of his life.

He couldn't go to meet Mariela now. He was too distracted, and she would only want to know why there was a tremor in his hands and why his mouth was so dry that it changed the way he spoke. Back at home, he poured himself a white wine spritzer and worked on a story until all the typeface began to run together on the page. Even then, if he rested his eyes for five minutes, the words would find their natural places again and he could go on writing. It was all a matter of the will, he told himself. If you willed it thoroughly enough, you could transform yourself into the kind of man you wanted to be. The thing was not to be a wanderer like Bernard. Bernard showed you what could happen if you thought life owed you. There was a lesson in that and Addison was going to hold on to it, even if he had to recite it to himself every hour he was alive, even if he had to stand face to face with his brother to remember what it meant.

———•—••———

MARIELA WAITED among the trees, nearly naked, her Bismarck gold lace underwear glowing with the remnants of a long-gone world. She had arranged herself in the blue lamb's wool afghan to look like a mermaid, with the corners of the blanket binding her legs into a smooth fish's tail, giant and sea-colored and swishing back and forth when she adjusted her knees. Addison would shout out his surprise when he saw her.

When Addison didn't come after half an hour, her legs got too warm and she had to unwrap herself at intervals to let the Santa Ana wind blow over her thighs with its currents that were muted and blind and consummately dry. She hoped he wouldn't come while she was unwrapped, stretched out prone and disheveled like a ruined present. It would be too awkward to wind herself up again while he was watching. It would be contrived.

They had always met there, between the eighth and ninth rows in the orange grove, but when a whole hour had passed without his coming, she suddenly felt that she might be waiting for him in the wrong place, that she might have miscounted the lines of trees from the border of Trafalgar Road. So she ran up to the edge of the street and numbered the rows on her way back to the spot. She found herself again between the eighth and ninth trees, imagining that the dark-haired specter of Addison was just about to reveal himself to her, that he was just about to jump down out of the branches above her head, his fingertips reaching out for her like wands, breathtaking and impractical.

She nursed a momentary anger and then let it give way to worry. He had to be coming to her, because if he wasn't, then there was something very wrong. The moon gave out almost no light; it was the dish of a pauper, its patina turned to ash. But

Mariela had eyes that could see through any darkness, and she used them to search Marbury's orange grove as if it had stolen her lover criminally, abducting him away to some parallel world of greenery and confusion that Mariela could enter only if she happened across the right invisible door. The trees shook out their leaves vainly, like so many women unfastening their hair. Mariela began to breathe like a panicked child, each intake and outtake an audible gasp. Her mouth became coated with a fine layer of August dust—hot, desert-tinted silt that made it difficult to cry; it was as if she had already died and could not prevent the soil from falling past her teeth. Oh God my God, she said. Don't let him forget me now.

ADDISON TRIED to shed all the ways he had thought about Mariela; he tried to forget all the likenesses she had brought into his mind. He had imagined her as the heroines of the best books he had read, as Tess of the D'Urbevilles and Emma Bovary, as Miriam Levers and Antonia Shimerda, all of them vulnerable and inspired, their magic dampened only by the limits of their circumstance. But all of these incarnations were romantic falsehoods as far as real life was concerned. Wasn't that true? Wasn't that what his father would say? That art was art and life was life and you had better not confuse the two, or you would find yourself living out a tragedy you had never intended.

He saw her a few more times after that, once for a dinner at McArthur's at which they had both worked hard to give the impression of eating, once when making love in the luxuriant, unmown grass that swallowed them whole one night on the de la Sendas' lawn, once by accident between the travel agency and the library downtown, with Addison holding an airline ticket to Las Cruces in his hands, all the carbon pages fanning open in the air no matter which way he tried to carry them, tangible evidence of his impending abandonment of her. He tried not to look directly into her eyes when they spoke; he couldn't stand to witness the soulful reproach that now inhabited them. Of course she never said anything accusational. She simply waited there in front of him, mysterious and mournful and letting life happen to her.

Addison, for his part, had had enough of sanctified passivity. He was going to attend a writers' colony in El Fuerte, New Mexico, where he pictured himself eating off a hot plate in a desert cabin there and typing every day until his fingertips bloomed with violet bruises on the ends. After six months, he would know whether he was worth his weight in effort. He wanted people to nod with some internal affinity when they read what he had to say. He wanted people to raise their voices and exclaim and argue over what he wrote about. It didn't matter to him how many people, but he wanted a few of them to do these things. And he wanted a few of them to turn to his work thinking *I can't wait*, and having a reason to think it. That was all he wanted. That was not so much to want.

———————

MAXINE RIDGEWAY thought she had lived through almost every misfortune a man could dole out to a woman, and then her purse was snatched. Vanity had made her prey to attack, although she could hardly fathom that vanity existed in her as an abiding weakness. It was merely that she had not received a compliment on her looks for too many years in a row. So that when she was on her way out to the car after a long evening's work at the pharmacy, a flattering criminal was the last thing she expected to meet. She had the terrible habit of staring down at the ground wherever she went, as if she were elderly and feared a fall that would break her hip, as if she thought she might tumble down into a steaming chasm without any forewarning at all. So by the time she noticed the man, he was already beside her, already descending on her with the clean-seeming, alkaline breath of someone who drinks too much vodka.

"Pardon me," he said. "But I can't help noticing your hair."

"What do you want?" Maxine said.

"You don't dye your hair, do you?"

"No," Maxine said.

"Don't ever start," he said. "It's stunning just the way you have it."

She stopped walking then. Certainly it was an unusual man who could appreciate natural beauty. Her hair had always been her greatest physical treasure, growing with a stand-up, luxuriant gloss, like the coat of an ermine. She had always told herself that to dye her hair would have been a travesty of its spirit, a frank and foolhardy domestication. And here finally was a man who agreed with that notion. She would have taken a moment to appreciate him if he had not just that moment shoved her off her feet and run, her handbag swinging behind him like a lumpy kite.

When the Cordojo Women met the next Sunday, Maxine insisted that all of them come outside to learn the ten basic techniques in self-defense while she narrated them from the text of a library book. India and Emily D. practiced half-Nelson holds delicately, draping their arms around one another's throats like flesh necklaces. Dove and Esther Lee played tug-of-war on either end of a satchel with broken straps, dancing around one another palsy-footed and shrieking. When Clifford Ettinger pulled his car into his driveway, Maxine spotted him immediately.

"Doctor," she called. "We need you here."

Clifford ran down the mowed slope with the definite impression that he was being called on to break up a fight. But when he arrived, the ladies stepped apart from one another on their own accord, greeting him with their polite lipsticked smiles and their hands still gloved from church.

"Anna doesn't have a mugging partner," Maxine said to him. "Will you work with her? Because our practice will really only be effective if everyone participates."

Clifford didn't understand how it had happened, but he

found himself with his arms wrapped insistently around Anna's shoulders while she elbowed him in all the ticklish dents of his ribs. The six of them rehearsed for cold calamity, with Maxine directing them on all the finer points. "Now pretend you're going to jab the assailant in the eyes!" she called out. "Curl your knuckles over so you won't really do any jabbing, but . . . India, I really think you should save your hyperventilating for a time when you're alone. Everybody! Everybody! Hyperventilating is not appropriate."

Clifford and Anna carried on a quiet conversation in between gasps.

"My Mariela is heartbroken," she said. Then she bit Clifford's finger gently, because it was required.

"Isn't it better now than later?" Clifford said.

"Maybe not," Anna said. "Who's to say what might happen later? Who's to say we haven't interfered with their fate?"

"I haven't forced Addison to do anything," he said. "I've simply guided him in understanding his choices." Clifford sat down on the ground and clasped his hands around Anna's ankle. She made a mock, pinioned struggle in front of him while he stared at her miniature, freckled toes, mummified in their stocking. He realized he hadn't looked at them like this since that day on Mount Carillon, when he'd helped Anna down the foot trail after her sprain. That was the day she had started to cure his grief, though he could only understand that now, in retrospect.

"I'm not sure I approve of your guidance," Anna said.

"But we agreed ahead of time," Clifford said. "Don't you remember?"

Anna shook her head. "What I remember is the way my daughter was before this summer ever happened," she said.

"She'll come back to you," Clifford said. "Wait a little while and she will."

Maxine Ridgeway commanded everyone to stand up and compose themselves. She waved her arms in vast, geometric gestures, as if airplanes were taking off over her head.

"Everyone take a deep breath and repeat after me," she said. *"You can't take what belongs to me, mister!"*

And they answered her in kind.

———•◦•———

ON THE night before he left, Addison tried to take stock of his unfinished business. He threw away half the clothes he had lived in that summer, either because they were indelibly stained or irreparably worn or because they had absorbed the scent of Mariela into their thousand fibers, sweet and decadent and overtly sexual, and what was he abandoning if not these things? He stripped the sheets off his bed and he emptied his wastebasket and he telephoned Rita to let her know there wouldn't be any more grocery deliveries.

At the other end of the line, her voice ran below the surface of the earth, graveled and ancient, like some fossil come alive.

"So you aren't coming back anymore?" she said.

"Not for a while," Addison said.

He could picture her mulling this over, her bandy legs twined around one another like the cords of a banyan tree, the cigarette smoke rising away from her with the convolutions of steam. From somewhere within her, she emanated a primitive melding of earth and fire and volcanic ash. All of which Bernard had inherited in brutal incarnation. Addison wasn't sure he could follow through with their enslavement of him, with their too-eager agreement that he owed them something. What had he done, after all, except escape some mutual deprivation in the impoverished desert of Baston? He was a survivor, not a savior. He would have to make that clear.

"We'll miss you coming over," Rita said. "You turned out so good, you know. That's something I like to see."

Addison mumbled something ineffectual into the receiver. He hoped she wasn't about to indulge her sentimentality, biting her lower lip while the tears ran into her mouth, forgetting like a child to blot them away. She surprised him by sticking with the details at hand.

"You driving to New Mexico?" she said.

"No. Flying," Addison said.

"Oh," she said. "Because Bernard told me you might let him have a try at your car."

Addison couldn't find the breath to reply. Bernard and Rita and the two other children could only hold themselves back from grasping at him for circumscribed periods of time, artificial moments of restraint, like a pause taken midway through a meal. Thank God he was getting away from all this. In El Fuerte, New Mexico, for as long as he wished to stay, he would be related to no one; he would be a conception sprung whole from his own mind, borne and shaped by only himself.

"Bernard hasn't had much in the way of his own things," Rita was saying. "He could do a lot with a car if he got a chance at it. He could get a job even."

"My mother gave me that car the year before she died," Addison said. "So I'm not in a position to part with it. Not at all." He listened to the emergence of his own voice as if he were listening to someone else speak. He didn't know how he had gotten through saying the word *mother* to the woman who had once passed his bones through her body, but there it was.

"Oh, you shouldn't give it away then," Rita said. "I never thought you should, only maybe you'd loan it. Did you ever think about loaning it?"

"I'm not sure," Addison said.

"For how many months did you say?"

"A few."

"A few would work out fine," Rita said.

Addison gave in because he couldn't think of a way to say *I don't trust your family,* seeing that he was part of it in an increasing and irrevocable way. He left the keys dangling from the ignition and then waited by the lookout point of an upstairs window for Bernard to materialize at the periphery of the security lights on the lawn, which, a little later, he did. Bernard slipped into the seat of the Volvo seamlessly, as if he had the power of passing through the driver's side door unimpeded by steel plates and hinges. Behind the glass from which Addison was watching, all of it transpired in impossible quiet, even the ending, in which the car progressed down Raborn Way without the usual sigh of its motor. Addison could hear the sound of his own pulse caroming through his ears, but that was all. Just his pulse and the way that it stampeded past his throat and his temples and the thoughts in his mind.

Clifford mistook the episode for an overabundance of his son's generosity, or else he would have said more about it. But the following morning, driving Addison to the airport through a dry, flushed desert sunrise, all the colors of the lower sky running down to the absorbent earth, he was filled with the satisfaction of having already saved his son from something, some indeterminate fall that had to do with a lack of self-discipline and a smothering sensual entanglement with the girl that had eyes like a saint. So what if he had made the mistake of loaning out his car? There was no permanent consequence to an error in judgment on that scale. It was just the kind of fault you could expect your child to make once in young adulthood and then never again—neat, circumscribed, an object lesson about the nature of lending something you didn't intend to lose.

"It's not hard to loan someone something they ask for," Clifford said. "It's hard to go collecting on it afterwards, when the last thing they're capable of is recalling what they owe you."

"I'll get the car back, Dad," Addison said. "I won't let it turn into a problem." He spoke earnestly, his words climbing in the steep determination not to turn out to be a disappointment. The bond that ran between the two of them was one of increasingly genteel regard. His father counted on him to do the right thing when asked, and Addison counted on his own fledgling ability to interpret what exactly *was* the right thing according to Clifford. There was a lot of love concealed inside of all his father's deft instructions for living. There was a lot of wishing on Addison a better life than his own and thinking he could simply narrate how to do it, one set of directions at a time.

In the boarding tunnel at the airport, with the weight of his luggage lengthening his arms and the turpentine smell of the air fuel swirling in through the portal seams, Addison had a sudden, knee-weakening realization that almost made him turn back. He had neglected to take the house key off the key ring that had swung silver and priceless from the ignition of the Volvo as it had sat in his father's driveway the night before. He could see its precise edge, saw-toothed and ragged and looking like the inside of the mouth of some young carnivore, and he could see it turning over again and again, cool against the heat that would rise up from his brother's hand. The house key, the house key. How could he have forgotten something that would be as tempting to Bernard as that? *Let him not see it,* Addison said, his eyes closed with the unfamiliar blindness of prayer. *Let him not see it at all.*

———•◦•———

ANNA GOT more than she asked for when she asked that God let her see into the heart of Mariela the Shining. Because as time went on, she really could see that organ of her daughter's, growing like a lavish iris, purple-headed and painful and contracting with a rhythm born of desperation and melancholy. Mariela's skin faded to near-transparency in the anemia of her longing, and when Anna looked at her in just the right way, with a glance of purity and tenderness, she could see everything her daughter held inside: the blue tendrils of her veins, diverging from one another with lacework urgency; the polished white edifices of her ribs, each one of them rising to the next, pearly and spectral, like the rungs of a rare ladder; the love that resided in the four quarters of her mind, the same love that knew and forgave everything even before it was asked, the same one that comprised the sole ingredient of the aura that flew a few inches above her hair; the fetus which clung inside the jeweled sack of her womb, a girl, curled over and bent-necked, as if the very act of her growth were an unfolding from the position of prayer—her eyes open in two wide black worlds, coverless, fathomless, without the hesitation present in the expressions of all who have witnessed a lesser earth. Anna could see all these things and wonder at them in her maternal silence.

The powers of her vision burdened her at times, and she could not help but wish that Mariela's bargains with life had been gentler ones. Oh, it was not the baby she minded, because Anna only had to look once at the miraculous, coral-bodied notion of a little girl to know that she would be an ineluctable gift. It was the secrecy with which Mariela carried the baby; it was the fact that Mariela could not bring herself to say, *Mother, something has happened to me, and I don't know what to do.* Mariela had run away from being herself a child without ever once looking over her shoulder for Anna's consent. Well, Anna knew what it was to find yourself pregnant unexpectedly—shocking and transformative and impossible and profound—and she determined to hold on to Mariela's secret for as long as she sanely could, out of a respect for her new and fierce privacy, out of an acknowledgment of her insistent pride. This was what a mother ought to do under the circumstances, Anna told herself. Hold her tongue and wait for her cue and in the meantime carry trays of soda crackers up to her daughter's room when she was too green to get out of bed.

At the end of September, Mariela got a job on Main Street downtown, working in a hand-dipped chocolates shop that had been newly opened by Dove Pairlee's mother. Opal Pairlee had forgiven all the wrongs committed under her confectioner's tent the previous June as soon as she had heard that Mariela had been abandoned by the Einstein-haired, wild-eyed young man who swallowed ice as nonchalantly as if it were air. Anybody could see the kind of influence a fellow like that would have on young girls, and the phrase for it was unbridled temptation. When Opal Pairlee spoke it, her cheeks trembled with a meaty indignance that made Anna smile. Opal would protect Mariela from all preventable ills, and that was all Anna needed to know.

Mariela came home at the end of the day with semisweet

smears on her apron front. The scents she carried with her became caramelized, frosted. Her breath smelled of marshmallows and sweetened coconut; and the heavy, dolorous aroma of fudge had woven its way into the strands of her hair. It was as though the essence of her, the ingredients that gelled together to form her amorphous soul, were in the process of being reduced on a cook stove, concentrated into a treacle of chocolate and liqueurs.

But Anna knew only too well how perishable confections were and she prayed for this metaphysical sweetening of her daughter to stop. She feared that the saints were preparing Mariela for something—her flight from the world perhaps—in the same way that the people of the Old Testament fatted the calf for Holy Days, out of calculation and design. And she was no less alarmed by the fact that Mariela's weightlessness was turning chronic, her form floating up to the ceiling and bobbing there above Anna's head at least once a day, as if she were practicing her earthly release, as if one day she would make her way past the roof of the house and keep on going, her hair spread out over the sky in angelic profusion, her arms reaching farther and farther toward the embrace of the angel who was sent out to claim her. To ward off such a calamity, Anna kept one arm around Mariela whenever she would permit, fastening her to the world with a determination that would not give way, not even to God, whom Anna knew she was supposed to love above all others, but also whom, in this singular instance, she did not.

Emily D. came over to the house on the day before she left for college. Someone had cut her camel-brown hair into a pageboy and it hung over the sides of her head in dutiful meekness, as if it were a borrowed hat she wished she could take off. She and Mariela sat on the window seat and whispered to one another like the children they remembered being. Anna could picture them from that time, and for a moment the image seemed no different from the way they were now. They had sat together in that same spot with their angular, fragile limbs and their narrow, white-shorted bottoms and their hair salted with the dandelion seeds that fell in through the window like a light summer snow. That was before the time that Emily D. had turned mousy and Mariela had turned haunting and their days were made listless by either their banishment from or their visitation to the country that love comprised. But the two of them were changing all the time now, their prospects shifting, their futures coming clear for an instant and then going blurry again. And Anna could see in her daughter's eyes that for the first time she was wondering what it would be like to trade places with her friend, to breathe something other than the sainted breath, to be innocent of the kind of longing that could cripple you if you thought about it for too many seconds in a row. And what would it feel like to be going to college tomorrow with your first kiss still out there waiting, undescended from the wheeling, furious world?

———

SOME KIND of parasites feasted on the Ettingers' rosebushes. They emerged out of cobwebs or chrysalises or secret egg sacks somewhere and they transformed the tear-shaped leaves of the plants into cerulean green swatches of vegetable lace. Much of the foliage faded to brown tatters and dropped away to the ground in insubstantial clumps, like so many hair nets thrown off by waking grandmothers. Clifford wandered in their ruined vicinity, spraying opaque clouds of sulfur powder into the air and then running away from them, holding his breath. Even so, he emerged from the task looking shell-shocked and shaken, as if he had just left World War I and a trench of mustard gas behind him. Anna looked out of her window at his trials and realized with astonishment that she loved even his fearfulness, even the way his hair flew away from his temples in two steel-colored wings when he was frightened by the exigencies of life.

The two of them went together to the Mozart concert which the Cordojo Women had given Anna tickets for. They went because Clifford was behind in his days-of-living to days-of-mourning ratio, which was a thoroughly supportable reason, and because they were hungry to sit next to one another in the nervous darkness, which was not supportable at all. They ate finger-sized pecan pies under the sounds that floated out to them from the throat of the Hollywood Bowl. Anna looked around her to see the way the faces of the crowd became disembodied in the stage light, all of their features suspended against the invisible, like the heads on copper coins lying still at the bottom of a wishing pool. Anna felt the same sense of ecstatic wakefulness that she did whenever she attended church, with everyone lined up in their seats in one palpable, nameless quest. Everyone wanted to rest silent awhile in the presence of what was meaningful, and there was a kind of redemption in simply wanting that. Anna had known this for as long as she could remember.

Clifford closed his hand over hers sometime during an adagio when the horns retreated to an enclave underwater, mournful and beckoning, like sirens beneath the break of the waves. Anna's fingers escaped to the far side of her purse while she tried to remember everything she had told herself in advance about the scope of professional ethics.

Clifford leaned over to her and spoke into her ear even though he didn't believe in speaking during Mozart, as he had mentioned to her earlier. "Hold my hand," he said.

"I'm your therapist," Anna said.

"Then hold my hand for therapeutic reasons," he said.

So, for no other justification than that it was what they both wanted, Anna acquiesced. Who could tell the difference in a crowd this size? The impropriety of the whole thing would have to be worked out later, with the two of them facing each other across a table under the stark, unmovable light of day. But for now, holding hands with the first man since Cristobal, the first man in twelve years, forty-eight seasons, four thousand three hundred and some odd days, Anna reveled in the discovery that she was still eminently touchable, that she did not break or wither away or show signs of rust from her prolonged disuse.

Twenty rows of seats above them, the Cordojo Women passed a set of safari-sized binoculars back and forth. The two lunar lenses contained for them a picture of delight, a positive proof of what Anna would later deny.

"Has he kissed her yet?" Dove Pairlee said, tugging on the cord of the glasses that encircled India's neck.

"No, not yet," India said. "And stop hanging on me while you're at it. You know it's not your turn." She passed the binoculars to Esther Lee, who accepted them with strange delicacy, as if she thought they might be carrying some germ of pornography within their construction.

"Well, I think he will," Dove Pairlee said. "Esther, watch his lips."

"I can't see his hips. He's sitting down," Esther Lee said.

"His lips," Dove said.

"I've already told you," Esther Lee said.

"Try not to be so rank-minded, Dove," Maxine said.

"Maxine, you're a woman of principle," Esther Lee said.

"Thank you, dear," Maxine said.

"Not at all."

———•◦•———

ANNA HAD anticipated that Clifford would fire her. But still, when he did it, she was struck with the force of her own raging disbelief. Once, when she was a child sitting in the stands of a baseball stadium with her father, she had watched while the ball whirled toward her, concussing her forehead like a falling planet. And that was what she felt like now, with his words still reverberating from one portion of her mind to the next: *I won't be needing any more therapy from you.*

Anna held a shallow breath. She kept her body wholly inanimate; if there had been vines growing close to her feet, they would have gyred around her legs with a greedy, green tenacity, anchoring her to the spot. "Do you really think you can make that determination for yourself?" Anna said.

"I can make it," Clifford said. "I've known for some time now that thinking about Marjorie wasn't going to haunt me anymore."

"You didn't know that in June," Anna said.

"Well, I know it now."

The two of them stood on the flagstones of Clifford's lawn. At night, each stone was turned to a meager, canescent island, a sea of grass encroaching on the circumference. Anna could smell the fringes of her own perfume, sifting outward in a careful cumulus of orris and sandalwood, amber and civet. He didn't need her help anymore. That was what he had said.

"All right," Anna said. She began to back away, her steps extending behind her precariously, as if she were balancing on a wire. "You'll call me if anything changes."

"Why would I have to call you?" Clifford said. He followed her down the walkway, placing his feet conscientiously in the exact spots where hers had been. "Why would I call you when you'll be right here?"

"Yes, that's true. I'll be right next door," Anna said.

"I'm not talking about next door, and you know it," he said.

Anna had prepared three objections to being kissed, but they fell away from her like too many loose coins when she tried to retrieve them as an offering against temptation. The words *clinical*, *dependency*, and *displacement* lay glittering in the lawn close to her feet, but they did not signify anything to her except a sweet and far-off familiarity. She allowed herself to be led inside the house, and it was only there, while climbing the white-shouldered stairs, that she realized she had walked right out of her shoes—her high, needle-heeled shoes that she balanced on as if they were a pair of sexy, treacherous stilts. They would still be standing on one of the flagstones outside, a polished, screaming signal to anyone who really thought about it that Clifford Ettinger had so desired the woman who wore them that he had lifted her straight out of their silk-cushioned insteps. If the neighbors didn't come to that conclusion, it would only be because they had decided on something more compromising. The baffling truth was that Anna really couldn't convince herself it was worth worrying over.

Clifford was leading her up to the second floor, into a part of the house she had never seen before. Here, as downstairs, the walls gleamed a supernatural white, cultivated and antiseptic and reminiscent of the way wealth bleached all surface imperfections into nothingness. But in the bedrooms, floral nosegays spilled off the wallpaper, backed by ribbons and latticework and English countryside wisteria. This was Marjorie's influence almost certainly, and Anna found herself relieved by it. She liked knowing that Marjorie, by being her generous, careless, clearseeing self, had succeeded in making herself so indispensably loved. In Anna's view, there was no use being loved any other way.

What Anna thought of in the morning was how she slept a different kind of sleep when she was bound up all night with the limbs of a gentle man. Her rest was more profound, as if she had been submerged for all those hours in a lake of breathable water, all her mind's images paddling by like a cloud of rare fish. Clifford's breath did not turn stale overnight, only faintly salted, like the breath of newborn things, still scented with the brine of their own genesis. Anna thought she could get used to waking up like this, in the midst of these vague, indeterminate echoes from the sea.

Her eyes settled on the crystal doorknob in front of her with the notion that she had located a clear jellyfish, faceted and mushroom-shaped, and she was not initially surprised when it twisted a quarter turn clockwise, in a motion that prismed the daylight into a dozen spectrumed shafts. But then, there was a woman entering the room. Anna saw a topknot of blond, overworked hair and two mannish, blush-backed hands which supported a silver tray childishly, the pinkies extended. Then there was a gasp, a gulping of the air, and the woman went out the same way she had come, her little fingers waving, as if decorum were the last thing she would let go of. It would have been Hanna, of course, bringing up the breakfast on a tray when Clifford hadn't come downstairs for it. Anna retrieved Clifford's long-tailed dress-shirt, collapsed in a spread-eagled flag on the floor, and slipped into it. She followed Hanna with the inten-

tion of explaining something to her, of making clear her own
identity and so dispelling her alarm. But when Anna reached
the kitchen, it dawned on her for the first time that the woman
was simply and seriously heartbroken, sobbing as she was over
a plate of tepid eggs, her hair bun dislocated onto the side of
her head as if it were in the process of dropping off. Hanna
could not leave behind her lisp, even when crying, and her
breaths came out in long, soughing whispers, *ssshhh, ssshhh,*
which sounded to Anna like she was telling the world not to
speak to her ever again.

———•—

AT JUST the time Anna emerged raisin-skinned and mesmerized
from an hour in her neighbor's bathtub, the bells of St. James'
Episcopal swung into sound in their clapboard tower over the
tremulous, fog-covered heart of Marbury Park. From a mile and
a half away, Anna had an intuition of the resonating peals. She
could not hear the sound so much as she could sense the stray
ripples of air that ran along its borders. The surface of the bath
water which had not yet drained from the tub seemed to rise
and shudder into minuscule peaks. It was Sunday morning, and
Anna had skipped her rounds of the local church services for
the first time in twelve years. Her phone would be ringing for
days with the calls of veteran parishioners who wondered what
incident or influence could have kept her away. "I had an accident on Saturday night," Anna imagined herself telling them.
"I remembered irresponsibility and desire at the same moment
in time."

It wasn't until she had dressed and collected her things and
hurried out under the shrunken, veiled sky that she realized
the Cordojo Women had already gathered on her porch. They
were peering in through her wide-open windows, rapping their
love-worn knuckles against the door frame. When they saw her
they did little dances under their exotic fruit hats; they clapped
their white-gloved hands together to make a series of muffled
pops, the sound of pillows being fluffed in the next room.

"You disappeared," Dove Pairlee said. "That was an astonishing thing for you to do."

"Actually, it was outrageous," Maxine said.

"I kept calling you on the telephone, but Mariela was home the whole time by herself," India said.

Anna moved past them to the front door, hoping that if she didn't stand still, no one would be able to focus clearly on her appearance, on the stockings which trailed like hollow snakeskins from the outer pocket of her purse, on the shoes which she balanced in her hands, precarious and bare and dappled from the sprays of water that still wafted in rhythmic curtains over the Ettingers' emerald lawn.

"Well, I can't stay in one place every minute of the day," Anna said. "You would all begin to take me for granted if you haven't already."

She ran upstairs to change her clothes while the Cordojo Women waited. When she looked into the mirror, she saw that she had slept on her hair strangely overnight, and now it refused to remember its natural shape. All of her auburn strands stood slightly apart from one another in muted alarm, as if they had just passed through an electrical storm and were still waiting to be struck. Her face demonstrated a certain sheen of exertion which she could not dull, even after dusting it twice with cosmetic powder, creating such a suspended, strangling cloud each time that she had to hold her breath.

There was no concealing the precious undoing that went along with physical love. Not even the saints, in their metaphysical love of God, had managed to keep free from the disarray of ardor. The statuettes that Cristobal had left behind all portrayed one imperfection or another. Saint Brigid had a bad haircut, with all the ends straggled into bird feathers. Saint Augustine's robe was two sizes too big, swallowing his hands inside its cavernous folds. Saint Margaret looked as though she hadn't slept in a solid month; there were circles under her eyes like blue half-moons, like twin shadows of the interventions which kept her from resting at night. So Anna did not feel entirely alone in her disheveled bliss. This was a small price paid for the opportunity of devotion. The Cordojo Women knew that as well as she did.

When Anna rejoined everyone downstairs, she found that her role as hostess had been gladly commandeered. Dove Pairlee had pulled five raspberry custard tarts from the refrigerator and was passing them out on as many paper doilies. Esther Lee had brought in the Sunday paper from the porch, and was now poring over its pages in her lap in search of the want ads. And Maxine Ridgeway had begun the afternoon's conversation, which had something to do with sexuality and nostalgia and how wasn't it a shame that the one necessarily meant the other.

"Men aren't supposed to be very much interested after the age of forty," India said. "But my husband was. He would put on some old Ella Fitzgerald record and roam naked from one room to the next until I noticed him."

"Lord, India! How long did it take?" Dove said.

"Oh, I never made him wait until the record was over," India said.

"Was it a forty-five?" Maxine said.

"A thirty-three," India said.

"I never realized you played so hard to get," Dove said.

"That's just because you can't fathom anybody showing a little restraint," Maxine said.

"I've never believed in restraint," Dove said. "I've never seen the point."

"Well, none of us can pretend to be shocked by that view at this late date," Maxine said.

Anna sat down in her favorite chair, the one in which the cushions gave way like liquid, leaving her half-submerged. On the coffee table in front of her, four pairs of white gloves lay piled together in a near semblance of a cabbage rose, mammoth-headed and fragrant, the fingers protruding with the grasp of vanity.

"The older we get, the less sense it makes to hold back, though," Anna said. "The chances for happiness with someone become so slight, and I don't think a timid person is able to fully understand that."

"Why is it that you sound like you're speaking from personal experience?" Maxine said.

"Everybody speaks from personal experience," Esther Lee said. "That's the only kind of experience there is." She had looked up from her place in the classified advertisements to speak, and now she went back to it, licking the tip of her index finger as she readied herself for the turn of the page. She had no idea of the subject that was being discussed, but she didn't approve of it, with its vagueness and giggles, flitting around the edges of her hearing.

"I think that Maxine was getting at where Anna was last night," India said.

"You all know where I was," Anna laughed. "I don't know why you want to make me say it."

But the women set down their forks of custard and gazed at her expectantly. India took off her mango-covered hat as if she had just then been asked to stay for the rest of the afternoon. Above their heads, even the mourning doves were quiet, rocking back and forth on their swings with solemn alacrity.

So what she said was: I was visiting Clifford Ettinger across the way.

And what she thought to herself was: I was visiting a place where my heart was unfastened. I was trying not to cry when I felt it come loose.

———•◦•———

ANNA AND Clifford became used to sneaking home in the early morning hours, when the light filtered onto the earth in the same way that smoke infuses a closed space, in dusky, amorphous plumes, airy and alive. They held their clothes in compact, protected bundles under their arms, as if concealing stolen goods, and they looked back over their shoulders with frequent and giddy compulsion to make sure they had not dropped anything—a sock or an undershirt or a jacquard silk camisole—onto the bare plains of grass they had just crossed over. Their working hours arrived with suddenness and immobility, and Anna and Clifford burst in on their appointments always slightly out of breath, with their coats turned inside out.

Anna realized that for all those years she had been alone, what she had called happiness was something less than it ought to have been. All those years spent with her friends and her patients and her prayers to the saints had simply been a single, attenuated reach for contentment. And now that she saw contentment for what it really was, with one day following the next with a predictable sameness, with no part of your own life to be passionate or angry or ecstatic or hysterical over, she wondered why she had ever considered it genuinely worth having.

Of course, the definition of a predictable life was subjective. What had been to her a peaceful decade of living would have been to Clifford unmitigated bedlam. But it just so happened that the particular nature of the confused, tender, outright, and overwrought affair they were carrying on managed to fulfill them both, and each of them looked back on the time they had spent alone as having been silently stunted, intangibly impoverished.

Anna thought of herself as having come fully awake for the first time she could remember, as if all of her past thoughts about love and loss had occurred to her while sleepwalking, with a night shade pulled over her eyes. There were two deciduous oak trees standing in the village park, and with the onset of late October, their glossy, seven-pointed, king-sized leaves all washed bright with the color of cardinal red. When she looked at the trees in a certain way, the foliage there seemed to consist of one thousand fluctuating, scarlet birds, ready to take flight. That's what is happening to me, she thought, staring at the oaks' vastness from the ground underneath. I'm changing into the bright-hearted color of love, all of me, and now there isn't any going back to the season I was in before.

On the day before Halloween, Clifford came over to Anna's house to carve pumpkins. The Cordojo Women were there, too, all of them wearing shower caps and knee-length aprons, holding their hands up in the air as if they had just been prepped for surgery. Anna slid tin sheets filled with buttered, salted pumpkin seeds into the oven for baking, and the air was suffused with their smell of balsa wood and bitter fruit, nutmeats and squash. Clifford carved a pumpkin face that was toothy and innocent, like a child with a snaggled grin, and when he held it up for display, everyone but Maxine Ridgeway gave their approval.

"I'm not sure," Maxine said. "I think it misses the point of Halloween."

"It does not," Dove said.

"What do you mean?" Clifford said. He was sitting cross-legged on a sheet of newspaper, his pumpkin cradled in his arms like a prize.

"Well, I just mean you've made it too cheerful," Maxine said. "There's nothing frightening about the expression. There's nothing ghoulish."

"I get your point," Clifford said. "But I can't see that there's anything wrong with a happy pumpkin."

"There certainly isn't," India said. "In fact, seeing the way yours turned out, I wish my pumpkin were happier."

"Do you want me to show all of you what I mean?" Maxine said. She forged her way over to Clifford, stepping carefully between pumpkin heads and piles of rind. Something about the way she reached for Clifford's jack-o'-lantern, with an honest, mother-of-the-earth assurance, made him give it up to her. She wielded her knife as if it were a harmless extension of her hand. It could have been a magic wand, pointing here and then there on the pumpkin's baby face, transforming its expression into something more appropriate for midnights and dark windows. When she had finished, the Cordojo Women saw that she had cut two dangerous eyebrows on top, so that the pumpkin now had the look of the wicked innocent, the bad seed.

"Oh, you shouldn't have," Anna gasped.

"That was criminal," Dove said. Her voice warbled with indignation; her eyes swam with delirious fervor. "How would you like it if someone disfigured *your* pumpkin?"

"I didn't disfigure it. I enhanced it," Maxine said.

"Then what if I decided to enhance yours?" Dove said. She

tilted Maxine's pumpkin so that its face was pointing upward, and with several short jerks of her knife, she extracted all of its teeth. They fell in damp, pulpy triangles to the floor, littered and bright, like pieces of a fruit salad. "There and there and there and there and there," she said while the teeth were dropping.

"You're a barbarian," Maxine said. And, since Dove could not think of any other way of responding, she picked up a handful of soft pumpkin mash and threw it at her, spreading it across her apron front in a stain that was reminiscent of the sky at sunset, all the clouds transformed into a weighty, viscous orange. There was a pause before the air in the room erupted with projectiles, cutting the space into quarters with the sweet, sticky, indelible mess. The Cordojo Women chose sides, wailing at the bitterness of war. Pumpkin seeds snagged in their hair like strange ornaments. Strings of squash dangled from their limbs like wet tinsel. Dove and Maxine ran in small circles, spanking one another with balls of bright mud.

"Give up," Maxine said.

"Make me," Dove said.

The ridiculousness of it struck them then and Maxine began helplessly to laugh. Dove simpered through her nose, her nostrils flared into two pinkening wells. The pumpkins stared at them from the floor, their expressions astonished, their mouths flung open. India and Esther Lee and Maxine and Dove huddled together in a chastened, giggling, gargantuan collapse.

"You're the most preposterous bunch of women in the universe!" India said.

"Count yourself part of us," Esther Lee said. "I saw you pitching pumpkin seeds overhand."

"Self-defense," India said.

No one noticed for a long time that Anna and Clifford were missing from the group. They had disappeared into the kitchen at the first opportunity and now kissed the pulpy, pungent taste of pumpkin off the planes of their faces and from the concealing depths of their hair.

"My friends aren't like this usually," Anna said, catching a breath.

"I don't care what they're like," Clifford said.

"It's just that I don't want you to think badly of them," she said.

"I'm not thinking of them at all."

Whatever happened in the presence of Anna, it was always unexpected. If Clifford managed to keep his eyes focused on her—on her gentle sensuality, on the seamless softness of her skin—then the chaos that leaped in the corners didn't matter to him at all. It was like riding a merry-go-round with someone, going very fast; the rest of the world spun away from you in cacophony and confusion. To keep from getting dizzy, you had to keep your mind fastened on the poetry of the ride, on the horses that rose up in pale, gilded dignity, on the music box accompaniment that sounded like discovery and love.

YEARS PAST, in the middle of an ordeal from which she would never entirely recover, Esther Lee gave up her hearing in the same way that someone might give up a painful habit—biting fingernails to the quick or eating spicy foods before bedtime. She gave it up willingly and without regret on the same day that her husband's erratic behavior was explained by a diagnosis of Alzheimer's. Before he died seven years later, he would give voice to unbearable accusations and nameless rages, the likes of which would have made Esther Lee walk out or give up or pickle herself in a deep tub of bath water, had she heard them properly. As it was, she could only see his lips move; she could only witness the clear, pitiable consternation that masked his face in his waking hours. *Where has my soul gone*, he seemed to be asking. But Esther Lee could not tell for sure.

In the beginning, they had both been able to laugh over his absent-mindedness, his inexplicable mistakes. He poured his breakfast cereal into empty flowerpots. He wore his eyeglasses upside down. He grew flustered at dawn and dusk, when the movements of light were ambiguous and the direction of the day indeterminate. Twilight madness, the doctors called it when Esther Lee had asked. Lunacy caused by shadows and equivocation. She had never known of anything more unlikely or more real.

Then later, there was the descent into an anguished semblance of life. There was the way he roamed around naked from one room to the next, in search of something behind the walls. There was the way he lost language, hundreds of words at a time, so that his phrases were left missing in the manner that vanquished armies go missing, their bodies left unburied in the same forest in which they have died. There was the way he ceased to know her, his wife of thirty-seven years, the way he startled upright in bed every morning and asked her *who are you, who are you?* She could read his lips as they released that simple question, so trembling and confused, so ancient and infantile.

The pity of his end still strangled her when she thought about it. She had loved him too meekly over all those years of clear-headedness. She had assumed too complacently that their old age would be spent together in put-off travel and constant hand-holding. If she had had it to do over again, she would have exhausted her middle age more recklessly. She would have installed candle-light sconces in the bedroom and she would have worn eye shadow that was the color of smoke and she would have taken a shower together with her husband at least two times a week.

None of these realizations would have been survivable without Anna de la Senda being there to lend them shape. Her consolations were received as easily as an elixir, soothing, spiritual, almost overdue.

"Just don't punish yourself with what you should have done," Anna said. "You helped him through a fearful, bewildering death. Any other lapses are made up for by this one gift."

When Esther Lee could not hear her, Anna would pull out a piece of notepaper and write her words down. At home, Esther Lee made a collage of these penned reassurances. They were taped to the wall, cluttered and rough-edged above the headboard of her bed. *Maybe part of living a good life is dying a good death.* And, *Love is never diminished. It is only transferred.* And, *Regret should be reserved for the long contemplation beyond this worldly life. Because the living have no use for it.* In the night, Esther Lee regarded her mosaic of wisdom and found that her loneliness was somehow eased.

The mystery was that, after her husband had died and Esther Lee wanted to listen to the comings and goings of the world again, she could not. Her deafness was entrenched and persistent and refused a miracle cure. Even with her peanut-sized hearing aid curled in the cup of her ear, she perceived all conversation as fragile and indistinct, as moving away from her on a current of intangible wind. People seemed to swallow their words out of some shameful ravenousness for the sounds of their own voices. More and more, she felt stranded in quiet isolation. Her rescue was improbable, but secretly, it was all that she longed for.

She had it in her mind that she ought to find a job. Something where she could count out change in people's hands or help small children cross the street. Something where she could relate to people simply, without having to ask them over and over again could they please repeat what they had just said. There weren't any ads in the paper for cashiers or crossing guards, but Esther Lee checked the classifieds every day all the same. Then, she found a listing for an office receptionist, with the requirements for the position being organization, efficiency, ability to send out the bills on time and keep the African violets alive. When she arrived for her interview in one of a set of professional buildings set back from Glenallen Square, she was stunned to find herself sitting across a desk from Clifford Ettinger, whom she had last seen wearing a pumpkin-stained shirt with her best friend's lipstick imprinted on his neck, but who now looked eminently professional in his white doctor's coat and his stethoscope necklace.

"I didn't know you were hiring," Esther Lee said.

"I didn't know you were looking," Clifford said.

In the end, he took her on not because of the way she answered his questions, which seemed distracted and incomplete, but because she emanated a species of deliberate and everlasting patience which he suspected would extend to ill people. He had had too many experiences with young receptionists who found the sick to be candidates for condescension and bleak distaste. Esther Lee, who hovered in her early sixties, could possibly supply just the compassion the office had lacked. She wore her hair in a cap of salted curls, just like nurses from an old World War II movie. And when she said hello, she cocked her head to one side as if she were utterly fastened on what you were about to say. Clifford approved of these things as signs of her dedication, and despite her myriad and trivial oversights, he never withdrew his initial esteem.

Esther Lee got all the patients' names and ailments wrong, but she was thoroughly consistent about it. Eileen McDonough with the wandering eye was Irene McCullough with the chronic stye each and every time she came. The athlete's foot of Calloway Levers was Anthony Cook's cat scratch fever. The female baldness of Sue Boria was Fifi Wallace's seborrhea. Esther Lee recognized all the returning patients as soon as they entered the waiting room. She never showed any confusion over who was who, and she exhibited an extreme, grandmotherly tolerance in the presence of anybody who did. The deafness would have presented a profound problem, except that Esther Lee had a talent for making infirm people adore her. She touched them with her hot, crepe-skinned hands, leading them into the examining room as though they were all her children or her grandchildren or the progeny of her borderless hearth. She held purses and briefcases secure in the central cavern underneath her desk in the same way that she provided cubby holes for schoolchildren, all the lunch boxes and windbreakers neatly sequestered. And when someone had just been given a lackluster prognosis, and the new knowledge of it had made them cry, Esther Lee comforted them with words of unabashed renewal, pressing her embrace onto them like the conduit of solace. Actually, though, the words were Anna's, borrowed from the slips of paper which fluttered above her through the dream-drenched night, learned by habit and by heart years ago.

———•—•———

FOR A few weeks, Anna concentrated on inhabiting the skin of love. She waltzed around the house wearing the black silk voile nightdress the Cordojo Women had given her, her shoulders reflecting the white of still, Italian stone, her skirts flaring outward in leaves of iridescent longing. Her head felt unweighted, as if she had all her life worn ropes of Rapunzel-length hair and had only recently shorn them off. Words and fresh laughter burbled out of her lips when she was all alone in the house, with no one there to respond to her except the wooden-faced saints, with their expressions of beatitude and their eyes that never shut.

But even in the midst of her ecstatic satisfaction with life, Anna began to be trailed by the shape of her daughter's devastation. Mariela's sadness permeated the walls with its scent of confection and self-sacrifice, of withheld mourning and martyrdom. How was it possible for a woman to be happy when the child she had prayed into existence was not? An invisible cord still tethered Mariela to her mother's soul and what ran back and forth along its pulsing loops was something more than sympathy; it was symbiosis. Damage the life at one end of the tether, and the life at the other end would cringe and scuttle and quake with pain. So Anna understood love and the absence of love at the same moment in time. It was as though she and Mariela had kissed one another full on the mouth, and, in that one instant, exchanged their very breaths.

Mariela had begun noticeably to gain weight. The heart-shaped cameo that was her face spread into an unfamiliar, womanly fullness, as if she were being fed generous plates of dairy cream in the hours she was gone from the house. Her abdomen extended just as far as her breasts, giving her a kind of natural, age-old balance when looked at in profile. Anna had the impression that she moved with the dignity of a giant egg, her center of gravity traveling down into the open, ivory cradle of her pelvis, the extreme delicacy of her movements showing that she knew just how thin her transparent skin was, just how tearable.

Opal Pairlee's hand-dipped chocolates shop was conducting a breathless business, and Anna had no doubt that the reason for it was Mariela, standing behind the counter in all her ripened, extravagant glory. Men came in off the street just to share in the privilege of seeing her. They settled their eyes on the blackness of the hair that grew like night woods, in secrecy and fury, all the daylight filtered out. They bore witness to the sainted face, the sweet fertility, the commingled reverence and sensuality that confused and enthralled them at the same time. Their palms grew numb in the places where she touched them while counting out their small change. The moisture in their mouths evaporated when she spoke. All of them went away feeling vaguely hypnotized and transported, their arms balancing great quantities of truffles and praline fudge which would be laid down as gifts in front of the women they went home to.

Anna could sense that sometimes it bothered her daughter, the hungry watchfulness on the part of the customers, the gasping and stuttering of the passersby. Often, she carried library books as a quiet defense. In the chocolate shop, she concealed her face behind their open bindings. On Main Street, she kept her head lowered, reading the same piece of dust jacket copy a dozen times over until she could turn onto a side road. She signed out all the same books that had passed through Addison's hands in the course of the summer: *Anna Karenina* and *Madame Bovary* and *Tess of the D'Urbevilles*, books in which the women always came to sudden, catastrophic ruin, as if a feminine longing could come to nothing else. Mariela did not just cart the texts around as props. She read them, really read them, poring over the lines as if she expected to find there variations on the theme of her life, as if she expected to find object lessons. She also read the critical essays in the back of the books, but most of the time she found that they were trivial. None of them directly addressed the question of why a woman could not look for love without finding the world's end instead. She would have liked for someone to explain that to her. She would have liked that more than anything.

At night, Anna would come to sit on the edge of Mariela's bed while she brushed out the long, cold-bodied cascade of her hair. In November, the invisible hours after dusk were filled up with the pressure of rain, and the two of them would listen to the sound of its sheeting through Mariela's open window. The drops collected in a permanent and shallow wishing pool on the floor, its hardwood shore speckled with tulip leaves and the small, purple-shelled snails that devoured them. Mariela liked to worry the buttons of her nightgown, one at a time, until they would pop off into the hollow of her hands. Then she would sit up straight on the mattress and toss the button into the water, where it rolled and settled like a precious, dislocated pearl. When she lay back down, she allowed Anna to continue brushing her hair, a momentary resolution in her eyes, as if she had decided something.

"What did you wish for?" Anna said.

"For everything worth having," Mariela said.

Anna reached up to her widow's peak, studying the downy whorl of growth there as if it were the keyhole through which she could peer into her daughter's desire.

"And what is worth having?" Anna said.

"You don't need to ask me that to know," Mariela said. She set her hands to work on the next button of her nightgown, twirling it with distracted determination, as if it were a withered tooth.

"He may not come back to you," Anna said. "Will anything be worthwhile then?"

By way of answer, Mariela turned transparent, the opacity of her skin fading to cellophane even as Anna laid her hand on its surface. Underneath her ribs, her swollen, iris-shaped heart was thrumming. And in the glistening, wide sack of her womb, her open-eyed baby rolled over, waving at her grandmother with two appendages that turned out to be wings, splay-feathered and fluttering and drenched by the closed sea in which they moved.

"You're wrong, Marielita," Anna said. "Life justifies itself, whether you believe it or not. And even if you had no one else to love you in the world—not Addison and not me and not the baby who swims inside you—even then your life would be a benediction."

Mariela's body paled one shade further. Her hair flickered through the lower spectrum and then settled on a color that was translucent and green, the color of fish scales and mermaids, of seaweed beds and salt water.

"Can you see my baby?" Mariela said.

"Yes," Anna said.

"What is she like?" Mariela said.

"She's like the angel of your daydreams," Anna said. "She's like the messenger of your old innocence."

ON MORNINGS when Anna invaded the Ettingers' kitchen, Hanna wandered in other rooms of the house wearing a look of listless, Germanic sorrow, her feather duster dangling from one hand as though she were carrying a boa she had worn in her youth. Clifford caught a glimpse of her thick-waisted shadow drifting over distant walls, and asked Anna whether she couldn't get used to letting Hanna prepare the meals. That was the kind of work he had hired her for in the first place, and without it she felt dispossessed, usurped, utterly unneeded. Still, Anna could not help the amount of territory which she herself required. There was something about plowing her hands into a bowl of bread dough once a day that made her feel that she was materially contributing to the world. She fried eggs and cheese and salsa in an iron skillet that was so monumental it required two hands to lift, and when she presented the meal to Clifford, he nearly cried from jalapeno peppers and boyish pleasure.

"This is unbelievably good," Clifford said. "Did your girl's father teach you how to cook like this?"

"Cristobal? Yes, he did," Anna said. She thought it was odd that Clifford had put the question that way—saying *your girl's father*, as if both the girl and the man had long since ceased having names. Probably he didn't mean anything by it, but his words contained an inherent distance, as if he were commenting on her life from a far-off mountaintop, his telescope focusing on her knobby knees. "You know, I've never heard you say my daughter's name," Anna said.

"Hm?"

"My daughter," she said. "You've never said her name."

"Well, we haven't talked about her in a while," Clifford said.

"No. It's true," Anna said. "We haven't talked about Addison either. Maybe we're just pretending the whole thing will go away."

Clifford regarded her indulgently for a moment. She seemed to be working her way up to an episode of crying, he thought. He could sense her distress, milling in the air above his food, changing its taste to something that wept at the edges. "What whole thing?" he said.

"Oh, all the pain they've caused each other," Anna said. "All that."

"Hasn't it gone away already?" he said.

"No," she said.

"I don't think I understand what you're saying," he said.

Anna disappeared behind her cup of coffee. She held her lips under the heated, velvet surface of her drink for such a long time that it occurred to Clifford she might be slowly drowning there. "Mariela's pregnant," she said when she took the cup away.

Clifford's eyes drifted past Anna's face toward the hallway behind her. He stared into the daylit passage, his expression suspended, as if he thought that just a minute from now someone would come rushing through it, wildly out of breath, with news of some medical emergency that he would have to see to. But no one came.

"Don't tell me this comes as a surprise to you," Anna said.

"You've seen her these last few months. You've seen the blouses she wears untucked from her skirts—all the new weight she carries underneath."

"I thought she was eating chocolates," Clifford said.

"What?"

"She works in a chocolate shop, doesn't she?" he said. "I thought she was eating too much."

Clifford's gaze was still fixed on the hallway, hovering in the cave of its sun-filled mouth.

"You were wrong," Anna said. "Very wrong."

Through the window, the late-waking birds sang songs of mourning, their voices cluttered together in thick-throated laments. Anna wondered whether the sounds came from the birds living under her roof, in the great copper cages that held their small lives.

"Pregnant," Clifford said.

"Yes."

"And you're sure," he said.

"Yes," Anna said. How many more times would he need to ask her the same thing? Well, he was a father, so the times would be innumerable. The Spanish word for question had always reminded Anna of pregnancy. *Pregunta*: to be filled up with longing, to be desperate with the desire to know.

"What we need to find out now is whether Addison loves her anymore," Anna said. "Does he even love her a little bit?"

"I . . . I really don't have any idea," Clifford said.

"Will you write to him and ask?" Anna said.

Clifford folded his hands together in front of him, all the fingertips touching in the way that children's do in prayer. "All right," he said, and his eyelids closed down over his eyes, turning them blind and unreadable. "All right. I will."

———•◦•———

ANNA REALIZED that being a lover and a mother at the same time meant forging an uneasy alliance with the needful world. On the one hand, she was willing to give up many things for

Clifford—her fierce secrets, her solemnity, the solace of her loneliness. On the other hand, she was willing to give up everything for Mariela—her laughter, her state of grace, the fragile substance of her life. Six months ago, it wouldn't have seemed possible to her that one attachment could exclude another. But now that Mariela was in trouble, she didn't know whether she could go on being in love the same way she had, giddily, magically, with the taste of wonderment filling her mouth.

For a while she thought to herself, if Addison comes back within two weeks, then everything will right itself. Because a fast return would mean that his heart had not forgotten Mariela, that his soul had never left her. But two weeks came and went and nothing had changed. Mariela had grown wider and her skin had stretched thinner and her winged feet barely touched the floor when she drifted across it, but nothing of substance had been altered. Her breath still reeked of sorrow and sugar candy, and she still floated up to the ceiling during her bouts of weightless, angelic despair.

Once, it occurred to Anna that perhaps Clifford had not written to his son with the news, that perhaps she was waiting for an answer that wouldn't come. Clifford wouldn't be able to hold her in his arms if this were true, though. He wouldn't be able to whisper to her in the lengthening, blue-edged hours after midnight that she was the reason he knew that God watched over the world.

———•◦•———

CLIFFORD WROTE,

Dear Addison,

The girl is pregnant, which is the very thing I worried about from the beginning. It's too late for me to tell you you've made a big mistake, but just soon enough for me to say you'd be making a bigger one by coming back here. Addison, think about it. Is the situation going to be improved by your throwing in your lot with her? Is it going to be turned into anything approaching respectable? And I don't mean respectable in the sense of what others think; I mean it in terms of what's right for you. Sometimes just walking away is the least damaging thing a person can do. I hope you'll understand that idea without having to find out what happens in its absence. Call me if you want to hash this out person to person. In the meantime, try not to let it throw you off balance; try not to let it disturb your work.

—Dad

It was only later, on his way to the post office to buy stamps, that Clifford passed by Opal Pairlee's hand-dipped chocolates shop and found himself wondering whether his letter contained more selfishness or wisdom. Through the plate-glass window, Mariela was filling a foil-lined box with decorated truffles. Her hair poured over both shoulders in identical waterfalls of blackness, reflective and in motion and separating into liquid locks at the ends. And in her face, there was something mythic and removed, as if she were the archetype of all men's longing, as if goodness and sensuality combined there in precisely the balance of each man's wish. Although her dress showed the melon shape of her pregnancy, she moved with a grace that was girlish and buoyant, as if what she carried under her clothes was in fact a helium-filled balloon that half-lifted her off her feet.

Clifford had looked in through the shop window hoping to confirm his every thought about the girl—that she would be ambitionless and swollen, attractive in a temporary, sullen sort of way, a perfect example of the teenaged tender trap. But what he saw instead was vulnerable beauty, shadowed hopefulness, wide-eyed wonder at the misfortune she was living out. A long line of customers curled through the interior of the shop, and Clifford felt a jolting impulse to run to the front of it so that he could apologize to the girl face to face, apologize for the fact that he still would not relinquish Addison to her, even now that he had witnessed her predicament first hand.

In the end, he walked away from the shop without having

uttered a word. Half a block away, he pulled his letter to Addison out of his pocket and tossed it into the public trash barrel. Staying out of things from now on would be his greatest gesture of contrition. Staying out of things would be the most he could possibly do.

———•◦•———

CLIFFORD ASKED Anna to go to the beach with him the following Saturday, but Anna turned him down.

"The Cordojo Women are taking me to a baby shop in San Patricio," Anna said. "Because there is so much to prepare for and we have hardly begun."

"Well, it won't take you the whole day, will it?" Clifford said.

"Oh yes, I think so," Anna said. "We need to pick out the wallpaper and the crib and the linens and the clothes. That will take us into the evening, I'm sure."

He was surprised not to hear a shade of regret in her voice, as if there were nothing she would rather be doing than buying cribs and rattles, as if there were no one she would rather be doing it with. After what seemed to him like too long a pause, she said, "Would you be interested in coming along?"

"No, no," he said. "You have your plans."

So the Cordojo Women went by themselves, led in a caravan down the interstate freeway by Dove Pairlee who drove with alternate passion and carelessness depending on the man who occupied her mind. In San Patricio, Jennifer's Baby Shop was populated with pastel moons and stars, hanging from mobiles in varying dimensions. When Anna looked from one end of the shop toward the other, she imagined that she had been transported to a foreign universe, devoid of harsh seasons and sharp objects, where the language was one of cooing and lullabies and where safety was as precious as platinum.

"I thought I was pregnant once," Dove said. "I went through morning sickness and week-long backaches and my tummy swelled out this far." She linked her plump, perfumed arms in front of her, as if improvising a basketball hoop.

"Really?" India said.

"Oh yes," Dove said. "But it all turned out to have been my imagination. Six months into the experience, I caught a case of the hiccups, and when it was all over, I had shrunk back to a perfect size seven."

"Hiccups!" Esther Lee said.

"Yes," Dove said. "I had been accumulating air in my stomach cavities, and then when I got the hiccups, all of it leaked out of me all at once. The doctor said it was psychological."

"Psychosomatic," Esther Lee said. "But the hiccups won't cause a miscarriage."

"It wasn't a miscarriage," Dove said.

"You're contradicting yourself," Esther Lee said.

At the center of the store, there was a giant-sized cradle that rocked by itself. Its woodwork was finished in white-washed oak, the color of sleepiness and vanilla ice cream, and from somewhere underneath, it let off an electronic purr, a continuous feline breath of satisfaction. India climbed inside it, despite the protests of the Cordojo Women, and held on excitedly to the lip of the sideboard. With her broad-brimmed pastel hat and her exaggerated, innocent eyes, she looked in fact like a strange species of baby, loose-throated and lipsticked and bobbling back and forth with delight.

"Would you give it your seal of approval, India?" Anna said.

"Not yet," India said. "I haven't got the complete feel of it yet." She laid her head back upon the king-sized moiré satin pillow, her hair spilling out of the bowl of her hat, and wriggled into a position of drowsy comfort. Her eyes shrank away from the bands of fluorescent lights that hummed seven feet above the cradle's hood, and she appeared to fall asleep; the faces of Anna and Esther Lee and Maxine and Dove all looked in on her the way grandmothers look in, with tender, earnest, unquenchable concern, with the unutterable curiosity over what it would all lead to.

Anna kept expecting that some saleswoman would discover them and then require them to leave before they had had a chance to purchase anything. But the only clerks she could see were all gathered at the back of the store beside a newly stocked mountain of bonnets, admiring a pattern that showed eight ducklings lined up around the rim.

"I hope Mariela's labor goes smoothly," Dove said. "I never could stand the thought of all those hours of agony."

"Not everyone knows it as agony," Anna said. "It's more like urgency . . . it's more like an urgent deliverance."

"I gave birth to Emily D. in two and a half hours," Maxine said. "That was urgent, let me tell you."

Maxine had her hands on her ample hips, cupped over their shape like two queenly brackets displaying a porcelain dish that was too fine to use at the table. This is where it happened to me, she seemed to be saying. Here, and here.

"My first husband saw it when she came out," she said. "He didn't want to see it, but he did because of the quickness, and then afterwards he was put off."

"What do you mean, 'put off'?" Dove said.

"It was too graphic for him, and he said it turned his stomach," Maxine said. "He never touched me after that, in a sexual way I mean. Not even once."

The Cordojo Women were stunned into a sudden quiet. They lowered their eyes, as if acknowledging the death of someone they had known long ago and in another place. Only India made a sound, a throaty, stertorous breathing that bordered on an outright snore.

"Men are so faint-hearted," Maxine said, her eyes swimming now. "That's been my biggest disappointment."

"Some of them are that way," Dove said. "Not all of them, though." She tried to speak delicately from under the trembling, diffused cloud of her blond-curled head. She always put herself in the position of defending men, she realized, but she couldn't help it. Most men were gloriously worth defending, and if she didn't make that point, no one would.

"Well, that Ettinger boy turned out to be faint-hearted, didn't he?" Maxine said.

"We're still waiting to hear," Anna said.

"A month since the doctor wrote, and you still haven't heard?" India said. She had sat up in the giant cradle now, disheveled and refreshed from her nap. A crease shaped like the letter L was pressed into one side of her face.

"You see that?" Maxine said. "That's just what I mean. Who could turn away from a girl like Mariela except a thoroughly faint-hearted man?"

———•———

THE MORE that time went by, the more Anna began to feel a certain tightening of the parts of her that had been free-moving up until now. Like a house in the rain, her doorjambs and window frames were swelling to the point of immobility; and she felt that if anyone wanted to enter where she lived with the intention of finding her, then they would have to do it by forcing their path, by damaging her entryways, by breaking sheets of glass. Because the only people she wanted to think about right now were the baby and Mariela and herself. She wanted to think about how they would live and what they would look forward to, the birthdays and the baby clothes, the revolutions of the days and nights. She wanted to think about the favorable glance of God, which she must not take for granted, ever, ever, no matter how much she wished that He had seen fit to make her family's place in the world a little more secure. She wanted to think about the kind of love that bound heaven and earth, however imperceptibly, with a few frayed and human cords.

When she lay in Clifford's bed in the early hours of the morning, she pictured her granddaughter's restless wings, wet and iridescent and sloshing in their nurturant sea. And when she kissed Clifford she thought, in her heart of hearts, of Mariela's melancholy mouth, of her lonely skin, of the wordless yearnings that lived inside her bulbous, vulnerable, buoyant self.

Mariela's heartache invaded her as surely as if it had been her own, and secretly, it appalled her that Clifford did not share their discomfort. Allowances might have been made for Addison, who was still at the age where selfishness and survival seemed to mean the same thing. But for a man such as Clifford, who had spoken the language of devotion and grief and the life that continued on after these things, the omission was all but inexcusable.

So when Anna began to avoid seeing him, it was simply because she had overlooked all the silences she was capable of. When he called her on the telephone, she was too busy to talk for very long, and when he asked her out to the movies, she was in the middle of baking a set of yeast-rising saint cakes. Once, when he looked for her nightgowns in his closet, he was astonished to find that she had removed them without his knowing, and in the space where they had been there were only three empty hangers, tinging their wire shoulders against one another in muted, overdue alarm.

He ran over to Anna's house right then and there, with his bare socks and his unshaven face and his hair that flew out from his temples like stray feathers. He crashed through his bank of rosebushes, which were now furiously overgrown, and tried to ignore the smell of fear that moved with him as he went, rising up from the straw-thick grass, pouring out of the empty eaves. He rang the doorbell, but no one came, so he jogged around to the side of the house and rapped his knuckles on the kitchen panes. Anna appeared behind the screen, her hands wet with soup stock or fresh lemonade or something she was making from scratch. She wore a pair of earrings that Clifford had never seen before, two sterling silver cornucopias, with all the fruits spilling out the one end.

"I need to talk to you," he said.

"I'm halfway through a gelatin salad," Anna said.

"So when are you free?" he said.

"I don't know," she said, and she held up her dripping hands in front of her, as if they were the proof of her plight.

Clifford was standing on the tips of his toes to see over the sill. The soil underneath his socks was sodden and movable, and he had the sudden sensation of balancing over a soft spot on the earth which at any moment would give way to a crater underneath.

"Anna, if this is about your daughter, I think you're making a big mistake," he said.

She stared at him silently.

"We're not living our children's lives," he went on.

"Of course we are!" Anna said. "That's what parents do."

The certainty of her opposition startled him. The cornucopias dangled from her ears like trembling exclamation points.

"So you're holding me accountable," he said.

"It's not a question of accountability," she said. "It's a straightforward question of love."

He felt the air stop moving through his throat. He wanted to say the right words to her, but he had the feeling that they would scatter before they reached her hearing, that they would be too large to fit through the netting of the window screen and would fall away to the tall grass where he would never find them again.

"Anna, if it's a question of love," he said, "well, you know that I . . . I think it's obvious that I . . . I love you."

"But I have to help Mariela to feel loved right now, and I don't think you can help me to do that," she said. "Can you?"

She waited for him to contradict her. The wetness filled up the rims of her eyes in the same way that he had seen it do when she woke up in the mornings, when her tears were some kind of involuntary offering to the world.

"I just don't know how to answer you," he said.

"No," she said. "Well. Come talk to me when you do."

PART FIVE

———◆———

*Other People's
Destinies*

ADDISON LEANED in the door-
way of his modest, stucco retreat and tried to determine where
in the unrecognizable world he was. The desert reclined on the
near point of the horizon in bold, striated shafts of color—in
the veiled-over purples of foggy-skinned grapes, in the damask-
hued reds of luxury and burials. The shadows seemed to rise
out of the sand itself, defying all the laws of obstruction and
light, and Addison liked to watch them gather and swell and
extend their edges while he said to himself that he would have
to remember how the darkness prefigured the actual night
here, running ahead of it in ragged-made pieces.

He had found out that, in the desert, the most memorable
part of life was the imaginary part of it. He had formed rela-
tionships with the nineteen fictional characters who populated
his stories, for example, but not with one person who ate and
slept and breathed the irrefutable breath of life as he knew it.
There was one blond woman he had spoken to, a painter who

worked in a set of adobe rooms next door to his, but she was self-absorbed and eccentric. She ate the half-moons of paint that collected under her fingernails, and she wore only her underwear when she knocked on his door to ask him a question. Her body looked as if it had been starved away, her bones protruding with a weary insistence, although to look at her face by itself, Addison would have guessed that she was a dedicated carnivore. Her lips were tinted a provocative orange-red, as if she had eaten meat for so many hours in a row that she had permanently stained them. He supposed she was sexy in a frazzled, lean, predatory kind of way; the other men at the colony were always grinning in her direction, silly grins, without language behind them.

Addison wrote stories during the hottest hours of the day, when the sun whitened the outdoor landscape into a picture of blindness, with all the colors leeched away. Afterwards, he went to eat supper with the other residents in the common dining room, everyone's eyes gone bleary and small from too many hours spent indoors. Daphne, the blond painter, always beckoned him to her table, her gestures emphatic, her hair kinked and dying. She liked to talk about coffee blends and irony and the makings of raw talent.

"I'm not really talented," she said one night. "I'm just clever. If you're clever enough, you can make other people think anything you want them to."

"What's the point of that?" a man said. He was moon-faced and his ears stood out, and it was rumored that he wrote poetry like an alien, perfectly, without any revision.

"I suppose you'd have to be clever to know," Daphne said. She waited for people to smile at her and then turned away when they did, pointedly, her lips the color of warnings. "Mostly, I can tell who has real talent without even seeing their work," she went on. "Like with Addison. I can tell that Addison has real talent."

"Let's not take this any further," Addison said. He pushed his chair away from the table, and it groaned for him, empathetically, its struts and pegs shifting in dread.

"You see? See what I mean?" Daphne said. "People with talent hate to talk about themselves."

"But you force them into it anyway," the moon-faced poet said.

"It's in my nature," Daphne shrugged. "I'm inquisitive."

Later that night, she knocked on Addison's door to apologize. She was wearing a cotton-knit shift and chewing her fingernails and her hair was tied back with a snippet of yarn that was candy-apple red, like a child's. "I shouldn't have gone on about you like I did," she said. "The truth is, I knew your work was good because I'd already read one of your stories. In the *Indiana Review*. The library here has two copies."

"Really?" Addison said. "So why couldn't you just say that?"

She collapsed into a low pocket of his couch, staring at her stained fingernails, regretful. "I'm strange," she said. "Sometimes I lie to try to make life more interesting."

"It's not interesting enough in itself?" Addison said.

"Not to me."

She came back on other nights after that, bare-limbed, insomniac, speaking in idioms of despair while the smoke of her cigarettes sifted its way through his rooms. She seemed to want something from him, but he didn't know what. She liked carrying his stories away and bringing them back the next day to say they had altered her blood pressure metaphysically, through a means she couldn't describe.

"So you're working on a book for someone, I take it," she said.

"For myself," Addison said.

"Who's your agent?"

"I don't have one," he said.

"Haven't you contacted anyone?" Daphne said.

"No."

Her cigarette wound astonished snakes of smoke around the ceiling lamps. She looked at Addison through emptied, sweeping, half-closed eyes, trying to decide what to believe about him. Finally, she slipped a pen from between his fingers and began scrawling a name and address in the notebook in front of him.

"My cousin works for a reputable place in New York," she said. "A boutique agency, very well thought of. Send him your material. Mention my name."

She left without waiting for a reply, sidling out past his open door, dropping old ash and embers at every step.

———◆———

HIS ISOLATION astonished him. It was so complete and dauntless and, when he allowed himself to admit it, demoralizing. He passed through the sequence of days unencumbered now by anyone who needed him, unburdened by any wants other than his own. There were no one else's groceries to buy, no one else's feelings to spare, no phone calls or appointments or rendezvous in Marbury's groves. There were only hours falling into line one after the next and the unbroken quiet that defined them. He had worked hard at being unattached; he had looked forward to it. But now he understood that being alone was not something worthy of manufacture. It was a sadness that descended on you. It was a regret.

The colony served ambrosia salad for dessert every Friday night, and Addison ate whole bowlfuls of it while he felt like dissolving. The recipe contained white peaches and walnuts, which was unlike any ambrosia he had had before. But still, it reminded him of something that had been lost to him, intentionally, out of a thought that he would be better off without it. He told himself not to think of Mariela, but he told himself too often, so this had the reverse effect. He thought of her when he saw desert finches or bowls of ripe fruit or lovers tangled together in public, and he thought of her in between, when there was nothing to witness but the view from his window, treeless and searing and blank.

There was a road close by that bent its narrow black neck toward the town, and occasionally people would travel it on foot, their lower halves twisting in the vapors from the asphalt, their upper halves disembodied and unaware. Some of the men carried coils of green garden hose or stacked burlap sacks, and some of the women, small woven rugs or bibles. Addison could watch them traversing his horizon one wavering step at a time while he wondered who they were. Once, a pair of wandering figures had turned out to be the parents of the moon-faced poet, their car having broken down several miles back. And the next day, there was a young woman with abundant black hair and a batiste peasant dress and an illumination above her head which Addison thought he recognized. The illumination could have been a mere mirage, but it could have been a sign, too, and he was not going to wait there wondering which. He hurried out to the road, following her, the soles of his shoes turning pliable and hot against his feet. She was a hundred yards ahead of him, the skirt of her cotton dress swinging back and forth like a lovely white bell. Twice, she turned around to look at him straight on, but her face was unformed by the distance, her features disorganized and concave. Nearer to the town, she disappeared behind the crumbling facade of a pueblo church, its doorways carved with faces of the holy virgin, beatified and grieving.

It was possible, wasn't it, that Mariela had come to El Fuerte to see him, that she had walked or driven or flown into the desert knowing somehow that he would be at the center of it, heat-struck and forlorn? That seemed possible to him in a crazy, blatant, fateful sort of way. Lovers were always coming together again over impossible distances and careless divides. It was part of their genius, that ability to transcend real geography.

In the nave of the church, the darkness enveloped him. He heard dislocated whispers from somewhere off ahead, rosary beads clicking together in invisible hands, the Spanish supplications of a dour-sounding priest. He spent a full half-hour scanning the backs of the parishioners' heads, searching for one that would look luxuriant and familiar to him, all the black hair growing in a gleaming, passionate crown. But the girl had disappeared, and it wasn't until the Mass concluded that he found her again, all but the white hem of her dress concealed under a yarn-fringed shawl. She hurried past him and out toward an unpaved lane that adjoined the church's stone-dotted yard. He ought to have turned back toward the colony, but something in him had been left unsatisfied. He hadn't seen her face clearly, and if he gave up now, he would always wonder about it. He would always be unmasking her in his mind, seeing her as sometimes Mariela, sometimes not Mariela. She loves me, she loves me not.

The desert lane vanished and then reappeared under his feet. Heads of cactus grew on the sloped terrain, swollen and lopsided, like thorny green gourds. All around him, the daylight collapsed into itself, falling downward onto the sand and then going deeper, into the salty strata underneath. Ahead of him, the girl quickened her pace, her sandals scuffing the hard-baked path, the corners of her shawl unfurled and snapping in her wake. She kept him at a constant distance, too far away for talk or recognition. When the forms of two trailers appeared, bottle lamps shining in each window, she broke into a run. Addison would have followed her up the cinder-block steps and past the narrow trailer door if he hadn't been stopped by two men who met him there. They were frank-eyed and alarmed and they had bodies like the bodies of tree trunks, thick and immovable. When Addison tried to push past them, he found it impossible.

"I think I know her," he said to them. "I just want to see her face, because I think I know her from . . . somewhere else."

"Step back, man," one of them said. He put his open hand on Addison's neck and pushed him backward into an old barbecue grill, the coals gone powdery and cold. There was something about their looks, Addison realized, something staunch and impassive that said they would solve all problems physically.

"I just wanted to see whether I knew her," Addison said, brushing himself off.

"She don't know you, she don't want to know you," the second man said. While he spoke, the girl's face appeared in the doorspace behind him. Her eyes were heavy-lidded and remote and Addison saw in an instant that she wasn't who he had hoped. She could have been Indian, he thought. Peruvian maybe. She was nothing like Mariela at all, not even her hair, which under the indoor lights looked coarse and tangled and left to grow wild.

"I'm sorry," Addison said. "I made a mistake."

"Yeah," the first one said.

They waited there, in front of the open door, while Addison wandered away. It was night now, and all around him the desert was bewildering and unlit, every direction looking like every other. The sand seeped into his shoes a cupful at a time, and the air turned his mouth into an open husk, all the moisture in it wicked away. By the time he made his way back to the town road, he was barefoot and gasping and he couldn't determine whether the colony would be north or south from where he stood. A car stopped for him, the driver of which turned out to be Daphne, wearing a child's dress and dark makeup and her cynical, lopsided smile.

"Are you lost, dear one?" she said.

"Yes," he said, settling into the car beside her. "Lost is what I am."

MARIELA WAS the only woman he had ever known to possess wonder and hopefulness and a physical quality that somehow transcended what could be touched. And he found that fact impossible to reconcile with the knowledge that he had willingly left her.

Addison had loved her with irreversible force; that much was apparent to him. He remembered lying next to her in Marbury's orange grove, confusing the scents of the fruit and her nakedness, because there was so much sweetness there, wrapped around her skin. And he remembered watching her submerge herself in the koi pond at the library. Whole bubbles rose out of her hair like great, silver eggs, and the flounces of her skirt glided away from him like the fanned tails of the fish underneath her. And he remembered telling her things he had told no one else, his nightmares that Bernard ate him limb from limb, his desperation over the fact that he couldn't recall the last words he had spoken to his mother. She had listened to his confessions with immutable and unflinching grace, never disappointed with his private uncertainties, never trying to make him fit the character of the surer person he should have been. And all of these memories were indelible in their essence, printed onto the workings of his mind so that he saw them in everything, the way he saw the shape of the sun in everything after he had stared at it for too long a time.

He tried to concentrate on what he had once criticized her for—the absence of her ambition, the indefiniteness of her plans for herself—but these didn't mean anything to him when he thought about them. They were not urgent or permanent faults, and he wondered why he hadn't been able to understand that when it still would have mattered.

People could slip away from you without your really intending it to happen. They could slip away in the space of a season or a moment when you were distracted or uncertain or looking in the wrong direction. And afterwards, there was no replacing them. There was no finding anyone on the whole unguarded planet who could make you feel about living exactly the way you used to. Affections were not to be traded. It couldn't be done; it shouldn't be tried. Addison had learned that much from Mariela, and he had learned it from his mother, too.

Now, there were arid, undivided days when Addison wondered whether someone like Mariela could forgive him for what he had done. He suspected that even the saintly had limits, although he couldn't guess what they would be. He wrote to his father, but never about the important things—never about the questions *how is she* and *have I done her a lasting harm* and *would she agree to see me if I came back.* Instead, he talked about his work and the technical problems it posed for him and every few weeks he enclosed his latest pages to illustrate what he meant. He always addressed the envelopes to his father's office, because he thought of it as an antiseptic, orderly, confidential place, having no idea about Esther Lee's arrival, or the warm-hearted confusion she carried with her or her fascination for the stories that fell into her hands.

———⋅•⋅———

ADDISON WROTE about the same things over and over again: devotion and enchantment and the rareness of passion. Most people caught glimpses of these in the course of their lives and then lost them again, out of carelessness, as he himself had. Now he spent all his waking hours submerged in the details of love, recalling what he knew and inventing what he didn't, recording and embellishing and crossing out what was hollow. His fingers grew longer reaching for dictionaries and typewriter keys and phrases with the right intimations behind them. He was distracted from the world at the same time that he was engaged with it intently. Because this was his fate, he told himself: to spend his life daydreaming other people's destinies. He wrote,

> *I found out that her hair was liquid after all. I sank my bare hands into it to find the strands cool and continuous. As in a waterfall, my fingers could never find open air on the other side. When I took it in my mouth, it tasted faintly of almonds.*
>
> *In the beginning, I tried to explain certain of her mysteries. I tried to find out why, after sleeping all night in my bed, she left no impression on the mattress. And why her presence altered the dark, her body illuminating whole rooms from somewhere underneath its surface. And why her touch was always cool in hot weather and hot in cold weather, as if she were an answer to nature itself. But the reasons were insignificant, whatever they might have been. What mattered was that I knew her mysteries by name. I knew her skin and her sinews and the weight of her floating soul. And a knowledge like that cannot be undone.*

There were ten stories altogether and Daphne's cousin managed to sell them as a collection for what he called a respectable advance. Since Addison thought that twenty thousand dollars was more than respectable—that it was in fact ample, even kingly—he had all the more reason to celebrate. He didn't need the money, really. He had enough money set aside for him in the family trust. The point was to have an audience, however fledgling or tentative, and now he would have one; by his sudden, improbable luck, he would. In the moments when he realized what had happened to him, he felt that the globe was revolving faster underneath his shoes, making him lose his balance. He was hurtling toward his fate at a quicker pace than the average person, and it made him giddy and vivified and gasping for air.

Addison wrote to his father to ask him whether he should come home, now that there would be a contract and a book and all the details that went with them. But even as he mailed the letter, he knew what Clifford would say: that a future in Marbury Park was a contradiction in terms, that writers had to find their own haunts, as lonely as they might be, that there was nothing for him to come back for, nothing worthwhile at all.

He wouldn't mention Mariela by name, only by implication. She was what Addison would again be warned away from —she, with all her guilelessness and beauty, with all her undisguised goodness in the face of the self-interested world. Addison ached when he thought about her—his throat ached low and at the back, as if someone had put a hole into his windpipe there and he was leaking out the breath that kept him alive. That must be what happened when you turned your back on what you shouldn't, he thought. Your soul developed punctures, infinitesimal, whistling gaps that wouldn't be checked or mended.

No one at the desert retreat seemed to notice. They all acknowledged him and congratulated him and asked him why he didn't go off somewhere exotic to celebrate. Everyone but Daphne, who argued that New Mexico was exotic enough. She had been showing up every night at his door, her clothes flung around her meagerly in jerseys and sheers and gauzes that hung like tissue paper. The last time, she brought a bottle of champagne with her, ice-cooled and dripping so that when she handed it to him, there was a damp cusp left on her blouse.

"We should have a toast together about your book," she said.

"I don't know," Addison said. "It's one o'clock in the morning." He stood in front of her, his hair driven out in all directions, careless and provoking in ways he was unaware of.

"Don't tell me you're too worn out for champagne," Daphne said. "Nobody is. Not legitimately."

When he brought her back a paper cup, she drank out of it fervently and two-handed, as if she were taking a potion. She closed her eyes to reveal two sunsets of eye shadow setting on her lids, abstract and uneven, like the pictures she painted.

"I'm drinking to your future," she said, in between swallows. "Not all of us can say we have one, but you are an exception."

"Everyone has a future," Addison said.

"It's that belief right there that sets you apart," she said.

They drank in silence for a while, and then Daphne lit a cigarette and paced the floor inside its sheltering smoke. It occurred to him that she was made out of a different set of elements than he was: old bones and molten rock and things that lay hidden underground. Hot vapors poured off of her, off of her breath and her disappointments and the combustible attitude with which she crossed a room. The ends of her hair looked like they had been set on fire and then extinguished, brittle and frayed and spent like straw.

"Let's pass a little time not talking," Daphne said. "There are other ways to say things." She pulled one of his endless, tapered hands out of his pockets and tucked it under her blouse. She moved so covertly, it seemed to him that she was stealing something, shoplifting his appendages, concealing them from view. Where his fingers lay, there were inclines of skin that filled him with restlessness and dread.

"Daphne," he said. "This isn't what's going to happen."

"Why?" she said. "Why not?" She pressed his hand harder when he tried to remove it. He could see her stained fingernails through the transparency of her shirt; they were five glaucous sickles, foreign and tenacious.

"Because I'm not free to take this on," Addison said. "I'd be thinking of someone else the whole time."

"I don't care," she said. She inclined her head toward the smoke circling above her, some part of her famished for it, eager to breathe it in a second time. He'd seen another person do this once. He couldn't remember who. "I'm not talking about an attachment, you know," she said. "An attachment doesn't mean anything to me."

"It does to me, though," he said. He disengaged himself from her with slow resolution, his unburdened arms falling back to his sides.

After she left, it came to him that she smoked her cigarettes exactly like Rita, his own mother, swallowing lakes of smoke into the well inside her desperately, unfathomably, out of a hunger he couldn't name.

PART SIX

———•———

Portals to Pray By

RITA DIDN'T like Bernard's taking the car out at night. She liked having it handy in case a boyfriend called, agitated and flattering and with a set of plans already in mind. But when the phone didn't ring, she fell asleep early, curled in a Q on the coverless bed, her makeup leaving traces on the pillowcase that looked like blurry wildlife. Then Bernard could drive away without her knowing, navigating himself toward the glinting, adjacent world with a recklessness he couldn't help. It rained that winter in swollen, plunging fits, like monsters falling onto the backs of each other, and Bernard liked the raucousness of it on the highway and in the neighborhoods, where the storms came and went with a will. In Marbury Park, the rain batted the citrus blossoms off the trees, clotting them at the street drains and the down spouts in ragged, fragrant mounds. The streetlights flickered on and off for reasons no one could guess. To Bernard, it looked like the town was slowly dissolving underwater, the flower beds flooded out, the real estate signs listing sideways, the cats mincing their paths from one doorstep to another. He moved through it all anonymously, no one peering past the cloudy glass of his windshield, no one stopping to wonder whether he belonged.

At the Ettingers' house, the key turned in the lock the first time he tried it. Inside, the residual rain fell from his coat, plashing in dime-sized drops wherever he moved. There were people close by. Someone was having a conversation in a room ahead of him and to the left, the voices rebounding toward him in soft, dislocated vowels. It sounded to Bernard like they would go on a long time, sleepy and unsuspecting, so he made his way upstairs to the bedrooms where the outside lights filtered in through the windows in silvery, diffused shafts that revealed the furniture. In the back of the top dresser drawer, he found a money clip, which amused him because he didn't think anybody used those anymore. But there was almost a thousand dollars there, and his breath shifted and quickened when he counted it out.

There was some ladies jewelry, too, arranged in layers inside a makeup case he found wedged under the frame of the bed. At first he thought it was nothing, since when he opened the lid there was an old hairbrush on top and it was full of stale hair. Underneath this, though, there were black velvet pockets doubled back on each other, zippered and plush and weighty. One of them hid a long rope of pearls that would have made a triple strand on a lady's neck if she folded them the right way. Bernard thought they were real, because his mother had an artificial strand and it didn't look anything like the one he took away with him. His mother's were yellowed unevenly, and sometimes the individual spheres would shed whole layers of shellac, just shed them without his even provoking it much, as if they were minuscule onions, peeling themselves in his hands.

There were other things, too. There was a diamond tennis bracelet that unwound itself in a brilliant white centipede of stones. There was an emerald pendant that felt cold and violent and priceless when he touched it, like a primordial egg, oversized and brutal. Something like that would always stay cold, no matter what the surrounding temperature was.

Bernard noticed that a lot of things in the house were the same way, impervious to climate. When he had first walked in the front door, he had felt the coolness of the marble rising up through the soles of his shoes. And someone had chosen everything in white, the walls and the furniture and the carpet, where there was carpet. White never held the heat either, he had noticed. He could have lived in a place like that and he could have been an entirely different person, with everything drawing the fever out of him wherever he went. Heat was a kind of madness when it lived inside your mind, and with Bernard it did. If he had been set up in the right way, though, in the way his brother was, with surroundings that left you cool and clearheaded enough to make your plans, he could've made a definite impact. He was sure he had the makings of impact closed up inside himself, sealed in by high temperature.

He didn't hear the movement on the stairs, because the sound of the rain against the house overtook all the rest. But he was only a few feet from the bedroom door when it opened up on him, and the old man came charging through it like he knew just what to expect. With all the lights turned on, Bernard shrank back, his eyes turning inward, stunned and searing.

"You left the car parked out front," the man said. "How long did you think it would take me to figure it out?"

Bernard began to see segments of him clearly, his cinched-up mouth, his fisted hands. There were tracts of color moving around from one part of his face to the next, migrating like an illness.

"I don't know what you think you've collected," he said. "But you're not taking it away with you." He was looking at the velvet sack, where the prongs of the gem settings pressed outward like dozens of animal teeth.

"You don't know who you're dealing with," Bernard said.

"I don't need to have seen you before to know who you are," the man said. "And who you are just makes it worse." He was about to say something else when Bernard went through him with a force that left him wheezing, dry-wheezing, hunting around the room for a way to breathe. That was one good thing about holding so much heat inside your head. It enabled you to pass through people like they weren't there. Bernard had seen it before and it was a definite benefit. On the staircase, a housekeeper melted away from him, too, her prim, dark dress fusing flat with the wall behind her. By the time the old man had recovered enough to follow him, Bernard was already loping across the streaming driveway, reaching for the handle on the car.

"You can't do this!" the old man called.

"I'm doing it," Bernard said.

The pepper trees above them were leaning and shuddering and tossing down sodden scraps of leaves. They looked like they were fighting with the earth underneath, straining to uproot themselves and flee. Through the windshield, Bernard could see the house careening away from him, its lights wavering in their places, its roof throwing off assaults of rain. The man was becoming smaller now, a miniature model, a toy version of himself. Bernard watched him in his rearview mirror, making tiny toy gestures of fury. He pressed the accelerator, waiting for what would happen. In a moment or two, the sight behind him would have shrunk so much that it would no longer exist.

———•◦•———

MARIELA FELT that windows were the perfect portals to pray by, especially at night, when the visions that presented themselves on the other side were shadowy and indistinct, and might comprise exactly the miracles she had requested from the beneficence of God. In fact, when she held her face in the rain that passed over the window ledges, when she felt the baptismal touch of the wetness running over her hair, she imagined that she was secretly being washed by the fingers of the saints, who were jealous, it was said, of what was holy and mortal at the same time. Under her knees, minor wishing pools rippled back and forth over the hardwood floor, and it seemed to her that it had rained so long and she had prayed so fervently that her supplications and the weather had become somehow related. Perhaps the sky had learned to weep from the weeping of her soul. She wasn't sure of the explanation behind her belief, but she was sure of its validity.

She was six months pregnant then and the baby was springing and toppling inside her as if she could not stand being bound. Her mother had told her that the baby had visible wings, and sometimes Mariela thought that she could feel them gliding against her womb, fin-like and slickened, and tickling her with their quills. The unborn child had become her mysterious ally, helpless and blessed, as Mariela had for some time felt herself to be. And it seemed to lessen the breadth of her despair to know that the baby continued to grow despite the wild fluctuations of the world that awaited her. Abandonment and recrimination, forgiveness and willing sacrifice, these things would signify nothing to her child, for whom the relevant world would be divided into moments filled with love and moments empty of it. There was a certain undeniable wisdom in someone who would value milk and caresses above any other thing that could imaginably be offered to her. And in a few months more, Mariela would have milk and caresses in abundance. Already, the colostrum was escaping from her nipples, requiring her constantly to check her blouse-fronts in order to see whether the two modest blossoms of stain had yet appeared.

The rain traveled through her window now with a steep, wind-swollen urgency. Outside, the oaks tossed their leaves behind their woody shoulders, the same way that women move their hair from front to back. The old gas lamps cast aureoles of wet light onto the pavement, but directly in front of the de la Senda house, where the illumination stopped, the street turned into a broad thoroughfare of blackness and ideas where anything might happen. Mariela looked across the gradual, balding knoll that bordered on the Ettingers' yard, across the unkempt profusion of the rosebushes, where the spearmint-like leaves trembled into susuration, over the glistening lawn where the waves of grass lay down flat as if to listen for the murmurs of the earth beneath them. For an instant she remembered what the house looked like when Addison was in it, all the lights on the second floor blazing, his Volvo standing in the driveway, the shape of his soul or his shadow held in portrait momentarily in one corner window. When she stopped remembering it, she was stunned to find that the car remained visible, a material reality, streaming water from the fenders, its antennae quivering in the wind. So this was the way of miracles, she said to herself. This was the way that prayers were made manifest—silently, discreetly, waiting to be picked out of the blurry, intemperate view from a window. The baby tumbled inside its glistening sack, as if it had just been injected by the same shot of adrenaline hope that Mariela had. In her veins, the currents quickened. In her iris heart, the purple quadrants flooded brighter. The air from outdoors smelled nascent and electrified, waiting for something like lightning to happen.

When the Ettingers' front door fell open, Mariela saw Addison rush out of it and get into his car. His hair was long, longer than she had ever seen it, as if he hadn't once been to a barber in the intervening months, as if in his absence, his life had become as unwieldy and nonsensical as hers. Suddenly, it occurred to Mariela that the whole of her loneliness had been the result of a misunderstanding, that for some reason Addison had thought his going would be better for her, for some reason his father had contrived because a father like that could bend the whole world to his way of thinking. Even now, Mr. Ettinger was following him out into the rain, badgering him about something, rapping on the car window with his swollen, knuckle-studded fingers.

Mariela ran downstairs and out into the liquid night. The wings that grew from her feet were fluttering with such an urgent speed that they had turned invisible, but Mariela could feel them beating at her heels, a pair of hummingbirds supporting her weight. The Volvo was tearing out of the driveway now with Mr. Ettinger baying after it. His pale hair was crested, like frosting on a cake, abundant and uneven. "You can't do this!" he was shouting. "I won't allow you to do it!" But the car was pulling away from him all the time. When it raced over the wet leaves in the street, the sound was like a celebration, like a thousand small packages being opened simultaneously, all the tissue paper falling away below into hushed unfoldings.

Mariela drifted out past the sidewalk, waving. Her hair was filled up with the rain, and the weight of it pulled on her neck, like a winter hood. The headlights didn't appear on the car, and she kept thinking they were going to come on any second. She was willing them to come on; she was concentrating on it, but the street remained dark, the place where she stood a quiet vortex of colorless wind and minor debris. In Saxon Hill proper, the gas lights winked, kindly and immobile like a row of elderly women, their circumscribed warmth and their postures still intact.

When the accident first happened, all Mariela could think of was that this must be what it felt like to fully depart from the wide, reckless world. This must be what it felt like to have your existence interrupted by God, whose gestures were all vast and unfathomable and free from attempts at explanation. There had to have been noise, but she could hear none of it. There was only a far-off, endless rush that filled her ears, like the sound of the ocean inhabiting an empty shell. Even in the instant before the car struck her, she had heard the shushing inside her head, as if she had been met by a prescience of eternity, as if she had been swallowed into the circle of its beginning and its end. The car tore away in animal horror, whining its fretted, fuming breath. Why would Addison do this to her, she wondered? There was no recrimination in the thought, only astonishment, young and open-mouthed. Why would he ever, after all the thousand hopes she had placed in his keeping?

Mr. Ettinger's face appeared above her, ashen against the dark. There was rain running down the trail of his nose, and his breath smelled of coffee, concentrated and nervous. "Good God in heaven," he was saying. "Help us now if you're ever going to." And then her mother was calling from the front porch, "Clifford? Is that you? What is it? What's happened?", some part of her already knowing the full extent of it, the desperate confusion that whorled through her daughter's mind, the red-bodied lake in which she had begun to float, the white, lidded heat that lit up in her abdomen, burning there insistently, like the eye of her fate.

Hanna trotted thickly down the Ettingers' drive, as if her legs had aged beyond the rest of her, as if she were trying to run with someone else's ankles. Mariela could hear her breathing alongside her own, labored and thickened, as if she were inhaling dark water. Hanna's hands held onto Mariela's face in a hot, rough-skinned frame of fingers. "Szomebody," she lisped to the sky, "szomebody call the hoszpital and tell them to hurry. If they hurry, itsz not too late."

———•—•———

IT SEEMED to Mariela that she couldn't understand what everyone was trying to make her understand: that there was no baby anymore, that the baby had left her. People kept offering her explanations of the event, that it hadn't been Addison driving, that it had been Bernard, who was now in jail waiting for the judge to set his bond. That between its immaturity and its trauma, the baby had never stood a reasonable chance, had never drawn in a breath or a whimper, had entered the world having already left it, a blue-tinged shadow of who she might have been. Mariela could understand the words themselves, but she couldn't believe that they were connected to what she had lived through, not in any way that was meaningful, not in any way that she could hold on to with her two empty hands.

She had been half-asleep during surgery, and the anesthesia had rendered her mind cumbersome and unwieldy, her thoughts melting into one another like remnants of butter and wax. Whatever the doctors were doing with her abdomen, their movements felt like rummagings through a bureau drawer, rough enough so that all the sweaters would be spilling out the opening. And for quite some time after the drawer had been closed, after all her sutures had zippered up the opening, she felt the conviction that the contents had been left in a jumble inside, that all her organs were in lopsided disarray, crowded together in some back, left-hand corner and forgotten. When she got out of bed to walk for the first time, she felt as though she were listing to the side from careless ballast. She would have fallen if her mother had not been there to catch her, her luminous, freckled arms extended, as they had always been, to cradle the weight of whoever needed lifting up.

After that, Mariela preferred the wheelchair to walking. She liked its fluidity, its safety, the sense that it gave her of being at rest and in motion at the same time. And more than anything, she liked the fact that there was always someone pushing the wheelchair from behind, a nurse that smelled of talcum, or her mother who gently zig-zagged from one side of the corridor to another, or one of the Cordojo Women with Kleenex and lozenges spilling out of her pockets. They were all angels of a kind, present but invisible, scented and sympathetic and hovering just above her head. It occurred to her that she had not allowed anyone to care for her in a very long time. Oh, she had let people care about her in a polite, well-intentioned, advice-giving sort of way. But she had not had anyone to give her succor or sustenance. She had not let anyone feed her dried figs from the palm of an open hand, the way India Perry now did. She had not let anyone massage baby oil into her skin after a sponge bath every other day, the way her mother now did. She had not let anyone brush her hair out on the pillow, the way Emily D. did on the day she came to visit. There was something undeniably healing in the gentle ways people placed their hands on her, as if she had suddenly become a small child again, unknowing of the world and needing help with all her minor forays into it. She did not want the touching to stop.

Everything about Emily D. was older than it had been the summer before. Someone had shown her how to use hair spray on her bangs to keep them off her face, and Mariela was surprised to see that her eyebrows, instead of being the same shy brown as her hair, were darker and hawk-shaped and made her look discriminating. She had a new pair of eyeglasses with frames that were precisely the same admiral's navy blue as her mascara, and when she was not using them, she pushed them backwards onto her head where they reflected the ceiling lights like daytime stars. The only thing about Emily D. that reminded Mariela of the girl she had been was the way she held the hairbrush, two-handed, with exaggerated care, as though it were a priceless or heavy or particularly breakable thing that was now her responsibility. She had always moved about in the material world with that kind of concentrated delicacy, picking up ice cubes as though they were diamonds, laying out her clothes each night as though she intended to get married in them the following day.

"You're so pretty now," Mariela said to her. "You're so pretty and I'm lying here broken into pieces."

"You feel like you're in pieces, but you don't look that way to me," Emily D. said.

"I don't know," Mariela said. "I feel like a part of me has been taken away, the best part of me, the angel part of me."

"The baby," Emily D. said.

Mariela nodded. Since September, Emily D. thought, her face had changed, not so much from a physical spreading as from a spiritual one. It looked as if her soul had enlarged, bringing along with it the widened proportions of her cheeks, her deepened widow's peak, her amplified eyes. "That baby was the most . . . the most . . . angel part of me there ever was," Mariela said.

You still have a halo, Emily D. thought, but she couldn't bring herself to say it. It wavered over Mariela's head, vaporous and iridescent, and after Emily D. had finished brushing out her hair, there was a curious dust that coated her hands, glittering and gritty, like tiny bits of mica. It could have been that these were pieces of asphalt left over from where Mariela had lain in the road, but it also could have been that these were cast-offs from the saints, chinks fallen out of an old aura, soot drifting out of a sacred hem. Whatever the case, Emily D. would not wash her hands for days.

"I didn't even get to hold her," Mariela said. "Afterwards. They carried her out of the room right away, and I didn't even get to see what she looked like."

"I could ask someone who saw her," Emily D. said. "One of the nurses or someone who was there. And sometimes they take photos even."

"My mother said she had wings," Mariela said. "So maybe they thought she was a monster and I wouldn't want to know." She turned in her bed, lying down on her own nest of hair. Her face against the darkness gave off its own particular light, a solitary planet, revolving far away.

Emily D. left the room, and when she came back, she was accompanied by a nurse who held a Polaroid photograph in her hand. She passed the picture to Mariela gingerly, as if it were a glass of water she was trying not to spill. There, in celluloid and gloss, was a naked, blue-green bundle, a creature who had spent the whole of her life underwater, just below the surface of the waves, waiting for the elements to change. Her skin did not fit her, but gathered in folds over her arms and legs as if it had been a coat sewn for an infant several months older. Her eyes were wide open, the color of slate roofs and rain, and they looked like they had seen the whole world from a very great distance with all its minor oscillations on view, with all its proofs of human kindness and folly. Underneath her, there was something dark and fringed, which could have been a tasseled blanket or a feather duster that was out of place, or which could have been a pair of wings, folded up so as not to be so noticeable, all of the quills pressed together in a tight cascade. It was impossible to tell, really, because of the ambiguous camera angle and the light that flowed in a weak fog out of the wrong corner of the room. But Mariela seemed to know what she saw and to approve.

"Oh, someone meant for her to have a life," she said. "See how carefully she was made?"

———•·•———

EARLINE ETTINGER, at the age of seventy-seven, dropped out of her retirement home due to problems of the heart. Those were the four words she wrote on the sheet of paper that asked, *What are your reasons for leaving Lord Tennyson's? Dissatisfactions with staff or facilities? Personal conflicts with residents? Medical disability? Please explain.* Earline did not feel the need to clarify whether problems of the heart meant angina or Stewart Souther, however. She simply arranged for an attendant to pack up her chess set and her Herme scarves and to deposit her self and her worldly belongings on the front lawn of 240 Raborn Way in a place where the pepper trees poured great lakes of green shadows onto the grass.

When Clifford arrived at home that evening, he found his mother pruning long, thorny stalks off the rosebushes with a snub-nosed pair of manicure scissors. The clippings made a raw haystack in her lap which an occasional oversized cricket would crawl out of, inspiring Earline to swear.

"Mother," Clifford said. "What on earth are you doing?"

"I'm trying to make up for your neglect, that's what," Earline said. "If you don't like looking after the roses anymore, I don't know why you just can't get someone to pull them out and haul them away."

"Why don't you let me worry about it?" Clifford said. He noticed that his mother's hands wavered through the air with an erratic tremor, as if there were an isolated weather that surrounded them, Arctic and frost-bitten. Every time she grasped a rose's stem, the whole bush quaked in sympathy.

"You used to take such pride in keeping up your property," Earline said. "I don't know what's happened to make you change."

He captured one of her hands in his in the same way that he would have captured a moth, by concentrating on its mercurial flights, anticipating its digression. "Mother, why are you here?" he said.

"Do you dislike my being here?" she said.

"No," he said. "I just would like to know why you've come."

Earline tilted her head back and stared at the far-off pearls of sky that the trees seemed to clutch between their branches. "It's different when you get old," she said. "You don't have so many places to go anymore." She sighed a certain two-toned sigh that she always did when a bout of crying was rising in her throat. It sounded as if a little man were standing inside her lungs sighing with her. "I'd like to stay here for a little while," she said. "Would it bother you too much if I did that?"

"No, of course not," Clifford said. He brushed the cuttings off her lap and carried her inside.

Earline didn't tell him what it was all about until the following day, after Hanna had washed and dried her hair for her and put a new pair of fleece-lined slippers on her feet. Then it was possible to speak of Stewart Souther's desertion, of the way he had taken up with Opal Pairlee without so much as a backward glance, of the fact that everybody knew the money was behind it, since Opal's hand-dipped chocolates shop had been earning five thousand dollars a month from the time it had opened and Opal had never harbored an interest in conserving her cash. That woman pulled out hundred dollar bills to buy her senior citizen movie tickets! It was showy and conniving and Earline had made up her mind not to forgive either one of them.

"Did you at least get your car back?" Clifford said.

"What car?" she said.

"The yellow monstrosity," he said.

"Oh, that," she said. "I wouldn't want to stoop to a repossession." Earline fished through her cavernous handbag and retrieved a wand of lipstick which she began to apply. She held her lips apart in earnest vanity, as though she were going to be photographed immediately afterwards.

"You've really had your feelings hurt, haven't you?" Clifford said.

"What kind of a question is that?" Earline said, without moving her half-colored mouth.

"Well, I thought you told me at one point that you could never look at a man like Stewart seriously," he said.

"That was my head talking," she said. "That was the part of me that could stand separate from my life and be wise about it."

"Oh," Clifford said. "I see what you mean."

After breakfast, Clifford wheeled Earline out onto the porch where they set up the chess table and disagreed over who should be ivory and who should be black. It was the season for rain, and the sky always looked like it was hunching its gray shoulders, holding something back. In the winter weather, Clifford's knees turned arthritic, swollen and soggy and soft to the touch. When he walked, he favored his joints by being bow-legged, hitching himself forward by rocking side to side. People who knew him stared at the spectacle, but Clifford went right on with it. What else could he do? He had spent too much of his life in the company of others' physical suffering to feel sorry for himself. Heartbreak was worse. He could say that firsthand.

Earline moved her marble castle piece while Clifford wondered whether Anna would ever kiss him again and mean it. He felt a creeping sort of internal paralysis every time he considered what had made her so disappointed in him in the first place. What was it that he had said? Something about not making the mistake of living their children's lives for them. That was the moment when he had lost her. He had known it at the time, his feet sinking away underneath him while he clung with his arms to the plank of the window sill. A few simple words and she had retreated far enough to be out of his reach. What was it precisely that she had wanted him to say? He told himself that he had no idea whatsoever, and then immediately afterward he suspected that this was a lie.

At the very moment he was pondering this, Anna's car slipped past on Raborn Way and curled into the mouth of her driveway. Today was the day that Mariela was to come home from the hospital, and now he could see the form of her in the passenger seat, dark and diminished and glowing, waiting for her mother to bring the wheelchair alongside. She stared straight ahead, like the prophets and the terminally ill, some part of them already focused on the world to follow after.

"What happened to the neighbor girl?" Earline said. Her neck pleated itself into delicate folds when she turned her head to see.

"A hit and run," Clifford said. His Adam's apple felt as if a stone had lodged next to it, permanent and painful. "She lost her pregnancy because of it," he said. The words came out desiccated and hoarse, as if they had fallen into dust the same moment they had been thought of.

"Her pregnancy!" Earline said.

"Yes," Clifford said.

Across the lawn, Mariela caught sight of Earline and waved her small, sparkling hand. It was a wave of genteel recognition, as though people in wheelchairs shared some particular knowledge of the world, as if they were friends by virtue of their common predicament, and even if this were all they had to talk about, they would never run out of things to say. Anna was trying unsuccessfully to navigate the wheelchair up the porch steps. Mariela leaned forward in her seat as if she thought that at any moment she might rise up off the canvas and fly the intervening distance, but her expectation didn't come to pass.

"Clifford," Earline said. "Who was the father of that baby?" She was sitting extraordinarily straight in her chair, her arms pouring down over the rests in conscious repose, as if she were studying to become a queen.

"Well, who can tell about things like that?" Clifford said.

The expression on his face reminded Earline of his petulant moments as a child, sucking his cheeks into a pucker, as if all the air inside his head had suddenly been vacuumed out.

"You've answered me without meaning to," Earline said.

"No, I haven't, Mother," Clifford said. He stood up too abruptly, toppling the miniature marble towers that made up his chess pieces, the bishop with his pointed coronet, the castle with its remote battlements. "I'm going to help that girl get to the top of her steps," he said, stalking off across the lawn.

"Generous of you," Earline said. But she hated the way the words tasted as they passed through her mouth, bitter-edged like citrus rinds, overripe like an old disappointment.

———•◦•———

MARIELA SUBMERGED herself in a world with blurred borders, where the distances appeared clearer than the near views, where slow daydreams took on more shape and substance than the objects in a room. She slept in the day and fretted at night, and she only wore clothes she could disappear inside of, sweat suits and flannel nightgowns and sweaters that swallowed her down to her knees. Gradually, her belly lost the ripeness of its curves and retreated back into the cradle of her pelvis. Her skin lost its character of transparency and became instead a screen through which light and darkness passed. So it was only occasionally that her mother glimpsed the outline of her chambered heart, glowing four-tongued and flickering, like a rhythmic source of fire.

Earline Ettinger came to visit every few days, her white hair gleaming and stacked on her head, two half-moons of dusty eye shadow colored in below her brows. She and Mariela sat in their wheelchairs on a flattened, easy part of the lawn while Earline described how she had ever reached the age of seventy-seven while still believing in the overwhelming goodness of life. Mariela slipped in and out of a state of earnest listening as fluidly as if she were slipping in and out of a coma, and Earline spoke to her as emphatically as if she were attempting to revive her. It was a kind of ritual that they carried out—the litany of the saved being continuously offered to the one who needed saving. It was the gift of the *recomendacion,* as Anna liked to call it—the testimonial of one person's survival in this world, the witnessing of one individual's enduring hope. The *recomendacion* was what the Cordojo Women had been offering each other all those years, revealing the humble, heroic turns of their lives as parable, as cautionary tale, as affirmation.

"My first-born baby was so beautiful that I thought mysterious forces had been at play," Earline said once. "He had eyes that were a green like clear, green glass, and his hair was a brilliant blond that grew into curls at the ends—the way the Italian painters made curls on little children. His favorite toy was a blue bunny with a very square, lumpy body, and the first word he spoke to the world was *love*. I thought that God was sending me a message by giving me a child like that. I thought that every choice I had made in my life up to that time must have been the right one, because they had all led me to this single little boy. Then, when he was three years old, he died of meningitis. Overnight, it seemed to me. I was long gone and lost. I couldn't stand to hear people speaking to me, telling me it was going to be all right. I wanted to shout obscenities at them, but I never did."

"Which ones?" Mariela said. Her face was dark with recognition. Under the reach of the kumquat trees, her eyes caught reflections of the motions of the leaves, a trembling mosaic of which she was unconscious.

"Oh, things like *You know what you can do with your good intentions*," Earline said. "*Put your condolences where the sun doesn't shine.* Things like that. I never said them out loud, though."

Mariela smiled. Behind her head, her halo shifted, like a parasol that a woman moves from one shoulder to the other. "But those aren't obscenities," she said.

Earline shrugged. "They were at the time," she said. Wisps of her hair had loosened from her bun and now trailed over her eyes in a thin, shifting veil. "The trouble is that most people aren't willing to let you have your sadness. There's an idea in our midst that sadness can kill you if you're left alone with it—but that just isn't true. I can say that certifiably."

"It feels lethal enough," Mariela said.

"It isn't, though," Earline said.

Out on the curve of Raborn Way, a couple pushed a stroller with a bonneted baby inside it. Mariela looked away and then looked back. The mother kept running ahead to the front of the carriage to adjust the bonnet for a more protective fit. She had a peculiar kicking stride, as if she were trying to shake something from her shoes. But Mariela thought it was possible that this had something to do with her parenthood, with the ecstatic way it so clearly made her feel, all her extra energy pouring off the end of her limbs. When a car passed by, the wind from its wake made the couple's hair stand up, first the woman's and then the man's, rising straight up into the air, as if she had passed on to him some grand, startling, revolutionary thought.

"That could've been me, in another universe," Mariela said.

"It could still be you," Earline said, and then her hair rose up, too.

MARIELA BECAME a member of the Cordojo Women involuntarily, when her losses grew too substantial to bear in solitude. When everyone gathered on Sunday, she sat among them with chastened disappointment, part of her still wondering over the turn of events that had brought her there.

In the kitchen, Anna had transformed the dining table into a *retablo* of the baby's passing, an altar filled with rose garlands and the christening coat, a lock of hair and the Polaroid of the winged little girl herself, breathless and beautiful and blue. And over it all stood the statuette of the Holy Virgin, whose disciples ushered children to their waiting place in heaven without a moment's hesitation. Because no child was a stranger to the conferred grace of God, no matter what the worldly circumstances. Cristobal had told this to Anna many years ago, and she clung to the memory of his several words as if he were still standing there beside her, laying out for her the ways of generosity and belief.

She had once promised him that she would never again mourn, that she would never again devote her days to a single, repeated sadness, as she had done when her father died. But now there was no color to wear other than black, no cloth in which to bind herself other than those somber, restful folds that made her think of sleep and dark soil and endings. Her fledgling grandchild deserved at least that much acknowledgment, and she was unwilling to withhold it. When the vermicelli noodles had spelled out *sorrow* the previous summer, Anna had never imagined what a momentous forfeit they referred to, had never conceived of what a precious payment they would require.

Now, beside her, the Cordojo Women ate saint cakes with almond-cream frosting, the wedges balanced on the end of their fingertips as if they were concocted with nothing heavier than sweetness and air. Close to the ceiling, the finches and warblers watched hungrily, their wings stuttering against their cage doors.

"I don't know what else to say, dear, except that I'm terribly, terribly sorry," India Perry said to Mariela. She looked sorry; the brim of her straw hat hung down in two starchless ears at the sides of her head, and the fruit that dangled off of it had been spotted by the rain.

"Thank you," Mariela said. She stared at the untouched saint cake in her hands, as if she couldn't remember what she was meant to do with it.

"Of course, we're *all* sorry," Dove said, "which barely needs mentioning *again*, India."

"If I think about it for too long, it'll make me furious all over," Maxine said. She shifted once in her seat, spreading out her skirt from side to side as if flaring the colors of her maternal wrath.

"What will make you furious?" Anna said.

"The way that boy took advantage, that's what," Maxine said. "The way he left town when the time came to face up to it. None of this would have happened without his taking advantage at the start." Above the corded gauntlet of her neck, Maxine's jaw was set. She looked like a woman warrior, feminine and undefeatable, her skin bristling with the conviction of war.

"But he never knew," Mariela said. Her words entered the room like a wish, plaintive, barely audible.

"What's that, Marielita?" Anna said.

"Addison never knew," she said. "He wouldn't have run away from me if he had only known." The saint cake still lay in Mariela's hands, perfectly whole and undisturbed. India Perry had the feeling that if even a single crumb broke away, Mariela would begin to break into pieces herself. Her dignity, her self-hood, the faith that held her upright in her chair—these would be the fragments that fell away first. "And he wouldn't have left at all except for his father," she went on. "It was his father who wanted him to go."

"Well," Maxine said, "I know I shouldn't speak out as much as I do." The line of her mouth was sympathetic, but unswayed. Never again would she willingly believe in the inno-cence of men. She had done that in the first half of her life, and she had paid what she thought was an unreasonable price for it.

A stark quiet had fallen over the room. The Cordojo Women were coming to their silent conclusions, washing them down with throatfuls of tea. From the copper cage di-rectly above, a hoarse-voiced finch sang a song of strangled exclamation. So she still loves him! everyone was thinking in one way or another. She still loves him, after everything! The reality of it dangled there in front of them, bulky and awkward and unmistakable. They would have reacted in the same way if Mariela had suddenly stood up and removed all her clothes, revealing to them the scars that existed along-side her beauty. What was a woman to make of such contrasts —of pain in the wake of sensuality, of love in the trail of abandonment?

"Listen to the bird sing," Mariela said suddenly. "He sounds so surprised."

MARIELA WOULD not have bothered with the birds at all were it not for the way their wings sounded at night, like the movements of many angels all soaring under the same roof. She thought she heard a muffled tumult of activity, as if her house had become a freeway interchange for the travelers of the next life; and the noises made her think constantly of her little girl, her new, folded wings untried and damp, searching out the way to a far-off heaven. She had the idea that the soul of her child might be trapped somewhere below the sky, tangled perhaps in the cross-hatch of a tree or snagged by the high-tension wires that strung the distances together as surely as a web. Would any strange angel stop to help her, or would she remain there, a bright spot lodged in the nets of the earth?

So when Mariela woke up one night to listen to the flop and bother of the finches and mourning doves, the warblers and the speckled sparrows, she determined with impenetrable conviction that they ought to be let go. Afterwards, she only remembered a few details about how it had gone. She remembered the way the birds dropped from the doors of their cages, as if they were falling, before climbing determinedly toward the blackened sky. She remembered the cool press of one dove's feet as it hesitated in her palm, its delicate forked claws feeling like the stamp of some hieroglyphic, mysterious and more ancient than all things she had known. She could not recall, however, how her legs had suddenly carried her around the house, for this is surely what they must have done, or how she had navigated her way down the staircase by herself. She had simply moved from one room to the next as a result of her intention, the way she moved in dreams, her legs floating underneath her effortlessly. Perhaps she had flown the distance or perhaps she had walked. When Anna asked her about it later, she could not say.

What she did know was that the birds' being wild again was a good and destined thing. When she closed her eyes, she could still see them pouring out of the windows of the house, fervent and sweeping, their lives clearly urgent to them. And when they had risen out of sight, she imagined them flying at the four corners of her daughter's soul and lifting it up, up beyond the lid of the world.

———•◦•———

THE BIRDCAGES lay upended and scattered across the living room floor, reminding Anna with their copper domes and un-latched doors of a fallen citadel, gilded and empty. The doll which had once represented Anna from the center of a cake was now tearless and scuffed, her dress hanging over her head in abandon. So Mariela now had the strength to wreak her own havoc, Anna thought. She had undergone a vast improvement. She had stepped out of her girlhood and grown a second skin.

Anna dropped to her knees in front of the *retablo* for her granddaughter and prayed as she seldom did, aloud, so that the mother Mary, whatever else she was attending to, could not help but hear. "Help me to see that love has its own reasons for continuing to live in the heart of my child," she said. "You can see, as I cannot, why Addison has made her existence a bereave-ment. I welcomed him into my house every day for three months, and I never saw the signs of his betrayal. But I ask you now to search his worthiness, wherever he lives and breathes and sleeps. Search the capacity of his caring for her; search its shape and mettle and weight. And if he is not lacking, send your saints to bring him back to us. Send him a vision he cannot overlook, with messengers from heaven crowding out his rooms. Not because it is my will, but because it is hers, still hers, after all this lonely time. She has loved him with a constancy that is less of my world than of yours. Grant her your grace in return, so that she may understand her losses even as she has accepted them. All this I ask in your name. Amen."

The doorbell had rung twice, but Anna had ignored it. Now, rising off her knees, she could see Clifford Ettinger staring at her through the glass in the front door. He seemed to be taking in the whole of her discombobulation—her surprise at seeing him, her stockingless feet, the birdcages she stepped over while making her way across the room. Anna felt for her hair as if to make sure it was still on her head.

"I'm sorry for the wait," she said, pulling the door open.

"No, I didn't mean to interrupt you," he said. Anna could not put her finger on it, but something about him did not look right. His hair was overlong and his eyes were shot with red and when she studied him closely she saw that the socks he wore were a mismatched pair, one of them pale gray and one of them dark.

"I can't ask you in," Anna said. "I have cleaning to do."

"Oh. All right," he said. "I just wanted to see how you were getting along."

"I'm getting along. That's about all I can say."

Beyond the lawn, Raborn Way was submerged in one of its early-morning fogs, the white, primeval air lapping at the rises in the land. With every exhalation, Clifford released a long plume, a dragon's breath, that seemed to have had as its source the same wistful place as the weather.

"I had a telephone call yesterday," he said. "From the mother of the boy who was driving the car."

"Bernard?" she said.

"Yes. She wanted to know whether I would put up his bail," he said. "She's tried for two months to bring the money together and she can't."

Anna's form looked to Clifford like it had been thoroughly frozen in place, like she had just taken a swim in liquid nitrogen and here she stood, inanimate and brittle and barely breathing. He looked down at her bare feet and saw that they, too, looked more like a replica of feet than feet themselves. Her skin tone was the color of some porcelain dishes he had seen, reflecting the light with a man-made brilliance.

"Of course I told her I wouldn't be inclined to help," he said.

"I see," she said, now living again, her chest releasing the breath it had held.

"I'm amazed that she called at all after what we've been

through," he said. "The tragedy of it. Somebody's got to take responsibility and Bernard's obviously the one. I've found it nearly impossible to convince the police that what happened had nothing to do with Addison."

In the space above Anna's shoulder, Clifford thought he saw Mariela come halfway down the stairs and then retreat again. So she has remembered the will to walk, he thought. On hearing the tenor of his voice, she had instinctively turned away, her eyes lowered, her humility shining. She was such a specter, it seemed, drifting around the periphery of their lives, confusing them beyond repair. How then had she managed to inspire his grudging approval, he wondered.

"Well, it's not as though it had *nothing* to do with Addison," Anna said.

"No, but you know what I mean," he said.

Clifford took two steps backward on the porch, his midsection disappearing behind a finger of fog as he did so. He batted at it mildly, trying to reassert his existence, but the fog hung unperturbed, curling itself around his ribs as thickly as before.

"Did the police speak with him?" Anna said.

"With Addison?" he said. "Oh, no. Nothing like that."

"So he didn't want to give a statement," she said.

"Oh, they didn't get to the point of contacting him about it," Clifford said. "I think I convinced them that that wasn't necessary." The fog was encroaching on him even as he spoke, cascading down the wall of his legs, bubbling around the tips of his shoes. He stamped and snorted and continued to disappear.

"Good," Anna said. "It sounds like everything has worked out the way you wanted it, then."

"Not everything," Clifford said.

"Well, I'm glad that most of it has," she said.

If there was anything that made Clifford dead with frustration, it was the way he allowed himself to forget what he had come for. He dimly remembered having set out for Anna's house with reconciliation in mind. A sphere of thought had floated above his head, one in which he and Anna were wrapped together in a naked, trembling kiss. He could have walked forward and kissed Anna at that moment, but she would have turned to porcelain again, all of her heat suddenly drained away. She would not come to life for him just because he wanted it.

"Anna . . ." he began.

"Thank you for stopping by," she said. She turned now, the screen in her hands.

"I didn't have a chance to say . . ." But he stopped speaking when the door closed against him. The glass in the fan light buzzed slightly, as though a charged current had run through it and then faded away. "Oh, well, good-bye then," he finished, talking with a startled, dignified air to no one.

He stood still for a minute, allowing the mist to shroud his shoulders and his head, as it had been promising to do all along. Inside the body of the fog, Clifford felt despair take hold. It seemed as if he had been exiled into a loneliness toward which he himself had conspired. It was unthinkable that he could have contributed to this state and yet at the same time it was ineradicably true. The weather reached inside his clothing and grasped him there, dispassionately. He stared into the opaque, hoary breath of God and wondered whether he would be able to find his way home.

WITHOUT REALIZING it, Esther Lee had held the secret in her possession for whole, unbroken, anguished months. It lay in her filing cabinet at work, tucked away under section S, for son or stories, she couldn't remember which. When she came across it accidentally in her search for the Hanna Stuttgart file, it was like finding a treasure on someone else's beach. She had the desire to be recklessly loud and cannily silent at the same time. If she had kept a gun in her drawer, she would have fired a signal shot straight through the ceiling. And yet, she wondered if there might be any way to close the office for a few hours, to rope it off with the thick gold-braided barriers she had seen in

LANE VON HERZEN

museums, until the point that her discovery was complete. There, in the upper left-hand corner of each of the envelopes containing his stories, Addison Ettinger had inscribed his address: Southwest Writers' Colony, 2011 Adobe Plains Way #17, El Fuerte, New Mexico.

Dr. Ettinger opened the door of his examining room just then and beckoned Esther Lee to join him. Inside, Hanna Stuttgart, the doctor's own housekeeper, cheerfully explained the details of her chronic back pain. She kept lifting her sweater to expose a midriff that was startlingly robust and white, identical to those of women who, generations before, must have driven an iron plow and borne nine children. Esther Lee handed her file to the doctor, but when she attempted to leave, he called her back. He seemed not to want to be left alone with the patient, and it was only gradually that Esther Lee recognized his attitude as being one of embarrassment. Hanna Stuttgart suggested several times that Dr. Ettinger could not accurately diagnose her pain as long as she kept her clothes on.

"Wouldn't it be easzier if you could juszt szee the problem for yourszelf?" Hanna said to him.

But the doctor held up his hands as if fending her off. "No, no," he said. "We're getting ahead of ourselves here. You know I'm not a specialist when it comes to back strain, Hanna."

"I'm not looking for a szpecialiszt," she said.

"Well, I'm referring you to one anyway," he said.

Hanna Stuttgart slid off the patient table with a dejected, heavy-set grace. She shrugged her way into her cardigan, used to having no one to help her. "We're having szweet-baszted ham for dinner," she said.

"You've always worked too hard," he said. "That could be the problem right there." He handed her a piece of paper with the name of an orthopedist scrawled over it, and Hanna held on to it until she reached the parking lot, where she let it fall into a pile of leaves that the gardener was heaping into drawstring sacks. Esther Lee watched her from the window while she dialed Maxine's number. Loneliness was the greatest epidemic

212

on the face of the earth, Esther Lee thought. Nobody liked to say so, but that was the natural fact.

"Hello," someone said.

"Maxine? Is that you, dear?" Esther Lee said. "How far is New Mexico?"

———•◦•———

TRAVELING WAS never any good unless you traveled in the name of love. This was the belief to which the four of them subscribed, India and Esther Lee and Maxine and Dove, and nothing had assuaged it in all their years of life. They could have stopped in Deming, which would have been halfway, but when they reached it, no one was tired, as India had been passing around thermos capfuls of marshy coffee from the beginning. From the backseat, Dove fished handfuls of chocolate-covered toffees from her purse and dealt them out in a clockwise fashion until they were gone.

"Why do you have so *many*?" Maxine said. The toffee clacked against her teeth when she spoke—tockle-tock-tack—like a lazy castanet.

"I asked my mother to make me a special order before she closed doors," Dove said. "The chocolates aren't making money for her anymore."

"But I thought the business was booming!" India said. "I used to see the customers lined up along the sidewalk."

"Not since Mariela left," Dove said. "Chocolates are chocolates. It was Mariela who made them something more." The cellophane wrappers sifted to the floor of the car and rested there, in decorative debris. Whenever one of the Cordojo Women shifted her feet, they scattered and resettled, like clear-bodied grasshoppers.

"Yes, well, Mariela makes ordinary things exceptional," Maxine said. "That has always been her gift."

They had stopped talking by the time darkness poured out of the horizon, suddenly flooding the parcel they crossed. The joshua trees and the two-armed cactus collected together in evocative groups, gesturing to one another with emphatic, motionless, lonely beauty, as if they would never see each other again. When Esther Lee looked at the sky in a certain way, it was almost as if she could see the constellations revolving above her in a magnificent, domed passing of the minutes, as if she could see the way her life had been measured out from the moment of its beginning, in the order of time that had pre-existed her and that would outlast her, that lent all human kindnesses their fierce and lasting worth.

In El Fuerte, at two in the morning, the desert took on the white-bodied luster of snow, sleek and momentous, a complete thing unto itself. Rock ridges pushed upward at velveted angles, brutal and harmonious at the same time. When India idled the car to ask someone for directions, she opened the window by only a shy sliver, as if she worried that all the air inside the passenger compartment would rush out onto the lunar landscape, obeying the laws of physics or entropy or some such unknown. At the writers' colony, apartment number seventeen was unlit and unlocked, and the Cordojo Women tripped in over the front step, embracing the walls like the newly blind.

"Feel for the light switches!" Dove whispered.

But the switches had been concealed in some clever way the women could not think of, because they were at a loss to find them. Gradually, the darkness dissolved into uninterpretable shapes—a clear lake on the wall which turned out to be a mirror, a poor cat hanging from a hook which turned out to be a bunchy jacket, a gun on the kitchen counter which turned out to be a single, black-skinned banana. Maxine found Addison asleep on a bed in the next room. His blanket was lumped into volcanoes over his knees and feet, and he slept with his mouth slightly open in an expression of leaking surprise.

"Sit up, now," Maxine said, shaking him. "I've come a long way to say this to you, and you're certainly going to be paying attention when I do."

Addison's mouth opened a small fraction wider. His arms,

where Maxine had touched them, were leaden and hot, as if someone had poured them into place.

"Won't he wake up?" Dove said.

"See for yourself," Maxine said. "I don't think he's faking."

"My son, Ethan, used to sleep through everything," India said. "The Apollo moon walk, the earthquake in Marbury Park, the fire drills at college." She leaned over Addison's face with exaggerated caution, as if expecting to find the features of her son there, familiarly unconscious. "We used to soak his feet in ice-cold baths," she said.

"Did it work?" Maxine said.

"No," India said. "But that's what we used to do." She sat down hard on a free space on the mattress. Addison's body sank and rebounded, but its preternatural stillness never left him. His eyelids rose a quarter of the way and then closed again, sealed, impermeable, apparently indifferent. Underneath them, though, he was dreaming a dream of apparitions and urgency. There were four transparent women encircling his bed, and they were discussing his fate among themselves. Their hair flowed out of their heads like colorless grass, rippling and faintly alive; and their breaths, when they leaned down over him, were confectionary and complex, and this was blissful and familiar to him.

They were angry with him, and apparently, they had reason to be. But he could not feel fear, knowing that whatever they did would be considered and right. It was like being visited by angels almost. They looked down on you while you were sleeping, and they knew every shameful, glorious thing about you without even having to ask.

"What are we going to do with him, then?" one of them asked.

"What *can* we do?"

"I'm not leaving before we've given him something to think about."

"Did we bring anything to write with?"

"To bite with?"

"To *write* with."

The sound of their voices came in a hypnotic, wavering cascade, as if the words were liquid and formless, carrying only their intent. When all of the specters moved about, the folds of their skirts glissaded together like women at a dance, all the taffeta talking. They left through the bedroom door, one after the other, their fingertips trailing along the walls like vines, like roots pointing at the places he had been.

When he woke in the morning, he remembered some of it. He remembered the toffee sweetness of their breaths, which still suffused his rooms, and the way they had peered down at him, piercingly, their magic hair floating wild at the borders. And he remembered a few pieces of what they had said: *I've come a long way* and *What can we do?* Apparitions, he thought. Mystical beings.

Except that, on the mirror in the living room, someone had scrawled four lines with a periwinkle eye pencil, most of them indecipherable, the letters careening into each other at ingrown angles. He managed to decode only the last seven words, which stood apart from the rest in a bellowing, flamboyant script . . .

. . . *asking you to come back to her!!!*

When he read this, he felt some piece of him tighten and swell and brace against his sternum. As if a live hope were writhing in the cavern between his lungs, filling up all his empty spaces, crowding out all his lacks.

———————

EMILY D. took Mariela away to college with her. Just for a sojourn, just for an overnight, just for the chance to be reminded that she was young. They had trouble fitting the wheelchair into the backseat of the car, and at the last minute, Mariela decided to leave it behind, half-collapsed and tottering, at a place in the driveway where the mica shone like loose jewels, extravagant and unreal. Anna noticed that by the time Mariela made up her mind that she could again walk, the fact was already accomplished. Like the resolutely faithful, she had reduced her healing to a simple question of belief.

All day long, as Anna went about her work, she imagined that she watched her daughter's movements through the space of a secluded window. She watched Mariela attend a history seminar and eat a gyro in the botanical gardens and float up and down the stairs of the library so many times that she became peaked and dizzy and had to stop for rest. At the end of the day, Mariela's hair fell out of its ponytail and coursed down over her shoulders in tender rivulets of black, and five students gathered at the door to Emily D.'s dorm room, thunderstruck and serious, offering advice about the world before they were asked. Later on, Emily D. made up a bed on the floor and slept in it herself so that Mariela would have the mattress. And Mariela dreamed dreams about a future, tentative and lambent, with which she was just now preparing to fall in love.

Anna watched all of this with the sight she had been born with, the sight that spanned across miles and weather as though these things existed in miniature when held up next to the expanses of her heart. However far away Mariela went, she still lived and breathed within the reach of her mother's thought; she still dreamed and wept within her mother's hearing. It seemed to Anna that this was the natural state of the child, always floating at one end of the tireless maternal tether, always suspended unaware in the clear, singing sea of a mother's worry.

At one o'clock in the morning, when Anna was looking at the wind pour in and out of her open windows in a transparent tide, the doorbell rang. She tied the sash of her green, velveteen robe and drank a glass of water at her bedside table before she went down. There, on her porch step, his long, tapered hands turning like gulls under the floodlights, Addison Ettinger waited.

"I need to talk to her," he said. He looked disheveled and

appealing and mildly desperate, and he was breathing very hard, as if he had sprinted some inconceivable distance in order to get there.

"She's away tonight," Anna said.

"Away?" He spoke the word uncomprehendingly, waiting for its implications to rise. His hands ran off into his pockets, self-conscious and shaking.

"But you come in and talk to me anyway," Anna said. "I'll tell you everything there is to know."

She led him into the heart of her house, where shadows from the votive candles stroked the faint walls. He paused in front of the statuary, fixed on the silent murmurings there, on the sense that in the very next moment, the figures would begin to breathe and sigh.

"Have the saints appeared to you?" Anna said. "Is that why you're here?"

He stared straight ahead in surprise, the pupils of his eyes falling open into great, guileless caves. "Yes," he said. "I suppose it is."

PART SEVEN

Breeze and Bone

ADDISON'S SUITCASES lay in the marble hallway looking like the coats of two hunchbacked men, wrinkled and lumpy and disproportioned along some fundamental seam. Hanna unzipped them searching for secrets, but all she found were loose manuscript pages and balled-up sweaters, and the pure, slightly singed scent of the desert rising from a hidden source. In the dining room, the daylight spilled over pecans and spiced waffles and a central, dripping mountain of sliced fruit, while Clifford asked in a dozen ways why his son had so suddenly come home.

"It was time," Addison said. He ate as though he were cross with his food, as though with each bite he were delivering a measured punishment.

"Do you mean by that that you have run out of work to do?" Clifford said.

"No," Addison said. He studied a piece of waffle that cried syrup from the edges and then swallowed it with a voracious rage. He breathed through his nose with noisy, animal-like huffs. Earline could see that it was an unintentional release, like a safety gauge for steam under pressure.

"Clifford, you act like you wish he'd stayed away," she said. "All those months spent in isolation and you'd just as soon he went back to it."

"That's not what I said." Clifford could not understand why after all these years, he was still sitting across the breakfast table from his mother, defending his motives. A man ought to be able to have his private intents without being questioned about them all the time.

"Dad would have preferred that I stay gone until Mariela had either killed herself or moved away," Addison said. "Wouldn't you say that's about right, Dad?" There was a peculiar stillness about him where he was poised in his chair. He had the look of someone who was being given a slow-exposure X-ray, for whom any movement, however slight, would mean a diminishment of clarity.

"What did you say to me?" Clifford said.

"Just so long as I didn't find out about the baby, which was the whole point, I'm sure," Addison said. His father's face was difficult to look at, mottled and flushing and blustery with offense, and at any other time, Addison would have felt responsible for it.

"You sit there thinking that you know what you're talking about. But let me tell you that disadvantaged girls play that game every day of the week," Clifford said.

"Disadvantaged girls," Addison said. "That's such an interesting way to put it. What does it mean? Someone whose parents are too poor to set up a trust fund or too ethnic to have an acceptable last name?"

"That girl could have told you anything and you would have believed her," Clifford said. He threw his hands into the air as if he were tossing them away, as if he never planned to use them again all the rest of his life.

"Why shouldn't I have believed her?" he said.

"Addison, I'm talking about paternity, and that's a very shady thing," Clifford said.

"Those are strange words to offer to your adopted son," Earline said. "Real fatherhood isn't shady at all." Clifford turned to look at her. Her eyes were veined and swimming, and she had that glazed-over, euphoric expression of someone who has been running a fever for weeks. She held on to her convictions as if they were the last great thing that mattered.

"I was that child's father," Addison said. "There wasn't anybody else."

"You don't know that," Clifford said.

"Yes, I do."

"No . . ." But Clifford hadn't finished his thought before Addison had lunged at him, his hands landing on his father's collar with the weight of stones, a plate of sausages sliding from the table to bound away across the carpet. The chair keeled over backwards, breaking its spine on impact, and it was some time before Clifford and Addison could wrestle themselves free from it. The wicker backing had torn partially out of its frame, and the mesh there was large enough to entangle their fingers, which were splayed wide and grasping and easy to snare. They tumbled over each other like adolescents, hot-faced and awkward, their shirts pulling loose from their waists. In the end, Addison sat on his father's chest, which heaved from the indignity and strain like that of a stiff, old, barrel-ribbed governor. Parts of his eyebrows stood straight up in gnarled, graying twists, like tufts of strange fur.

"You did everything you could to ruin this for me," Addison said. "God knows why you did, but you did. And now you're going to call a stop to it. Okay, Dad? All of it, all at once. Okay? There's no other way to go." When he spoke, his voice was shattered and hulking, and it came out in pieces the size of bricks. He rolled off of Clifford and stalked away, his shoulders slung forward like an unformed boy's.

In his peripheral vision, Clifford could see his mother and Hanna, staring at him from the far edge of the room. What had ever happened to women as enforcers of the peace, he wondered. In the last five minutes, he hadn't heard either one of them utter a single word, not "stop," not "don't," not "I've had just about enough." They had merely waited at the sidelines, their manners tucked up neatly underneath them, looking toward the outcome with an interest that was maddening. When he got to his feet, a moment from now, they would tell him that this was what happened when you stood in the way of a young man's wish.

———•◦•———

FROM INDIA Perry's roof, it was possible to see everything, if only you leaned out over the rails and looked. It was possible to see the wind that riffled through other people's gardens and the windows that sulked and blinked in the daylight and the animals that trotted across the mown grass leaving tracks behind them like shallow wakes. On Saturday morning, though, Mariela and Emily D. were oblivious to the small movements of the world. Mariela's application to college lay spread out page by page over the knotted floorboards of the deck, weighted down by clay pots of impatiens, brilliant and frothy and in bloom. A bowl of wooden ladybugs sat next to a crooked tower of black straw hats, waiting to adorn them. Below, the fig trees tapped against the side of the house, indolent and newly green, as if pointing at something they wanted to possess.

"But what do they mean by 'an overview of accomplishments'?" Mariela said. "Accomplished grades? Accomplished wisdom? Accomplished growing up?"

"All of that maybe," Emily D. said. "You have to stop worrying what they'll think of you and just write as compellingly as you can."

Mariela knelt over the exposed pages, scrutinizing them for clues. She wore a new dress in a blue that was the color of tropical water, primal and jewel-like; and when she sat down, its hem was long enough to enfold her small feet, the toenails of which were polished the pink of floating shells.

This was the first thing Addison saw about her when he emerged onto the roof at mid-morning—the way her feet lay nestled in between the folds of blue cloth, still and self-contained in the shapes he had not allowed himself to forget. Anna and India stood to either side of him, waiting for something inexplicable to happen, like the flowerpots upending themselves or all the breathable air draining out of the neighborhood.

India announced herself. "We've all come up," she said, and then Mariela turned her head.

What surprised Mariela most was that she had stopped waiting for this to happen, stopped imagining the thousand and one ways Addison could possibly have stepped back into her life, stopped thinking that a reunion with him was a prerequisite to all other hope. Sometime in the recent past, these things had fallen away from Mariela without her realizing, like clothes fall away when they are two sizes too big; so that when she looked at him, it was with a kind of helpless nostalgia that originated at the fringe of her iris-shaped heart; it was with the folded recollection of love.

"Hello," she said.

"Mariela," he said. His hands would have liked to fly away from him to perch on the edge of the white-posted railing, but he carefully held them back. He tried to understand what he ought to say first.

"Addison stopped by the house to see you," Anna said. "So I brought him over." A sweater of Addison's was folded over one of her arms, as if he were still a boy whose sweaters needed holding.

Mariela nodded, and when she did so, her widow's peak appeared, gleaming and delicate, like a curl of dark frosting. Addison began to feel that the deck underneath his feet was sloped toward where she sat. He had to lean back on his heels to keep from falling through the air that separated them.

"What are you working on?" he said.

"Essays," Emily D. said.

"I'm going to college," Mariela said. "Next January."

The deck now tilted at the angle of a ski run. One more degree, and Addison would have been hurled off it. "Good! Good!" he said. Somewhere, in a corner of his mind, he understood that he was shouting.

Across the street, children were drifting out of a house after a birthday party. Lemon-yellow balloons bobbed above their heads, and their shoes shone like gumdrops, polished and black above the clear lawn. Emily D. and India and Anna collected at one corner of the roof, looking after them. They commented on the cowlicks and the leftover smudges of ice cream, and they kept their backs carefully turned toward Addison and Mariela, as if by doing so they erected a discreet wall around the two of them, an invisible, wind-filled room.

Addison staggered across the length of the deck, fighting against the incline of the uneven world. Gravity had slipped away from him, and he could not repossess it. The sunlight struck things with a perceptible impact, as if each particle of it had been launched. There, in front of him, Mariela was the only sight that soothed the ache behind his eyes.

"How are you?" he said. He strained to separate the words in a way that would make him understood.

"I'm better than I was," Mariela said. Her hair was blacker than he'd recalled it, iridescent black, like the feathers of ravens. It made him think of crying, somehow, of burying his face inside it and crying out loud.

"Well, I'm sorry for everything," he said. "Everything I did to you that I shouldn't have, and . . . and all of it put together." At the railing, the women were no longer talking. Their heads were slightly bowed, out of embarrassment or a desire to be physically smaller, he thought. When he spoke the next time, he was whispering, his voice comprised of one long wavering breath. "I can't stand to think about how it must have been," he said. "Your mother told me about the baby."

Mariela didn't answer him, and he wondered whether she had heard. The white tips of her application pages quavered in the wind. He thought he saw her float up off the deck for a moment, but then she reached out and took hold of a flowerpot, descending directly back to the same spot she had occupied. She wouldn't look him in the eyes after that. She avoided it, conspicuously, letting her hair fall forward in two impenetrable veils.

"You might go up to the cemetery when you feel like it," Anna said, turning suddenly toward them. "We had the burial at St. Lawrence's and there's a stone there. Mariela might take you."

"I'd like that," Addison said.

"Monday might work," Anna said. "Mariela, would Monday work out for you?"

Mariela embraced her clay pot of impatiens, her knuckles drained white with the effort. The blossoms bristled upward in a bank of animate fuchsia, and above them Mariela nodded her head, barely, but deliberately, as if she had only just made up her mind.

"I'll come over, then," Addison said. When he left the roof, the air became hot and unbreathable. His ears popped as if he were changing altitude, and he steadied himself by rushing up against the walls when there was a wall available. Outside again, the sunlight seared across the open spaces, confusing him. He tried to put a name on what he was feeling. Vertigo, vertigo, he thought. But then Anna called out to him from the railing and tossed his sweater down, and he saw the four women lined up on the roof smiling at him, and he thought, love, love.

THE HILLS were covered with markers, marble and granite, like the teeth of giants, discarded in old age. There were gardeners carrying sacks of white pebbles in their knotted hands, and whole flocks of people wearing bolts of black cloth who pressed against one another, wavering. Mariela walked ahead of him, the funnel of roses he had brought her held up like a torch against the unthinkable. She had stopped smelling of orange groves and grapes, and the scent that rose off her hair now was merely young, like bay leaves and cut hay. It was redolent of

possibilities, devoid of languor, and Addison strained to interpret all its parts.

Addison knew which was the particular headstone when
they were still twenty yards away. It was too small and gleaming
to belong to anyone other than an infant. There in the row of
a dozen mansion-scaled memorials, it was a little girl's doll
house, rose-pink and polished. Two sprays of open-mouthed
irises poured out of sunken vases at either side. The epitaph
read *Angela de la Senda. Born January 8, 1993. Died January 8,
1993. Missed in Heaven before she left.*

"I couldn't come to the burial," Mariela said. "The hospital wouldn't let me out for it." She had sat down on the grass,
her skirt spread out around her in a rumpled lake. She began
unfurling the florist's tissue from the roses, coaxing it free
gingerly, as if someone might use the untorn pieces again.
"Mother took care of everything," she went on. "She has a
talent for that."

Addison sat down too, then, careful not to settle too close
to her. Mariela's being there at all with him was a tentative,
breakable thing. She could have been a wild deer that had wandered into a garden while he was waiting in it. One inexplicable
gesture on his part, and she would have fled for her life.

"What color was her hair?" he said, needing somehow to
know.

"Black," she said.

"Like yours," he said.

He thought he saw the light surrounding her shift to a
different hue. Behind her face and shoulders, there was a burnished, reflective aureole of air, as if the atmosphere were
blushing on her behalf. "She had your long fingers, though,"
she said. "Her hands were two miracles. That's what all the
nurses said."

An old man trundled by them carrying a photograph and
some Scotch tape with him. He favored his knees, keeping them
bent through his stride as if he were in a permanent state of
sneaking up on someone. Addison wished more than anything
that he could be alone with her there, on the shoulder of the

hill, secluded from strangers and their strange griefs. He cried because he couldn't help it, understanding now for the first time what had lived and died in his absence. The trees and gravestones all melted and lay in molten pools on the grass. The words on his daughter's marker were illegible—unknown messages in a foreign language. He groped for Mariela's hand and found it resting beside him.

"Can I?" he said, taking hold of it. "You know, would it be all right?"

"Addison . . . I . . . I'm a different person now," she said.

"Okay," he said. "That's perfectly okay."

He couldn't make out the expression on her face clearly enough. It traveled in between pity and some feeling that was more urgent, depending on the way he strained his eyes. Her hand was curled inside his in the shape of hesitation, all the fingers pressed together to make a seamless, gathered wing.

"I can't just give my life over to somebody else anymore," she said.

"That's right. You can't," he said.

"I'm going to go to college," she said.

"Yes."

She didn't take her hand away, though, her furled, magical, sightless hand. She left it in his keeping where it gathered weight and the pressure of heat, like something about to unfold in its place, like something about to come undone.

No ONE talked to Clifford anymore, and so he was forced to start talking to the dead. Addison and Anna and his mother and Hanna and Esther Lee and even some of his patients regarded him warily, through half-open doorways and windows that glittered like dark lenses, their faces lit in cameos of remoteness and concern, their lips moving only in conversation with someone else, hidden away in the unrevealed spaces behind them. The loneliness settled around him like a sinking air pressure, volatile and dense and circumscribed by reproach.

The scent of his banishment was miasmic and musty and hot—like the air left over by hounds penned inside a cellar. He kept waiting for someone to open a window with a breeze on the other side of it.

He asked certain questions of Marjorie, because, living in heaven, she was in a position to know. Had he been as wrong as all that, really? Couldn't his actions exist under the headings of protection, wise intervention, parental guidance? The words spilled out of him unpredictably and aloud, and when he spoke he always threw his head back to stare at the sky, which was omniscient enough to answer him, if only it would. Marjorie was up there somewhere, doing whatever people did in the afterlife. There were moments when he felt like she was trying to get a message to him. Once, on the northern edge of the village park, a child had walked by him with a talking doll that said, "Why did you pull my string? Did you want to see what would happen?" in a voice that was both cheerful and accusing. And a few days later, he had broken open a lone fortune cookie in his cupboard that read, "He who feels abandoned has himself walked away from the world."

He could try to justify what he had done for a thousand and one Sundays, and still no one would be satisfied, not even himself. For all his life he had believed in the careful ordering of the moral world, in the ordained difference between a good intention and a bad one. Never had he allowed for the possibility of an indefinite error, a silent misjudgment, a selfishness concealed under the hood of charity. His life no longer fit into the immaculate compartments of a defensible past. His history was now circumspect and complex, all of it reeling with motive, surging with concealment.

Someone might accuse him of dooming his own grandchild and not be far wrong. That thought came back to him, especially at night.

He rolled over in his cavernous bed, and tried to imagine feeling unafraid for his own soul. The night noises of the house ascended and descended the stairway that led to his door, like thieves of things invisible, carting away notions about his life that only he would miss. He crept to the door of Addison's room and looked inside it, and sometimes his son lay there, smooth-faced and forgiving in his sleep, and sometimes he didn't. Once, Clifford found him walking at the borders of the lawn wearing only his underwear, his hands brushing the leaves of the gargantuan roses in one, long, languorous reach.

"You've let the garden go wild," Addison said. "After all those years of having everything in its place." He paused there, half-naked and elemental, surprising his father again with being, quite impossibly, full grown.

"Your mother was the one who kept everything tended," Clifford said. "In the garden and elsewhere."

"You were keeping up with it," Addison said. "I saw you out here with your pruning shears, your insecticide."

"I tried for a while, but I did it for all the wrong reasons," Clifford said. "You can't turn living things into a monument. They resist."

Below the light of the remote, still-eyed planets, everything in sight looked vaguely haunted and underwater and blue— Addison's face and his agitated, beautiful hands, and the tips of Clifford's own toes where they warmed a small wedge of grainy earth. It was as though the two of them had turned color from holding their breaths for too long a time, waiting for the right thing to be said.

"It's hard to admit when you get to my age that you don't know the things you once thought you did," Clifford said. "I used to think I knew almost everything and now . . . look at me."

"Dad, it's not . . ."

"No, no, it's perfectly true," Clifford said. "I used to think I knew how to heal people, you know, how to keep them alive, and then your mother died in spite of that. And I used to think I knew how to be a father to you, but then I forgot to notice that you weren't in need of my fathering anymore. Everything's changing all the time, and there's nothing you can do to make it stop. It's taken me fifty-three years and a few recent knocks on the head to figure that out."

"Well, I'm sorry about the knocks on the head," Addison said.

"No," Clifford said. "No need."

They walked lazily around the periphery of the house, staring up into the hollow eves and into the lacy hats of the trees where the shadows grew impenetrable and appealing. The outlines of strange figures appeared and receded on the clapboards beside them—toothless beasts and three-legged men and birds with human faces. On a night like this, anything was possible, Clifford thought—confessions and forgiveness and even crying in the sight of your own son. Any or all of it might happen, and the knowledge of this made his skin prickle and thin, as if it were about to be exchanged with someone else's.

"I don't know what I thought I was saving you from," Clifford said. "A life I hadn't planned for you . . . that must have been it." He allowed his voice to fill with some internal fog, and then spoke again in spite of it, thick-throated and hoarse. "Love is better than planning, though, and I guess that's not news to you now."

———

AFTER MEMORIAL Day, Mr. Marbury and the chamber of commerce installed a carousel ride in the village park. The town needed an attraction over the summer months, something that would play music and light up at night, something that would fill up the minds of the children. Mariela the Shining was hired on as manager. She collected purple pickets and held babies upright on glossy saddles and sometimes made conversation with the parents who ringed the platform, waving, their children's ice cream cones melting in their spare hands. Everyone loved her, even the pranksters who tried to ride without paying, even the toddlers who screamed when their horses leapt too high. The air wavered at her ankles, where invisible wings were beating. And her skin shimmered into translucence when she laughed, so that the light passed through from its source inside her, brilliant and bashful and enchanting to everyone who looked.

When Addison was not working on the revisions of his book, he was hovering at the edge of the merry-go-round, waiting for Mariela to revolve into view, her hands occupied with a task that would look like magic to him, whatever it was. He brought her small gifts: icy drinks in thermoses on days that were hot, insiders guides to college life, a lawn chair to rest in whenever she got tired. Sometimes, after closing, she would let him walk her home, past Main Street and McArthur's and down the long, fragrant stretch of Trafalgar where the orange groves fell away to either side, carefully fertile, as if that were possible. At other times, she rode home in a car with someone already waiting for her—her mother or Emily D. or one of the other Lovelorn Women, their kindly kisses falling onto her cheeks when she came close enough.

By the time Mariela closed the merry-go-round each night, darkness had already settled. Away from the lights strung around the ride's apron, the world dropped off into spectral views and floods of gray. Addison stood next to Mariela and helped her to polish the dust-covered horses, their manes splayed out in bright, wooden locks, their hooves suspended in ongoing flight. When she spoke to him, she turned her head away, as if she were speaking to one of the sculpted animals lined up behind her.

"Why do you come here all the time?" she said once.

"To help with the small things," Addison said. "Do you mind?"

There were smudges of grease on the backs of her hands, tender and haunting in what they made Addison think of. He didn't want her cleaning carousels in the dark. He didn't want that at all.

"I'm fine now, you know," Mariela said. "I'm fine on my own."

"I know," he said.

"Because I don't want anyone feeling sorry for me," she said. "Coming around here just feeling sorry."

"No."

"I'm fine on my own now," she said. "I really am."

She would not look at him. She wandered a few yards away to the ticket booth, her white skirt wafting behind her like a parchment, like a declaration. Out on the street, a sedan pulled up. Dove Pairlee leaned out of its window, her plump arms beckoning.

"You don't need me anymore," Addison said. "I know that. It's just that I thought maybe I could be someone you could still want."

Mariela held still. She hesitated there, equivocating, deciding something in the moment. Then she waved the sedan onward.

"It's all right, Dove," she called. "I'm staying late tonight."

When she walked back to where Addison waited, the two of them polished the same horse a second time, stroking its neck and its withers by turns, unaware as they were that it already shone.

CERTAIN PLACES on the earth had mind and memory of their own; and if you knew these places as a girl and then returned to them as a woman, the land would rise up and embrace you and kiss the ropes of your unfastened hair. This was what Anna de la Senda believed to be true; she could see it for herself through the space of her northern windows, where the two lawns beyond held Mariela and Addison in a windy, green cup, remembering them with what looked like touch. They ate bread torn off from the loaf in coarse, jagged pieces, and a salmon pie that Anna had made, with a sour dill dressing zig-zagged over the top. Addison had brought along an ambrosia salad which was pieced together in a bright mosaic of marshmallows and fruit, but Mariela had learned about ambrosia, and she refused to taste it again, no matter how many times she was asked.

Anna knew what they talked about as surely as if she had been close enough to hear. They talked about loss, irretrievable and lasting, and they wished out loud that they had never known the name of it until they had been old enough to see that it could be survived. Now, they knew that it could be survived, but they weren't sure what came afterward. How much of their former lives could be recovered whole in the aftermath—a reflection, a parcel, a calling-back of love? The answer lay in the way they passed time together on that small, rounded place on the lawn that recalled them to themselves. There, on that spot, Mariela's hair floated above her shoulders in that same weightless liquid black that had always encircled the rarity of her soul. And there, Addison tried again to free himself from the hands that wandered away in the embarrassment and exhilaration of talking to her like this. Around them, the shallow knolls rose and fell in a private wilderness of green. Cristobal would have called it their carpet of remembrance, *alfombra de memoria*, if only he had been there to speak the words.

Later, Addison switched on the radio that crouched on the tablecloth next to him, and he and Mariela danced to songs that were wishful and open-hearted, with all the end-notes rising up like fragments of prayer. Mariela danced with her feet off the ground from weightlessness and wonder, her toes pointed into two girlish crescents which skimmed only the fringes of the grass. Once when Anna glanced away, she caught sight of Clifford, defined and intent behind a window of his own house. His face was magnificent and abstracted in the distance, all the surfaces of it coming together at angles that were changed and strangely reconsidered. Sometimes he looked at their children, and sometimes he looked at her, mostly at her, she thought, from the particular tilt of his head. At a little after six, he turned on the lamp beside him, gold-headed and benevolent, and for some reason she was unsure of, Anna lit a single votive candle in response, setting it on the window casing where he would notice. It was as though they had found themselves sitting in opposite balconies during the same play. The drama was about reconciliation, as miraculous a thing as that, and Anna had longed to be a witness to it, believing as she always had that witnessing would be enough.

———•·•———

THE PASSING of summer urged everyone's front yards into tangles of beauty, tended or not. The jacaranda trees and the bottlebrush pulsed with the act of blooming, and their colors appeared so suddenly and with such extravagance that passersby were torn between looking at them and looking away. It was as though everyone could see forward to the time when the flowering would have to stop, and it made the trees beautiful and mortal, ecstatic and sad. You wanted to stare at them for whole hours put together, but at the same time you wanted not to want to.

And there were other, more singular transformations that took place. After Mariela had opened and read her college acceptance letter, her hair began growing from the top of her head in shades of iridescent green, the color of wishes granted, of supplications answered. Everyone who saw her agreed that the effect made her more rare and vibrant and unearthly than any other human being they had ever glimpsed or known. Strangers reached out to touch her when she walked by them, lurching toward her impulsively, unthinking, their arms raised from their sides in bold, empty embraces. She was as near to a sanctified vision as most people would ever get.

Lovers had trouble that particular year in containing what they felt inside the boundaries of their skin. There wasn't enough room for their enchantment to circulate in and, by way of response, their bodies expanded in peculiar ways. Full-grown men added three inches in height or their belly buttons popped out or their feet stopped fitting into their shoes. Addison Ettinger went barefoot for two entire weeks, out of necessity, until his toes halted at a men's size twelve. The whole of his feet were a luminescent white, and he walked in them awkwardly, as though he were dragging deep-sea flippers. But that was the way that love mingled with the time of year, largely, insistently, invading breeze and bone.

On the day of the wedding, two dozen birds came to sit on the ridge of Anna de la Senda's roof, resting their heads under their wings, waiting for something to begin. Dove was plainly wary of them; she held a ceremony leaflet over her hairdo every time she approached the front door. But Anna recognized their spindly legs and their crooked wings as those of the birds she had once healed. If she had raised her wrist, they would have flown down to perch there. If she had sung to them, they would have known to sing back. Every small charity returned to you in some way; it was part of a design that escaped clear understanding, but she sensed it nonetheless, imprinted there, upon the unknowing neighborhood.

The Cordojo Women lined up as bridesmaids in green, bare-necked chiffon dresses that ended at their calves in frothy, transparent waves. The hats which India had made for them were careful nests of dyed-to-match netting and sewn-on pearls, with couplets of fresh white roses glancing over the brims. Dove had placed an extra rose at the base of her burgeoning cleavage until Maxine had made her remove it. Her bosom would attract plenty of attention all by itself, Maxine had said. She didn't need to hang out a sign. But a moment later, Maxine was making up by tucking stray rose petals into the instep of Dove's shoes; she would release the fragrance when she danced, and her new boyfriend, whoever he turned out to be, would fall in love with her cachet. Dove laughed, the fingers of one hand plunging into the careless tunnels of her hair. Anger evaporated into ethers no one could trace. It was in the nature of the day itself, pristine and expansive and prayed for, dedicated to memories not yet made.

The reception unfolded under a white, resplendent palace of a canvas that arced in three broad domes across the Ettingers' lawn. In the shade provided there, champagne flutes multiplied like a beautiful species of mushroom, crystalline and fragile and hunted. Crickets hid under misplaced handbags and engraved cocktail napkins and chirped through what they

LANE VON HERZEN

thought was persistent night. And the pink-headed roses forgot to fade, standing in their centerpiece vases with a strange, vain innocence, their wraps peeled off their young shoulders to reveal a beauty that was unchanging.

Anna passed through the whole day with the feeling that she had died and drifted out of her skin and was now looking on from the vantage point of heaven. Her vision seemed clearer than she had ever remembered it. She felt as though the edges of the daylight had been honed down to their gleaming rims. She saw Stewart Souther appear out of nowhere and begin kissing Earline Ettinger's hand behind the drape of his linen napkin, when he thought no one would notice. She saw Dove Pairlee tucking petit-fours into her purse whenever she went without a dance partner for two dances in a row. She saw Clifford Ettinger wondering where she, Anna, could possibly be, always returning to her vacated place at the head table, his eyebrows melted together in a single, thwarted, bristling line.

Finally, he found her by herself at the buffet table, which was empty now except for a few desultory grapes and melon balls and a life-sized ice sculpture of a swan that cried clear tears of water as it shrank. On the dance platform, Stewart Souther was waltzing with Earline and her wheelchair, trying to keep his feet out from under the tires. He looked awkward and infatuated, his broad, checkered tie flapping over his shoulder while Earline smiled.

"He came uninvited, but that's all right," Clifford said.

"You don't mind?" Anna said.

Clifford shrugged. "He jilted my mother a number of months ago. I minded that," he said. "Now he's trying to make up for it and it seems like that's just what he ought to be doing."

Anna nodded her head. She petted the back of the ice-bodied swan in front of her, trailing her hand over its slushy feathers and into its surrounding lake. Clifford watched her movements in silence, waiting for their patterns to emerge. She was standing in a curious breeze which soughed through her hair and the gathered places in her dress, moving as though it

238

had eyes and judgment and a longing that mirrored Clifford's own.

"You look beautiful," he said.

"The whole world looks beautiful on a day like this," Anna said.

"Yes. Yes it does," he said. "They're making their start finally, and I guess that's why."

At the far end of the canopy, Mariela and Addison paused by two separate tables of well-wishers. They turned away from each other for a moment, but Addison's fingers found and grasped a corner of her veil, floating in the blind spot behind his back. The white tulle stretched between them like transparent hope, sailing upward in a generous, private, inexhaustible ellipse.

"You're being very generous in helping them," Anna said. "All this today. And Mariela's tuition. And I saw the apartment you've rented for them on the West Side. All that space! I told Mariela that those high ceilings will give them room to dream in."

"Room to dream in," Clifford said. "I've missed hearing you say things like that." His eyes turned shielded and squinting, as if she were suddenly too bright to look at.

"Well, dreams are necessary to people, just like bread and water," Anna said. "You'd die without a few of them flourishing somewhere." Her wet hand gestured toward the unseen somewheres of people's hearts, drops of water scattering from her fingertips in slight, disappearing arcs of light.

"Oh, I don't doubt it. Not at all," Clifford said. "I have some dreams, two of them actually, that have been the only things standing between me and despair recently."

"You do?" Anna said.

"Yes," he said. He bent toward her, now flushed and fever-skinned and compelled, his face coloring in anticipation of his own embarrassment. "Do you want me to tell them to you?"

"All right," she said.

A crowd of ladies began to cluster out on the slope-backed grass, the Cordojo Women forming a close, ecstatic knot at its center. Some of them stepped out of their shoes and plucked at their sleeves and rearranged their pearls so that they dangled down their backs and were out of the way. Any minute now the bouquet would fall into the hands of one of them, extravagant and pink-flocked and portentous. Clifford watched them while he spoke.

"The first one," he said, "the first one is this dream I have that if I apologized to you—I mean really apologized for all the mistakes I made, for all the self-righteousness and everything behind it—that you would be able to forgive me."

In the distance, the bouquet rose and spun above the outstretched, quavering arms of the hopeful-hearted.

"It's not realistic. I know that," Clifford went on. "That's why it qualifies as a dream."

Then the bouquet shivered and fell, and suddenly Esther Lee was doing a merry dance on the grass while the other women applauded. In her arms was the spray of tender-headed roses, their necks as wobbly as babies', their blooms stunned and voluptuous and filled with the substance of luck.

"I would forgive you," Anna said. She glanced up at Clifford and saw that his face had gone slack with wide, wordless surprise. His eyes swam in a clear, sudden water that he tried to blink back toward its source, as if it were a matter of mere concentration.

"What's your second dream?" Anna said.

"The second one is that if I asked you to come out to dinner with me, you'd say yes," Clifford said. He blinked in the direction of the melted swan, in sympathy it seemed for what it felt like to dissolve into a transparent lake.

"Yes," Anna said.

"Yes?"

She nodded, the glossy, rose-tipped brim of her hat nodding with her.

"Oh, Anna," he said.

Clifford looked around him and could scarcely believe the pressing beauty of the world. A two-year-old girl was dancing in a daffodil-shaped dress while keeping one hand clutched to her mother's taffeta hem. Earline was being lifted by Stewart Souther into the seat of his canary-yellow convertible, her hair already loosed in anticipation of the wind. Esther Lee was running toward Clifford exultantly, her hat and her hearing aid missing, pale roses the size of teacups frothing in her embrace.

"You two need to run up to the house!" she said. "Your children are waiting to tell you good-bye!"

Later, Anna couldn't remember what she'd said to Mariela in those last moments, when her daughter had stood on tiptoe in her honeymoon suit to plant a kiss on her cheek that made a sound like devotion. *May the saints bless every hair on your head,* she would like to have said, but of course they already had.

And when the dark rolled itself out over the neighborhood, Anna couldn't comprehend the idea of going home to a house without Mariela in it, without her rare iris heart and her blessed green hair, without her levitations and her sorrows and the scents of her changing breath. She couldn't comprehend the idea even when she had reached her front walk, shoeless and mystified, a great white wheel of wedding cake held up before her like a charm against the dark. A breeze of pastel confetti sifted against the near side of the house, falling through its open windows like ghosts and summer snow.

Anna could have spent the night wandering lost were it not for the thought of Clifford, and the Cordojo Women, and the fourteen statuettes of the saints and the little birds that perched on her roof even now, folding and unfolding their feathers, watching for her to give them a sign. Love would be bountiful in her life even in the quiet spaces, even in the lightless nights, when her daughter lay asleep a hundred miles away, dreaming dreams she could no longer guess.

Anna set a gleaming wedge of cake on the lawn and, calling to the birds above her, waited for the sound of wings.

℗ **PLUME**

ABSORBING NOVELS

☐ **LOUISIANA POWER & LIGHT by John Dufresne.** In this hilarious and highly original novel, the last survivor of the sorry Fontana familial line, Billy Wayne Fontana, strikes out on the rocky road called life and takes us all on a wild, hair-raising ride through the Louisiana backwaters. "Both raucous and wise, it lures us into introspection with humor, and amid guffaws brings home serious truths about faith and heritage, chance and genealogy."—*Chicago Tribune*
(275024—$11.95)

☐ **GOODBYE TO THE BUTTERMILK SKY by Julia Oliver.** When twenty-year-old Callie Tatum saw the man from Birmingham coming up the road to the farm-house, she knew she shouldn't talk to him. Her husband was at the mill. Only her invalid father-in-law and her baby daughter were home, and Callie had no business socializing with a stranger . . . or beginning an affair. "A compelling novel of illicit love against a steamier background."—*Anniston Star*
(274257—$10.95)

☐ **TUSCALOOSA by W. Glasgow Phillips.** In the simmering heat of 1972 Tuscaloosa, 22-year-old Billy Mitchell returns from college to live and work on the grounds of the mental institution run by his psychiatrist father. But soon he's overwhelmed by memories of his mother's disappearance years before and his growing passion for one of his father's inmates. "A strong, moving nar-rative . . . subtle and lyrical . . . draws the reader in with his classical Southern voice while eloquently questioning some of society's labels and prejudices." —*St. Louis Post-Dispatch* (274397—$10.95)

☐ **THERAPY by Steven Schwartz.** In this extraordinary and deeply affecting tale of lives that crisscross in and out of therapy, the author draws us achingly close to his characters. An intimate, absorbing novel about hope and hope-lessness, about the endless ways in which we can hurt and heal one another, and about the light and dark places in the human heart. "A supreme literary gift . . . triumphs spiritually, intellectually, humanly."—Bret Lott, author of *Reed's Beach* (274311—$12.95)

Prices slightly higher in Canada.

DUTTON

LITERARY FICTION

☐ **UNDER THE FEET OF JESUS by Helena Maria Viramontes.** This exquisitely sensitive novel has at its center Estrella, a girl about to cross over the perilous border to womanhood. What she knows of life comes from her mother, who has survived abandonment by her husband in a land where she is both an illegal alien and a farmworker. It captures the conflict of cultures, the bitterness of want, the sweetness of love, the power of pride, and the landscape of human heart. (939490—$18.95)

☐ **WHEN THE RAINBOW GODDESS WEPT by Cecilia Manguerra Brainard.** Set against the backdrop of the Japanese invasion of the Philippines in 1941, this brilliant novel weaves myth and legend together with the suffering and tragedies of the Filipino people. It shows us the Philippines through an insider's eyes and brings to American audiences an unusual reading experience about a world that is utterly foreign and a child who is touchingly universal. (938214—$19.95)

☐ **THE UNFASTENED HEART by Lane von Herzen.** Anna de la Senda possesses an extraordinary empathy that draws to her a marvelous collection of lovelorn souls, who form a mischievous chorus and play matchmaker between Anna and a lonely widower. While Anna is rediscovering passion, her daughter Mariela in encountering it for the first time. Anna wishes to protect her from all worldy disappointments, but she cannot. "Evocative . . . a story of love and longing in a near-fantasy setting."—*Boston Globe* (272904—$15.95)

☐ **ENTERTAINING ANGELS by Marita van der Vyver.** Griet Swart's life is not exactly a fairy tale. Her once marvelous marriage has ended in divorce. She has lost her husband, her home, and her baby in yet another miscarriage. But late one night an angel appears on her doorstep and breaks her spell of sadness with a joyful sexual adventure. A modern-day fairy tale that is outrageously witty, unblushingly candid, and magically moving. (939180—$20.95)

Prices slightly higher in Canada.
